Patty

ALSO BY SCOTT LASSER

Battle Creek

All I Could Get

All I Could Get

A NOVEL

Scott Lasser

ALFRED A. KNOPF  NEW YORK 2002

THIS IS A BORZOI BOOK PUBLISHED BY ALFRED A. KNOPF

Published in the United States by Alfred A. Knopf, a division of Random House, Inc., New York, and simultaneously in Canada by Random House of Canada Limited, Toronto.
Distributed by Random House, Inc., New York.
www.aaknopf.com

Knopf, Borzoi Books, and the colophon are registered trademarks of Random House, Inc.

Library of Congress Cataloging-in-Publication Data
Lasser, Scott.
All I could get : a novel of Wall Street / by Scott Lasser.
p. cm.
ISBN 0-375-41325-1 (alk. paper)
1. New York (N.Y.)—Fiction. 2. Wall Street—Fiction. 3. Success—Fiction. I. Title.
PS3562.A7528 A79 2002
813'.54—dc21 2001038911

Manufactured in the United States of America

FIRST EDITION

To Deborah

Contents

All I Could Get

Prologue

We lived then in a prefabricated unit that sat on a sandy, sage-covered plateau just north of the Roaring Fork River. Our home, like the twenty-one others around it, was made to look like a log cabin; to me it brought to mind the Lincoln Logs I played with as a kid. One day I was out walking with my son along the old railroad bed that ran between our subdivision and the river canyon. My son was just four, bouncing along in a pair of new Stride Rite shoes that had set me back forty-three bucks. We were terribly short of money. I looked up at the ski mountain of Snowmass, where, in mid-June, the snow was finally fading from the upper slopes, and then back to my boy, who was pulling at a sage bush. A private plane rose from the valley. I covered my ears with my hands and watched the jet tear at the sky. I'd had enough. I don't know why I picked that moment to decide it, but I knew I'd had enough of putting off purchases of basic foodstuffs like peanut butter and bread, had enough of driving a pickup truck with duct-taped fenders and a flaky transmission, had enough of fearing the heat and electric bills, to say nothing of the rent. I grabbed my son and went to tell my wife, who, in her own way, had had enough, too.

And so that's how it all got started. I was thirty years old, and I wanted to make some money.

1. Bid Without

I last saw weekday-morning light in October. Now, as I crest the hill on Route 172, I spot a bluish-gray strip of sky along the horizon. Dawn, or at least the hint of it. It looks to be a fabulous day. For one thing, the air this morning has that special charge you sometimes get in the spring. I felt it when I left my house, my face tingling and raw from having just shaved, the breeze soft and warm on my cheeks. There was the smell of moist earth and the first few bars of morning birdsong. I took a moment to stand perfectly still in my driveway, where I took a deep breath and listened; it's such acts that can give ballast to the day. Right now I am driving with my nose tilted in canine fashion to my cracked and rattling window.

I'm going to miss this air at work, though I'm looking forward to getting in. I'm on a bit of a roll. I've just finished my most profitable month and am trading with confidence. Last week a mutual fund did a billion-and-a-half-dollar trade with me, and I actually made some money on it. The other guys on the desk are starting to take note. Also, it's my birthday, thirty-five. Old still to be the low man on the trading floor, but it looks as if my luck may be changing. I turn left into the parking lot by the interstate, where every day I meet my carpool mates. I coax the Escort's gearshift into reverse, ease the car into a parking space, and check my watch. It's 5:59.

Seconds later, Chip McCarty backs in his BMW 540 next to me and gives me a little salute, like the navy aviator he once was. This background gives him unquestioned stature on the trading floor. He flew submarine-attack planes, not fighters, but Wall Street doesn't make much of a distinction, and now Mac is the best-known U.S. Treasury five-year-note trader on the Street.

We get out of our cars, and I breathe in the smell of cut grass, mixed with a tinge of exhaust wafting over from the interstate.

Mac and I nod at each other, but don't speak. He stretches, reaching his long arms above his head, as might a football referee signaling a score. It's just light enough that I notice the hair on the back of his head, how it stops its descent to his collar in a neat, razor-cut horizontal line. He got a haircut over the weekend, though it's not easy to tell. He keeps his hair so short that I have to notice the difference around the edges.

"Good weekend?" Mac asks.

A Little League game, burgers grilled on the deck, my wife, Rachel, and I curled up on the couch Saturday night, watching a movie, a Sunday-morning bagel run with my daughter.

"Are they ever bad?" I say.

"Never," he admits. He looks at his watch. "Where the hell is Dino? Can't that guy ever be on time?"

Just then Dino Corsetti's Infinity comes squealing into the lot. He swings the car around and lunges it to a stop in front of us. The car does a little jig on its shocks. I climb into the back seat; Mac takes the copilot spot. Bloomberg Radio is maybe thirty seconds into its 6:00 a.m. financial-markets update.

"See," Mac says, nodding toward the radio for proof, "you're late."

"Eat shit," Dino replies. He pulls out of the lot, and runs a red light to turn onto the I-684 entrance ramp. He reaches around his tie, which hangs from the rearview mirror, and engages the radar detector. It responds with its normal routine of beeps and squeaks, and we're off.

The news on the radio is dire. Stock markets worldwide are crumbling. Panic selling has rolled through Tokyo, Hong Kong, South Korea, Australia, and Singapore. There are rice riots in Bangkok, strikes in Seoul, bankruptcies everywhere. Two market-related suicides have been reported this morning in London. It's midday there, and most stock traders are cowering under their desks as if awaiting a nuclear blast. The trading day is about to begin in New York, and fear is oozing out of the radio reports and, I'm sure, e-mail updates from Tokyo and London. In an age of instant communication, panic is never localized. U.S. Treasury bonds, with their excellent credit and guaranteed (albeit low) return, are on fire. Chip McCarty and I both trade U.S. Treasury bonds. The radio announces that the thirty-year bond, a benchmark issue, is up in price by twenty-seven ticks. This is a big move.

"Hee-hee!!" says Mac, who's gone home long. He raps out a drum roll of glee on the dashboard, taking special satisfaction in making money by betting against the Japanese, whom he hates for reasons that have never been clear to me.

I can tell from the vibrations that Dino has reached cruising speed: somewhere between eighty-five and ninety-five miles per hour. Outside the window, the day is fading in. We slip under a stone bridge—we are on the Hutchinson Parkway now—and past the glow of a Mobil service area.

"How come you never stop for coffee?" Mac asks Dino.

"How come you never come prepared?" Dino sips at the mug he always brings from home.

"There's no place to buy coffee in Bedford," Mac complains.

"Make it yourself."

"Yeah, right." Mac turns to the back seat. "What do you think, Barry? Wouldn't a little coffee for the ride be nice?"

The radar detector screeches, and Dino stabs at the brakes. Right now I feel I would donate a spare digit for a cup of coffee, but I'm tired of this routine. Dino and Mac have several running arguments, and this one is the oldest; they've been bickering over coffee for three years.

"You guys work it out," I say. It's my standard line.

"I knew he'd say that," Dino says.

I lean back on the leather seat. I have things on my mind. Today I will take the offensive with Court Harvey, the head of my trading desk. This year, I want to get paid. A lot. This means I have to work on Court Harvey now. As traders, we never know what we will earn. Instead, we're given a token "salary," and then a year-end "bonus," or "number," which is a trader's real pay. The bonus criteria are subjective. Trading profitably is important, but no more so than one's image as a vital member of the desk. The main thing we do is lobby management for pay. It's a sad but true state of affairs that we have to start this lobbying in April. If April isn't too late. I've seen Mac in with Court Harvey twice in the last month. Perhaps they were talking about something other than Mac's number, but I can't imagine what.

It will take forty more minutes to reach lower Manhattan. I close my eyes, and try to get some sleep.

I wake to find us stuck in traffic two blocks from our building. It's ten till seven, the light still gray and hesitant, as if the sun were unsure whether to shine on the city. Back at home I know that Rachel is curled up in bed with Jane, who's no doubt sucking on a bottle of milk and pushing her tiny feet against her mother. If Rachel listens carefully, she can hear our son, Sam, snoring in the next room. I wish it were still Sunday.

"What a shit show," Mac says. I look up. We're stopped dead. Construction crews have been working this area all winter, tearing up the street to lay pipe, paving it over, tearing it up, paving again. This morning it looks as if they're in a tearing phase. Ahead I hear and then see a huge piece of yellow machinery pounding away at the pavement like an overwrought dinosaur.

Dino slams his fist down on the horn, then laughs. At the futility of it, I suppose.

It takes ten more minutes to reach our building. Dino maneuvers the Infinity down a long series of ramps in the underground garage, descending four layers into the bedrock. Only senior vice-presidents (or managing directors, the one higher rank) can obtain spots in this garage, and in our carpool only Mac is an SVP. He lords this privilege over Dino and me, and sets the prices we pay for the commute. Dino and I suspect that the firm deducts the parking payment pretax from Mac's paycheck, but that he doesn't pass this savings on to us. Dino's

Infinity has one of the two stickers awarded Mac, who always threatens to remove it for tardiness.

"Crowded," Mac says when we reach our designated level, and it is. Our usual spot and the one next to it are taken by a single Hummer. We prowl the row, looking for an opening.

"Would you look at these cars," Dino says. "Beemer, Beemer, Beemer, Mercedes, Beemer, Lexus. Beemer, Lexus, Jaguar, Beemer . . . What's that?"

I tell him it's a Bentley.

We park, and pull our suit jackets on for the trip to the trading floor. At the elevator, Mac says to Dino, "Are you ever going to pay me your commuting money? You owe on six weeks."

"You want money from me?" Dino says, affecting a Brooklyn accent, though he actually grew up in Kingston, a couple hours north of the city. "Get in line. Besides, it's only been five weeks." Dino puts his tie on in the reflection of the stainless-steel elevator door.

"What about this week?"

"It's only Monday."

The elevator arrives. "You know," Mac says, stepping inside, "I never have to ask Barry. He always pays on time."

"Barry's still new at this," Dino says.

I keep my eyes on the panel above the door to hide my embarrassment. This is not an issue of money. Dino probably carries three months of commuting money on his person at any given time, but he realizes that he can keep one up on Mac by owing him. This is trader mentality. It's all about leverage. I feel like a chump.

Five floors above, at the security turnstile, I run into Gretchen Barnes. Black skirt, white blouse, black blazer, put together like an ad from the Sunday *New York Times Magazine.* I know Gretchen from Dartmouth. At UCLA or Florida she would have been a goddess, but at Dartmouth, in the early eighties, she was worshiped for her beauty in a way that made her something other than human, like a piece of art. The intervening years have diminished nothing. I find myself openly staring at her. Her jet-black hair is now cut short, but she still has a lean, athlete's body—she ran middle distance for the track team—and those enormous black eyes that have probably gotten her whatever she's wanted from the time she was a baby. Her beauty is legendary among men at the firm. When they say "that girl from equities," they mean Gretchen.

"Barry," Gretchen says, "how you been?"

"Great," I say. No need to get specific—or even truthful—before seven in the morning.

"You still the bill trader?" she asks.

"Yep." I slide my identification card through the security scanner and follow her in. I have to hurry to do this. I've often noticed that having a conversation with Gretchen means doing it on the run. I can hear heavy breathing and the hurried jingle of pocketed change and keys as Mac and Dino struggle to keep up.

"I need something from you. I'll stop by your floor today."

I nod while she breaks off to go to the newsstand. I pause to watch her walk away, then continue on to the elevator bank.

"What could she possibly need from you that I couldn't give her?" Dino asks.

"Best legs in the firm," Mac says.

"Best everything," Dino gushes.

I shrug. I met her freshman year, on the weekend my girlfriend, Sarah, came to visit. Back then, Dartmouth still seemed ambivalent about being coed, and there were so few women that it was far easier to ship them in than to find a date at the school. At least that's the way we looked at it. Gretchen and Sarah made fast friends. When Sarah left, Gretchen latched on to me. I came to understand that she had no one in whom to confide. Her girlfriends were really rivals, and there wasn't a guy on campus who wouldn't have sacrificed his right arm to spend a night with her. Because of Sarah, I fell into a different category, even long after I'd given Sarah the boot. It was a sterile, neutered, and often difficult role, but years later I had a connection on the Street right where I needed one.

There is a moment, just before the elevator reaches the trading floor, when I can almost remember what it was like to wake in the morning and not have a thought about the markets, but the moment passes quickly. The doors open and I walk with Dino and Mac and the other traders across the wooden parquet floor of the reception area to the coat closet, a long, narrow, dead-end hallway lined with nonremovable hangers and dark, almost identical suit jackets. I hang mine at the end. It's April, so everyone wears navy or charcoal. Pinstripes are the allowable variation, though in this dark phalanx I do notice one glen plaid, standing out like the year's first robin.

On the floor I glance out across a football-field-sized space devoid of interior walls or partitions, an open field of nothing but row after row of computer screens, all of it coated in that odd, trading-floor light. The light has a fuzzy quality to it, produced from the combined efforts of ceiling light fixtures that shine back up at the pocked ceiling tiles; of thousands of computer monitors and phone boards; of a couple hundred televisions and desk lamps; of the few natural photons that manage to make it through the grime-encrusted exterior windows. I also notice the trading-floor smell. It's a faint but musty odor, one heated by all the electronics; it smells as if an electric oven has been turned on that hasn't been used in years. Later in the trading day, it will take on the stench of a locker room.

I see some activity in foreign exchange, where there is already a huge demand for the U.S. dollar, a phenomenon known as "flight to quality." When people get scared, George Washington, Ben Franklin, and the other founding fathers are somehow a comfort. The day the world really does go bankrupt, everyone will own U.S. dollars.

Other than foreign exchange, the floor is mostly empty. I walk to my seat, log on to my two computer systems, and check out my broker screens. I have stacks of broker screens, all arranged in a semicircle, a trading cockpit. On the left side of the broker screens, traders place their bids (the prices at which they wish to buy bonds), and on the right side, their offers (where they want to sell them). On this day it is early yet, but already, given the overseas panic, everyone wants to buy treasury bills. Right now people only care about safety, and t-bills are the safest place to be. In the short term, trading is all about emotion, and, looking at those screens, I can almost hear cries of desperation. Guys need to buy, and can't. One treasury-bill screen has bids for every bill but not one offer. Every bill is bid without.

"Why are we here?" asks Mac, whose desk is across the row from mine. After riding in together, we spend the day three feet apart, sitting back-to-back. "We live the farthest away, but we're the first ones in."

"Dedication," I say.

"Stupidity," he replies.

I am just about to get up for a cup of coffee when a voice comes over the Hoot and Holler, an intercom system that can be heard simultaneously in any of the firm's far-flung offices. We all have hoot buttons on our phone boards. I will never forget the first time I used mine and my voice was literally heard around the world.

"Barry Schwartz?" the voice asks again. It has an English accent and a slight reverberation, an echo across the ocean.

"Yeah?"

"Can you offer one hundred million U.S. Treasury one-year bills to Citibank, London?"

Try to understand my predicament. The world is crumbling. Crumbling. Everyone is selling stock all over the globe, and whatever cash is left over from those sales is being converted into U.S. dollars, and those dollars are flowing like the mother of all tsunamis right at the treasury-bill market. Everyone wants to buy; therefore, I want to buy. Still, I must show the account a price at which I will sell. I must: this is how the game is played. Customers call us because we always make a price. It's just that right now, at 7:07 in the morning, with the globe in financial meltdown, with a tidal wave of cash bearing down on me, I'm not sure what the price should be. The trick is to show a price high enough that the account will not buy, but not so high that the account might later complain to my manager that I was trying to rip it off. That would make it hard to ask for a raise.

I clear my throat, hit my hoot button, and give a price.

"That's done," says the salesman immediately. "You sell one hundred million."

I feel my bowel slacken.

"Oh," Mac says, "you are fucked now."

The trading day has begun.

13

Wall Street was always a dream for me. Not that I ever really wanted to work here—I grew up in the Midwest and couldn't imagine it—but in the surreal images I had of it. As a kid I often listened to the stock report with my grandfather, and when the announcer stated the number of shares that traded that day I thought he said "chairs," and pictured a room full of them, stacked up in large piles that were shoved around by men with the physiques of piano movers. Wall Street was, in short, a bizarre, fantastic place. My grandfather, meanwhile, invested what little money he had in American steel companies, and thus died almost penniless. So there was danger, too.

I met my future Wall Street boss when I was sixteen. Court Harvey was a year and a half older than I, but the summer before he went to college we played on the same traveling baseball team. This was in Michigan. In high school he'd been all-state in baseball and football for Royal Oak; he graduated third in his class. Even the Detroit papers wrote about him. It was said that he passed up a huge baseball-signing bonus to accept a full ride to the University of Michigan, where he was to play baseball and football. He played shortstop on that summer team and I third, and I thought it something of an honor to play next to him. It amazed me, then, to find he was poor. His father was an unemployed autoworker. I had my own lawn business and lent him money when he needed it—five bucks here, a ten-spot there. He took the money reluctantly, always promising to pay me back. I didn't really believe him, but Court was so talented—and with his help we won so easily—that it seemed that we all owed him something. In the end, though, he sent me a check for $118, along with a strict accounting. He even paid me 10-percent interest, the going money-market rate at the time.

Court's athletic career ended abruptly. In his junior year at Michigan he broke his leg on a punt return, the type of break that required two metal plates and a half-dozen screws. I'd been following his exploits from New Hampshire, but after the injury he fell from my sight. Years later, when Gretchen Barnes set up an interview for me, I asked if this Court Harvey might possibly be the guy I'd known.

"Describe him," Gretchen said.

"Six two, very fair. Great athlete. Quiet, intense. He's from Michigan."

"That's the guy," she said.

At nine-thirty, the stock market opens down 180 points. Behind me, tiny speakers called squawk boxes sit on Chip McCarty's desk. The squawk boxes give play-by-play commentary on futures trading in Chicago. "At even Merrill," says the S&P futures squawker. "At" means someone—in this case Merrill Lynch—is offering, or trying to sell. "Nine bid locals, at even. At nine half Merrill. Merrill hits the nines, at nine Merrill. At eight half Merrill. At eight even Merrill, at seven half Goldman." The voice becomes excited as a roar grows in the pit, what with Merrill trying to sell stock on fifth markdown. "Locals hit the six evens. At five half Merrill, at five. At four half locals!! Locals hit the three evens!!!! The pit's in front of Merrill!!"

My stock screen is flashing red. This stock selling is giving added force to the tsunami; it's a signal to buy treasuries. I manage to grab twenty-five million two-year notes. Behind me I can hear Mac saying, "Pay it fives, pay it." Court Harvey is screaming at his broker, "Those are my fucking tens!!" Meanwhile, the salesmen are on their feet, asking for offerings.

"Barry!" yells Derek Lane, a lanky salesman who once told me that the main reason he'd been hired was that he'd been all-American at lacrosse. "Offer Cutthroat a hundred year bills."

Cutthroat is a small arbitrage account. They claim they take their name from the species of trout, and during quieter times we find this funny. I show them year bills ten basis points richer than I sold them to London. Cutthroat buys. I waive in more two-year notes (bills stop trading in the frenzy). I'm now long two-year notes and short year bills, a trade that I will need to reverse. The trade itself is bullish for bonds, and bonds are trading great, because the rest of the world is engulfed in financial turmoil. Thus, the worse things get for everyone else, the better they are for me.

"At seven half, Solly," shouts the S&P squawker, while the squawker from the bond-futures pit yells, "All buyers, all buyers . . ."

"What a shit show," says Tom Carlson, our two-year-note trader, who picked the line up from Chip McCarty.

Around the world, large corporations and small countries teeter on the edge of bankruptcy; on every news wire, experts are questioning the soundness of the global financial system. An emergency meeting of finance ministers is planned for Geneva. For the first time in twenty years, people are buying gold. In the long run, say a week, this situation could put me out of a job. But right now, I'm trying to make money on a trade, and for my trade to work, I need things to get even worse. I take a deep breath, wipe the dampness from my brow, and hit a button on my phone console. I pay a ridiculous price for another fifty million two-year notes, and pray for world collapse.

A little after ten-thirty, my wife, Rachel, calls. The stock market is now down 346 points; the last time the ten-year note traded at these yields, Eisenhower was president and most of the traders on the desk—myself included—were not yet born. I lost a fair amount of money on that first sale to London, but made it back buying two-year notes at stupid levels, because the market is now even more stupid. ("A stupidathon," Stevie Vollmer, one of our traders, calls it.) I'm ready to sell out my long now, fifty million twos.

"The repairman's here," my wife says.

"What repairman?" I use my broker microphone to offer out half of my twos, which other traders snap up as if these are the last twenty-five two-year notes available on the planet.

"You sold twenty-five million," my broker's voice comes through the speaker on my phone console. In the background I can hear other brokers howling for more. "You could sell a hundred," says my broker.

"Just twenty-five," I tell him. Traders rarely bother to say "million."

"Are you there?" asks Rachel. I tell her I am. "For the stove," she continues. "The repairman says it's going to cost two hundred dollars."

"Two hundred dollars!! For one burner?!"

"You want to talk to him?"

"No time, but . . . jeez."

Two hundred dollars is commuting money for almost a month. It's a nice dinner out with Rachel, sitter included. It's the blazer she wanted to buy a month ago but didn't, on account of the cost.

Cutthroat comes back for more year bills. Two-year notes are now a full tick better than where I sold them, less than a minute earlier. Had I waited, I'd have pocketed an extra eight thousand dollars. The S&P squawker is frantic, his voice scratchy and desperate. "At six half Lehman, no bid, no bid, no bid, at five half Lehman, at five . . ."

I offer the year bills at 4.37, six basis points richer than I've seen them trade. On a normal day, the year bill trades in a three-basis-point range. I listen to Derek Lane reflect the level. Cutthroat buys.

I'm entering the trade into my computer when I hear my wife yell my name.

"Rachel, it is truly a bad time," I say into the headset. "I'll call later."

"Can you just give me an answer on the two hundred?"

"The two hundred what?" I ask, realizing as I say it that she's talking about the stove.

"Dollars! For the stove."

There was a time, not long ago, when we didn't have two hundred dollars for the stove, or for anything else, when Rachel and I would argue over money that Rachel said we needed to spend—clothes for the kids, a few more pieces of silverware—and that I said we didn't have. Of course, we both were right. I used to think there was nothing wrong with our marriage that couldn't be fixed with a bank account of seven or eight hundred dollars.

"Fine," I say about the stove, now that we do have some money. "How's Sam, the baby?"

"They're fine," she says. "You know, calling you is—"

"Great," I say. "I gotta hop."

My broker screens are flashing with buyers. I wish I hadn't sold those twenty-five twos. I still own twenty-five, so, given the second sale of year bills, I'm not really short the market. I check my P&L, which shows me down four thousand dollars for the day, which is like being flat. Behind me I can hear Court Harvey yelling at his broker.

"Fuck you, Ziggy. You're hung. No, fuck you. Those are my fucking tens!! Those are my fucking tens!! If you ever want to work another miserable fucking day in your miserable fucking life, those are my fucking tens!!!"

At eleven-thirty, sixteen large pizza pies arrive, courtesy of Brian Zigfeld, Court's broker, who realizes that he has a relationship problem. As there are only seven government traders, plus a couple assistants, we invite the sales force and the derivatives desk to join in. Activity always slows around lunch, when traders have their hands and mouths filled with pizzas, sandwiches, Chinese food, or sushi. Not that anyone ever, ever, leaves the desk to eat.

It's about this time that Gretchen Barnes comes by and touches me on the shoulder. I turn, my mouth full with a bite of mushroom-onion-and-pepperoni pizza. I can smell her perfume. Lilac, I think. Lilac is the only flower I can recognize. It's an exotic smell for the government-trading row, a gulch rarely traveled by women. I put down my pizza. Gretchen has removed the blazer she was wearing this morning, and when I swivel my chair I come face-to-face, as it were, with her breasts, small and round and, like the rest of her, beautiful. Behind her I notice that Chip McCarty and Tom Carlson are leering at Gretchen in a way that, according to company policy, could be interpreted as sexual harassment.

"I need data on the three-month bill," she says. "You're the man for that, aren't you, Barry?"

"Yes, I am."

I download the data onto a floppy disc and hand it to her. Just then Court Harvey comes out of his office, where he often goes in the middle of the day to take care of whatever managers take care of in their little offices. He sees Gretchen, and an uncertain look comes over his face. Call it embarrassment.

"Hi, Court," Gretchen says.

"Gretchen," he says.

"How have you been?" she asks him.

"Even bid Goldman," says the S&P squawker.

Mac and Carlson swivel around in their seats for a brief look at the screens. With stocks ticking up, bonds are ticking down.

"Fuck," Carlson grunts. He pounds his hand on the desk. No one turns around. Such outbursts are too common to be noticed.

"What brings you to governments?" Court Harvey asks Gretchen.

"Visiting my old friend Barry," she says.

"You know Barry?"

"Sure. We went to college together. You know that."

"Really," says Court Harvey.

Stocks tick up again.

"Ah, fuck me!" This time it's Colin Dancer, the ten-year-note trader.

"We should catch up," Court says. "Maybe after work."

Gretchen kicks at the floor, her black pump working at the reddish-orange carpet tile. Court is my boss, and I don't want to see him get rejected by the most beautiful woman in the firm. I swivel back to the screens and try to sell out my two-year notes, which suddenly nobody wants to buy. Then Derek Lane is yelling at me again, this time to bid (buy) a hundred million year bills from Cutthroat. When I have a chance to look up again for Gretchen, she is gone.

At three o'clock we mark out books, as we do every day at three, when bond and Eurodollar futures stop trading in Chicago. "Marking" is a kind of snapshot of the market, the time when we establish for the record the daily relationships between securities and measure out profitability, or lack of it, for the day. Trading usually pauses at this time, while bond traders around the Street take stock.

Stevie Vollmer, who trades the long bond (the thirty-year bond, the longest maturity available, hence the name), comes down to the front-end guys. Vollmer was captain of Princeton's lacrosse team when they won the Ivy League championship two years running. That was thirty pounds ago, but he still lumbers down the row as if he's suited up. When he gets to my chair he begins bouncing on his toes. It's a habit of his. The floor is bouncy because of the carpet tiles, which cover bundles of computer and communication wires two feet thick, the ganglia of the trading floor.

"Hey, Meat," Vollmer asks me, "who was that girl?"

Even though Gretchen left almost four hours earlier, we all know whom he is talking about.

"Gretchen Barnes," I say. "From equities."

"From fucking heaven," Vollmer says. He turns to Mac, who has swiveled around in his seat. "Did you see that bod?"

"USDA prime cut."

"She married?"

"No," I say.

"Well," says Vollmer, "that's her choice, I'm sure. She's gotta be bid without."

Tom Carlson stands up from his seat and joins the conversation, if standing up is what anyone would call it. On a good day you'd say Carlson is five foot four. That he has the belly and girth of a Russian mobster doesn't help him to look taller.

"How's the diet?" Vollmer asks. Last week Carlson started on a new diet plan—his ninth since I started at the firm—that calls for the eating of fat. I suppose the idea is similar to the one doctors employ when they give speed to hyperactive children.

Carlson looks at his gut. It's so round and expansive, especially compared with his frame, that I consider it a wonder of nature. When he stands, he must arch his back, lest he topple over forward. It's the kind of girth that a certain type of man—not Carlson—could be proud of. "Lost six pounds already," he says. He looks at Vollmer. "How'd you make out today, Stevie?"

"Lost only money," Vollmer says. "I got fucked so hard I coulda been a hooker. How 'bout you?"

"About like you. Right in the crevasse, all day long. I got lifted, I couldn't buy. I got hit, I couldn't sell, the market sank like the goddamn *Titanic.* A real clusterfuck."

"What I want to know," Mac says, "is why the best-looking woman in the firm wants to talk to the bill trader." They all look at me. In the hierarchy of government traders, no one is lower than the bill trader. It's as if the head cheerleader came by to visit the water boy.

"What is the world coming to?" Vollmer asks.

Court Harvey comes out of his office then, and calls across the tops of the computer screens, "Barry, you got a minute?"

"Looks like bossman wants an answer, too," Vollmer says.

I take a seat in Court Harvey's office. The office looks out over the eternal construction site with which the carpool has to contend every day. There are shelves on one wall; the wall that faces the trading floor is glass and equipped with vertical blinds. ("Harvey closes the blinds, you know it's serious shit," Vollmer says.) Court Harvey isn't much for decorating. The shelves hold a plaque commending him on fifteen years with the firm, and a firm directory that is two years old. There is not a single picture of a family member, or a loved one, nor are there photos of golf outings or fishing trips, as there are in most managers' offices. There's a phone console and a Sun workstation that flashes market data on his desk, along with position reports, research papers, and a few résumés, the latter a reminder to his underlings that there are plenty of people lining up for our jobs.

"How's it going?" he asks. He has a lean face, with small, narrow-set blue eyes beneath almost translucent eyebrows. His skin is very fair. Sometimes, under the color-leaching lights of the trading floor, he appears albino.

"Good," I say. I figure this is a good opening, so I go right to the point. "I'm making money, the sales force is happy, I'm sure the market-share numbers are up. I actually wanted to talk to you about what I could expect at year end."

"Year end? Barry, it's April!!"

"I don't like surprises," I say. "And, frankly, I've had a couple."

"Don't worry about it. Just keep doing what you're doing, you'll be fine."

I remind him that he said the same thing the year before, which hadn't been so fine.

"All I can tell you, Barry, is that it's too early even to think about it." He just looks at me. I don't know what to say, which is obviously the point he is making with his silence. "So," he says, "remind me how you know Gretchen Barnes."

"Dartmouth."

"I forgot about that," he says. "You went to Dartmouth."

I nod. I don't know where he's going.

"You were good friends? You dated?"

I just stare. Court Harvey is not one to ask or care about your personal life, or even acknowledge that you have one. This is out of line, and, for Court Harvey, out of character.

"We never dated," I explain, to break the silence. I let him fumble around for several seconds, then give him a brief history of my relationship with Gretchen, emphasizing its platonic nature.

His face brightens, as if he's stepped out of a shadow. From outside I can hear the "beep beep beep" of a construction vehicle backing up.

"I just bought a house in Bedford, you know," he says.

"Really? Where?"

"Guard Hill Road. You know it?"

I know it: a ritzy stretch of dirt road dotted with huge manor homes, stables, and the occasional helicopter pad. That Court Harvey can afford such a spot gives me pause. I know he makes a lot of money, but . . . *Guard Hill Road*? Now I'm pissed off. What I'm making wouldn't pay to pave a driveway on Guard Hill Road. And what on earth could Court Harvey want with such a place? A single guy, secluded on an estate forty-five miles north of the city. It's a little weird.

"Awesome property there," I hear myself say.

"You should come over. Check it out. Bring your wife and kids. I've got a pool."

"Sure," I say. What does he want from me?

"What day works for you?" he asks. "The weekend after this one, maybe?"

"I hope it's a heated pool," I say.

He looks out the window, as if to check the season.

"I guess it's early yet for swimming. But I've got a couple of horses, too. Kids like horses, don't they?"

"Wow," I say, "you've hit the big time."

He blushes. For Court Harvey this means that red blotches appear on his cheeks and neck. It's an odd look. It helps me to remember him from Royal Oak, when he was just a great high-school athlete in need of a five-spot, not some tycoon with a Guard Hill Road estate.

"It's not as big a deal as you think," he manages to say.

I hold in a laugh.

"It's done, then," he says. "I was thinking of having Chip and his family. And Stevie, if he wants to come over from Rye. You know, the guys from north of the city."

"Okay," I say. He's making me nervous now. I don't want to be a party planner.

"Let me ask you something," he says.

"Sure."

"Do you think Gretchen Barnes would come?"

"Beats me," I say. "Why don't you ask her?"

"I was hoping you'd help on that. I want to invite her son, too. It's what this is all about, after all. Kids."

"Her son?" I ask. "What son?"

"Yeah, she's got a son. He's, I don't know, seven?"

"Seven! Is she married?"

She's not, according to Court Harvey. The father is some musician she met who didn't want to have a baby. I know it should surprise me that I don't know this most basic detail of Gretchen's personal life, but it doesn't. She works in a different division. Months go by without our passing at the elevators. In the three years I've been at the firm, we've never had dinner. We've chatted over drinks twice, and on both of those occasions we ran into each other at a bar, unplanned. When Gretchen helped me land my job, I assumed we'd renew the friendship we had in college, but Wall Street doesn't work that way. Faced with the time demands of our jobs, we drop from our lives all that is nonessential, without even making a conscious decision on just what that is. Friendships are usually the first thing to go.

"I can't really invite Gretchen to your party," I tell Court.

"I'm not asking you to invite her. Just call her up, let her know I'll be calling. Smooth the way."

"This is starting to remind me of junior high," I say. I stand up. Court Harvey follows my lead. Meanwhile, he frowns, and that shadow again descends over his face.

"Forget I asked," he says.

"Don't sweat it," I tell him. "I'll make the call."

"You don't have to," he says.

"I know." I think of what Chip McCarty would do, and smile at my position. I have leverage now, and I intend to use it. I leave the office before Court Harvey can say anything else. Down the trading row I can see Tom Carlson holding a hand over his left eye as he steadies his right on his broker screens. On some people this business can be hell.

At ten to six, the carpool emerges from the bowels of our building, where the street lamps glow and all the cars have their lights on, though I suspect that up north of the city my son might be getting the day's last few tosses in with his friends. I think of how Dino and Mac have indoor garages; they leave their homes in the morning, get in their cars, and don't get out again until they are in the firm's building. In winter they don't bother to wear overcoats. It's odd how we live our workweeks in the world's most famous metropolis: six months of never seeing daylight, or even breathing fresh air.

We take an alley to get away from whatever mess the construction crews have left for the night. Mac has checked the traffic on his Bloomberg machine. There's a stalled car on the West Side by 42nd Street, and another just ahead of the George Washington Bridge. We decide to take the FDR. It isn't any better. We're part of a parking lot by the time we make it under the Brooklyn Bridge. The radio then informs us that there is a "distressed person" on the Triborough Bridge, and the police effort to talk him down has shut down most of the Triborough, the traffic from which is spilling back onto the FDR.

"What a shit show," Dino says. "I wish the guy would quit dicking around and jump."

"Nice," Mac says. "The guy probably owns stock on margin. After today, I'm ready to get up there with him myself."

"At least you wouldn't tie up traffic. A trader wouldn't dawdle," Dino says. "It's fucking rush hour. How inconsiderate is that, to commit suicide right out in the open when everyone's trying to get home from work?"

"So, Barry," Mac calls into the back seat, changing subjects like a trader, "you spent a lot of time today locked up with Harvey. What were you guys doing, reminiscing about your golden Midwestern youth?"

"Something like that. Do you know he's bought a place on Guard Hill Road?"

"He actually find someone to marry him?" Dino asks. Dino was Harvey's support man, way back, before Dino got promoted to being a trader in a different department. "I suppose you government guys will insist we let him in the carpool. We'll have to be polite."

"Do you good," says Mac.

Dino, meanwhile, is executing a dick move. A dick move is any move that flaunts traffic laws, rules of the road, and/or common human decency in order to get to where you want to go more quickly. In this case, we scoot up the right shoulder, then cut left around a station wagon filled with shoulder-to-shoulder Hasidim, effectively covering in one minute what would have taken twenty. I slide down in my seat, lest someone behind us pull out a gun and start shooting.

"Not bad," Mac says. "Not bad at all."

An hour and fifteen minutes after we pulled out of the garage, we finally approach the Triborough. A police helicopter hovers overhead like a giant insect, while five police boats bob in the East River below. I look for the suicide case, but can't make him out. Maybe he's already in the water. We cut under the Triborough, pick up the rickety Willis Avenue Bridge, and then, finally free of Manhattan, scoot onto the Deegan, which, miraculously, is moving. No one mentions this—to do so would jinx it—and in the silence I have a chance to think about Gretchen.

"Why doesn't he call and ask me?" she said when I got her on the phone that afternoon.

"My guess is that he's nervous. Besides, he is going to call. I'm calling to give you the heads-up."

"Men," she said.

"Gretchen," I asked, "do you really have a son?"

"Uh-huh."

"You could have told me."

"You're obviously not involved."

"What's your son's name?"

"Buster."

"A good name," I said.

"Thanks."

"So—will you come to Court's party?"

"If he invites me."

"He will."

"So what are you, Barry," she said, "Court's pimp?"

I laughed. "Let's just say he pays me."

"Then I'll see you a week from Saturday," she said.

2. Making Economic Injustice Work for You

I wait two minutes—it feels like an hour—to pull onto Route 172 from the Park and Ride, so heavy is the traffic. I'm in evening mode now, shoes off and stocking feet on the cool of the pedals, an old Led Zeppelin cassette I made in high school blaring "Black Dog." It's funny the things you never lose.

I feel great. The air is still warm, soft as a tissue on the hand I stick out the window. A crescent moon hangs in a clear sky. I realize I haven't noticed the moon for months. My mood is lifting. Money—lots of it—seems within my reach, and I keep my hand out the window, as if I might catch a few bills on my way home. This is a different feeling from the one I had when I first came east. Back then, I was just tired of being poor.

In Colorado we lived in a prefabricated unit owned by the county and rented to us at a quarter of the market rate, and even then we struggled against eviction. The architect, if there'd been one, designed the place to have small windows and few electrical outlets, and so we lived in relative darkness, even though the home itself sat on a treeless plateau that saw three hundred days of sun a year. We couldn't afford drapes; Rachel covered the windows with old flannel sheets, held up with tacks and pulled back during the day and hooked around nails we pounded into the Sheetrock. She also hung a few small Mexican rugs on the walls, to liven up the place. Bizarrely, the developer had laid carpet the color of a manila envelope; by the time we moved in it was rusty from the red dirt of our street and parking space. We had no television. By day our bed served as the living-room couch; Sam had his toddler's bed in the one bedroom. Our luxuries were a washing machine, a radio, a view of Mount Daly to the south, and the many mornings I'd be sipping my morning coffee when the narrow view out the kitchen window would offer up the figure of an elk or a coyote sauntering by.

We might have been happy there—on many levels we were—but about us there were Land Rovers and private jets, eight-million-dollar homes, and five-hundred-dollar dinners, while we strained under the weight of the utility bills and the rent. I had no career, just a series of seasonal jobs that paid the bills until Sam came along. After that, things got tight. If something went wrong with the pickup or Sam needed to go to the doctor, it meant debt. The more time went on, the more Rachel and I argued about money. It wasn't that we started off mad at each other, but we got mad at the crushing meanness of poverty, the trite cliché of it: the baby needs shoes, there's no money for shoes. Soon, for lack of other targets, we aimed our anger at each other. It got so I couldn't talk to Rachel about money, because I couldn't take the crying. I'd put the bills in my jacket pocket, as if taking them out of the house could help me find the money to pay them. One day, walking to a bus stop in Aspen, I actually found a twenty-dollar bill on the street. I spent the next three months walking around with my head down.

Eventually, Rachel and I talked about leaving, but for a while we did nothing. We liked the mountains and the air, and we didn't want to be poor somewhere else. Then I read about Wall Street.

The way I looked at it, I'd never make money faster than I would on Wall Street, and that was a big appeal. And when I read about the trading floor, it reminded me of a locker room. I'd been in a lot of locker rooms, and I knew I could do well there. I realized even then that to think that was hubris. I knew that I understood nothing of what

I was getting into, but I also knew that I had to do something or stay poor forever. The Street seemed like the best opportunity we had.

And so, one day, I walked into the house and told Rachel I was ready to make the move. It was late spring. I could study for the GMAT, collect my college transcripts, shake up a few memories for recommendations, and go to work on the applications. By early next year I'd be accepted somewhere, and we'd make plans to move.

I found Rachel folding laundry. She was sitting on the floor in frayed bike tights and no socks, an old turtleneck with a fleece vest over it. Each folded piece of clothing she placed on the bed, which was a mattress with no frame or box springs. There were little piles of jeans, T-shirts, and shorts spread across the coverlet. I told her my plans.

"Do you really think you can go back to school? You're thirty years old. Is this going to work?"

"It'll work. I'm good at school."

"And then we're going to live in New York City?"

"Not the city. Outside it. We'll find a place. This isn't a permanent move. We're going to go, get a pot of gold, and come back. Six years, eight tops."

"And Sam? He'll just about be a teenager."

"And he'll have health insurance and a college fund. He's the main reason we need to go."

She stopped folding clothes, and sat with her back to the bed. I could tell she wanted to believe in health insurance and money for college. She just couldn't picture it.

"We'll get a house," I said, "with a yard for Sam to run around in and a bedroom for us to sleep in. There will be lighting and windows and trees out the windows. We'll have a fireplace. When the end of the month comes, we'll write checks without having to wonder if there's enough money in the account. When we go to the doctor, we'll have him send the bill to our insurance company. Cars—we'll get two of them, and neither one will have duct tape. You can look after Sam, get him off to school and home again, and I'll come home and we'll have dinner in our dining room and then lounge around in our living room. We'll go out to restaurants. It will feel like we have a huge weight off of our shoulders."

"I'd really like a house with a fireplace," she said.

"I'll get you one."

"Health insurance would be nice."

"We'll have it."

She crawled over to where I was sitting on the floor and whispered, "New clothes wouldn't be bad, either."

"Yours."

"And a new car. With seats for all of us."

"Sure."

"What kind?" she asked.

I wanted to tell her that she'd be able to get whatever she wanted, but I knew there would be limits. I didn't know what to say.

"I'll worry about the car," she said at last.

Now I'm driving my normal route home, downshifting as I make the McClain Road cutoff. I speed down to Route 117, cut past the Boston Market and Burger King and the Manufacturers Outlet Center, travel over the Metro North train tracks to Kisco Avenue and the Ford and Volvo dealerships, then turn up Croton Lake Road, where the squalidness of American retailing gives way to large homes, horse estates, and endless stone fences. I live in a little dead-end community tucked between the estates and New York City's Croton Reservoir. The homes in our neighborhood were originally built to house schoolteachers, small cottages on quarter-acre wooded lots. After driving past the mansions and stables, I can't help thinking of our neighborhood as the serf quarters.

I'm in a hurry to get home. Ever since we moved to New York, it has been the hour following my return home in the evening that I hold most dear. It's the one hour every day when I can sit with Rachel and the children and remember why it is that we made this move in the first place. The hour is filled with parental duties, of course, but spoon-feeding the baby and trying to impart some notion of table manners to Sam are chores from which I can glean value and enjoyment. I'm building a family, after all. In my business, a lot of guys talk about what's "important," meaning their families, though at year end, when it comes time to get your number, no manager ever brings up your family in discussing what kind of year you had. So most guys work or stay out late and experience family life between weekend golf games. I've been working hard, though I do come home almost every night, unless there is a business function. My weekends—that glorious time when there are no financial markets open anywhere—I give over to my family.

Tonight I pull into the drive and find that our Escort wagon isn't there. The house is dark. I stumble inside, grope for the light switch, and spot a note on the dining-room table. It instructs me to "meet us" at the Grill.

I smell surprise. The last time Rachel left a note on my birthday was for my thirtieth. We still lived in Colorado then. I'd been doing some late-season skiing and arrived home to find instructions to go to the Woody Creek Tavern, a spot of local legend down the road from Aspen. On that night I drank tequila to excess for the second and last time in my life, and I remember little else. The Grill is not Bedford's equivalent of the Woody Creek. Newly opened in a mini-mall on 117, wedged between a bagel store and a kosher butcher in one of those spots where restaurants go to die, the Grill is the third eatery to open there in as many years. On the ceiling is painted an Italian countryside, with stacks of wheat, wooden carts, wells, and farmhouses in the European style, all of it heavy on yellow tint. It's an elaborate effort, one that harks back to an older, simpler time, and the new owners don't dare change it.

Surprise it is. There at the big table in the center of the restaurant sit Rachel, Sam, Jane, plus my childhood buddy Dan Connelly and his wife, Amy, and Tim Traxler, who is Sam's best friend. It occurs to me that it's lucky that Dan and Amy live so close; Rachel and I haven't made many friends over the last three years. How could we? I'm always working or too exhausted to make the effort, and Rachel spends all of her time looking after the kids.

I take the open seat, between the baby and my buddy Dan. He'll turn thirty-five in May. I haven't seen him in several months, and, looking at him now, I realize that I haven't really looked at him in a lot longer than that. I often see him as the bright-eyed kid I met at thirteen. In the last twenty-two years he has aged in the typical ways:

there is a loss of hair and a gain of flesh. He hides his receding hairline by keeping his head shaved to a dark stubble. He wears baggy pants and a loose shirt, but when he turns his head I see the hint of a double chin. In the last year he's put on twenty pounds, at least. Of course, he's a salesman, and so for him eating and drinking are important career activities.

"Jesus," he says, "you're old."

"But still virile," I tell him.

"Market got killed today, huh?"

"Stocks did. Bonds were on fire."

Dan nods. He works in the software business. His main concern about the financial markets is that tech companies fetch outrageous prices, so that, if one of the little companies he always works for ever goes public, he can retire a "tycoon." "Tycoon" is one of his favorite words.

"I lost a deal today," says Amy, who sells real estate. "Wall Street buyer."

"What other kinds of buyers are there in Greenwich?" Dan says.

Rachel leans over, across the high chair. "Let's talk about something, anything, but Wall Street."

"Like sports?" Dan says.

The baby then earnestly begins to talk, saying "Da-dee, Da-dee," and waving a book about a steam engine named Chuffie, which I feel obliged to read to her. My mother, who raised me alone, was fanatical about reading, and now I find that I can never withhold books from my children, even Jane, who can't yet talk.

Later, Dan leans close to me and tells me that he thinks his company is about to get bought out.

"That's great, right?" I ask. "You've got a couple percent?"

"More like one percent, which is a crime, since I've been selling this product and it doesn't work. Who else could do that?"

"Only you, Dan. Only you." This is true. Dan is good. He has a smile and exudes a confidence that people accept with ease. He could have been a bond salesman or a politician, though selling software—a weightless and invisible product—is hardly a waste of his talents.

"When are we going to do something together?" he asks.

"Business-wise, you mean?"

"Yeah. You're still one of the smartest guys I know. We should be rich. Hell, I bet you're still paying off student loans."

I am.

"My point is, we're a couple of guys on the ball. There's no reason we can't be tycoons."

My life experience has led me to conclude that the relationship between wealth and brains is tenuous at best. I tell this to Dan.

"That's why you need me," he says. "Every smart Jew needs an Irish guy out front."

I chuckle. It isn't much of a business plan—there isn't even a business—but it's the model we've followed since high school.

"Seriously, Barry. How much longer are you going to work on the Street?"

"However long it takes."

"To do what?"

I look at him. It's a question with an obvious answer. "Get rich," I say.

"And then what?" he asks.

"Then I declare victory, move back to Colorado, and live like a rich guy."

"Do you really think you can win?"

"Hell, yes, I think I can win. Why else would I be here?" I say. I know how this sounds, but if there's one thing I've learned from working three years in the markets, it's that there is no room for doubt, even when you know better. When you make a trade—and our move to New York is a big trade—you must make it with the courage of your convictions. It's only normal to feel doubts, but, then, normal people don't tend to be rich or successful. It sounds funny to say, but you have to believe so hard that you create a favorable reality out of nothing more than your own will, as if you were a god. Which is how you feel when you're right. And if you're not, then you take your hit and convince yourself of your infallibility all over again for the next trade. In realizing this, I've often wished that faith came easier to me. God and myself—I have a bad habit of doubting both.

"You really believe the American-dream thing," Dan says in a voice both kidding and serious. "Didn't you read *Death of a Salesman*?"

"Yeah, I read it. It convinced me to be a trader. Traders don't have to be well liked."

"Barry, it never hurts to be well liked. It's just not enough. You've got to be in the right place. Let me say just one word."

"What?"

"Software."

"What about it?"

"It's where the money is. You want to 'win,' you're in the wrong business."

I glance over to the lobster tank, where Sam and Tim are pointing at the glass. "Hey, Dad," Sam yells, "come look at this!"

I walk over to the tank. Lobsters are bouncing off each other in pinball fashion. All of their claws are held shut by thick rubber bands, except for one. This lobster has a free left claw, and he's giving the others hell.

"Oh, jeez," says the waiter. He rolls up his sleeve but can't bring himself to stick his hand in the roiling tank. Instead, I stick my hand in and pull out the marauder by grabbing him on his body behind his claws, as I learned to do when I was a waiter. God, I've got some useless skills. The lobster is the color of an old penny. He bats at the air like a sparring heavyweight; he hasn't been long in captivity.

"Cool, Dad," says Sam.

By now the manager has arrived and he relieves me of the lobster. Later, midway through our entrées, the lobster reappears on our table, gratis, bright red on a platter decked out with romaine leaves and parsley and wedges of lemon.

We're waiting for dessert before Rachel and I lean over the high chair and have a few words. It's often like this. What with the two kids and my hours, we can go a full week without really talking.

"Having fun?" she asks, cocking one eyebrow at me, just the way Sam sometimes does.

"You bet."

"It's not the Woody Creek," she says. I stare at her smile. That smile was the first thing I noticed about her, a big, wide-mouthed smile that accentuates the brightness of her eyes and the highness of her cheekbones. It's those cheekbones that often make people ask if she has Indian blood, even though her hair is blondish with a hint of auburn, and she is more Irish than anything else.

"You did great," I tell her. "Maybe we could do my fortieth at the Woody Creek."

She raises her glass. "I'll drink to that," she says.

I think about our return west. It's something we often talk about, and even when we don't it lurks in the background of our lives. We moved to Philadelphia and New York like miners, intent on exploiting the opportunities and heading back on our own terms. While our friends upgrade their homes, join country clubs, and drive German cars, we live in a cramped house that went for a quarter of what Dino and Mac paid for their homes. We drive Ford Escorts, join nothing, save whatever we can. At the present time that is very little, but I'm moving into the sweet spot of my career. Keep going, I tell myself, just keep going. Things will come to me, I know they will. I just have to have some faith.

"Can you believe this guy?" I hear a voice say.

Dan's voice. Then a poking. Someone's poking me. What is this? And then I look up to see Sam and Tim laughing at me. In fact, everyone at the table is laughing at me, except the baby, who's just laughing.

"Nice, Dad," Sam says. "You fell asleep again."

And so I have, sitting up in my chair. Not that falling asleep is terribly unusual for me. I'm so run down that I've made dozing off an art form. I do it all the time, in the back of cars, watching TV, standing in the shower, or sitting on the can. I doze off in midday and sometimes in mid-sentence. I once found myself dozing on a quiet Friday afternoon, my belly filled with a broker lunch, when I was supposed to be trading. But, as yet, I've never fallen asleep in a dinner chair in front of my family and friends, on my birthday. Standing at my side are a waitress and two busboys, the former holding a birthday cake, candles burned away by half, wax all over the icing. I've hit a new low.

35

We travel Guard Hill Road every time Rachel and I go to the movie theater in Bedford, but it isn't until I'm looking for Court Harvey's house that I start to get a feel for the wealth in my midst. Perhaps it's the slow speed at which I'm driving that allows me to notice just how widely spaced are the driveways, or how many of these drives disappear into property so large that it offers no view of a building of any kind.

We cross a bridge that spans I-684, and then we pass a clock tower, which informs us we are ten minutes late. This seems about right. You don't want to be too punctual for an afternoon party, but you also don't want to be too late for your boss, and today I desperately want to get things right. At a party like this, I know there will be opportunities to advance my career, to become one of the boys. It's something I need to work at. It's always been easiest for me to be a loner.

I adjust my mirror to get a look at my kids, who are being far more subdued than I know them to be. Jane, in fact, has fallen asleep.

"So look, Rachel," I say, "I think it's best if we're mellow at this party." It's the first time we've been out to a Wall Street event. She has no idea what she's getting into.

"Mellow?" she asks.

"You know, these people, they're not like you. Most of them grew up around here, haven't really lived anywhere else. To them, this is the pinnacle of life, being part of a crowd going to an afternoon riding party on Guard Hill Road. Riding horses, drinking Bloody Marys, you know."

"So what are you saying?" She has her hair pulled back into a chignon, and she's wearing a string of fake pearls that we bought on the street in West Philadelphia. Perhaps this is a bit fancy for a riding party, but she looks elegant, really.

"Rachel, all I'm saying is that these are not people who have played country music in honky-tonks in the outer reaches of the Canadian north. If they've been on a horse, it's been around here, on some Thoroughbred. These are English-saddle people, you know?"

"Honestly, Barry, what do you think of me? That I'm going to get shit-faced and dance on the tables? Look at you. You're a few years from being a ski bum, and you have an estranged brother who's a heroin addict. How can you talk like you're a Rockefeller or something?"

"I'm just asking that you play your part. I'll play mine. I'm not saying it's not a part."

"You never were into playing parts before. That kind of phoniness used to drive you crazy."

She's right about this. Phoniness did drive me crazy, till I realized I could get paid to accept it. "There's money at stake now," I say. "And events like this are crucial. Time off the desk, that's where perceptions are made. You've got to sell yourself a little."

"Sell out, you mean."

"There's nothing to 'sell out,'" I say. "Just remember where you are."

"Okay, Barry. Just as long as you remember *who* you are."

Court Harvey has a mailbox with his name on it, so I don't miss the turn. The driveway is practically virgin asphalt, with granite stones fitted along the edge as a curb. We drive a quarter-mile through natural woods without a house in sight. Then we dip right and down, travel over a small stream, then around a berm, and the house comes into view.

"Whoa!" says Sam from the back seat.

Rachel chuckles.

Before us, set on an immense expanse of freshly cut lawn, stands a Tudor mansion not unlike the clubhouse of the country club where I caddied as a kid. Certainly Court Harvey's version is no smaller. I count four conical towers. Wings jut out from the center as if the building, large as it is, is trying to stretch. The many lead-paned windows reflect a hundred suns. There's one slate shingle missing from the thousands visible. I can see it high on the easternmost tower, subtle but noticeable, like the flaw purposely sewn into a Navajo rug.

"One guy lives here?" Rachel asks.

"Part-time," I answer.

I park between Chip McCarty's BMW and a new Mercedes sport-utility vehicle. The cars here are similar to the Teutonic models found at the firm's underground garage, except for a 1968 red Mustang convertible parked on the grass, its top down to show off its white leather interior.

A sandy-haired man with a droopy mustache answers the front door, introduces himself as "Matt, a friend of Court's," as if it is easy to believe that Court has friends. Matt leads us past an open-aired atrium around which the house is designed to a large room with a roaring fireplace at one end, a large bar at the other, and, as Rachel would say, a bunch of Wall Street weenies in the middle. We come first to Chip McCarty and Stevie Vollmer, who are standing together and sipping Bloody Marys with large stalks of celery sticking out of the top. Sam is already clamoring for a Coke, so Rachel takes him to the bar while I stay with my colleagues, my sleeping daughter on my shoulder.

"What do you think?" Mac asks.

" 'Bout what?"

"This," he says, waving a hand at the fireplace, the vaulted ceiling, the French doors that opened first to the swimming pool, then, farther out in the distance and down a hill, an expanse of woods.

"Amazing."

" 'You had a good year, Stevie,' " Vollmer says archly. Mac and I immediately know what he is doing: mimicking his bonus discussion. " 'And what's more important, we feel good not only about your year but about your future at the firm. So—your number is twelve cents. We worked very hard to get you to that number, because we feel so strongly about your future with the firm.' "

Trader humor, cut short by the approach of Court Harvey. He wears jeans, a black turtleneck, and, I can't help noticing, a pair of pointed cowboy boots that seem to exaggerate his limp in a way that tasseled loafers never do. Call it the cowboy-poet look. Soon he's leading me away from the group to a guest bedroom, where I lay Jane on top of a bed, surround her with several large pillows to keep her from rolling off, and cover her with a fleece blanket that Court has pulled from the closet.

"She's not here," he whispers, a little desperately.

"Who's not here?"

"Gretchen."

I look at my watch. "She's not even a half-hour late. That's customary."

"Everyone else is here."

"They work for you," I tell him.

He sighs.

"Court," I say, in an attempt to change the subject, "you've come a long way since Royal Oak."

"Yeah," he says dismissively, as if the move from a guy who never had five bucks to one who owns a multimillion-dollar home were no accomplishment at all. "How old is your daughter?" he asks.

"Not quite a year and a half."

"She's very cute."

These are words I never expected to hear from Court Harvey. I say nothing.

"You're lucky," he says. "My parents wanted to have lots of kids, but they only had me."

"You never know with such things." I can't come up with anything better. I'm nervous. I have the feeling he wants to unload on me, to tell me some inner truth that I do not want to know. Being one of the boys shouldn't be too personal. I suggest we leave the room, lest we wake Jane. We aren't three steps back into the party when Court asks me if I think everyone is happy.

I almost say no. On Wall Street, when people ask if you are "happy," they are referring to your pay. There is an earnestness in Court's expression, and I realize that he is using the word in its conventional sense.

"Happiness is relative," I tell him.

The room is more crowded now. I spot Tom Carlson with his wife and infant son. Carlson wears bright gold, green, and red triangles sewn together into a sweater, over which he has donned a harness in which his son is sleeping, the child's tiny legs splayed across his father's enormous gut. I don't know what to make of this, but it's quite an act.

Court excuses himself with a comment about his duties as a host, by which I'm sure he means he wants to go look for Gretchen. In my previous life, before my M.B.A., I would have spent the next hour standing off to the side of the room, waiting for someone to talk to me. I've always been shy, content to stand at the outer reaches of a party and observe the proceedings. I know now that this will not do. I must remake myself into someone quick on the uptake, cutting, cynical, funny, and thus worthy of inclusion.

I'm soon talking with Brian Zigfeld, Court's broker. Ziggy, as he's known, stands about five ten, and weighs maybe 220 pounds in a way that seems less fat than just wide. He has a low rumble of a voice, and if you didn't know better you'd peg him for an auto mechanic or a plumber. In fact, he's been covering traders at the firm for seventeen years. He picked up Court at the start of his career and still calls him "the Judge," a play on his name. Court yells at Ziggy all day long, but he also uses Ziggy more than any other broker. Thus, Ziggy owns a large home in Bronxville and drives a Lexus. The carpool often speculates on Ziggy's pay, with the low end of the range being three times what I make.

"It's good to be the king," he says to me. When I stare at him blankly, he explains that he is talking about the house. Court Harvey has done all right for himself. "I knew him when he used to go out with me so he could get a decent meal. Hell, so he could just plain eat."

"I knew him when he was in high school."

"Well, yeah. I forgot about that. You win on the history thing. Where's your family?"

I point to Rachel and Sam, who are standing together across the room. Sam is looking up and smiling at his mom, and I don't think you'd have to know them to recognize the love. I ask Ziggy about his kids.

"Mine? I wouldn't bring my little hoodlums here, with the damage they can cause."

"Seriously, where are they?"

"Seriously," Ziggy says, "they're with their mother at their grandparents' on Long Island, and I'm not kidding. I don't need my kids tearing up the Judge's new home. Business is tough enough."

"You're actually worried your kids could break something here and Court would cut you off?"

"Barry, I'm standing here now because I don't take chances, especially with Court."

"Court said the party was for kids, for families."

"It may be okay for you, being an employee and all. Me, though . . ." He shakes his head. "How'd you make out last year, anyway?"

He means my bonus.

"Don't depress me," I tell him. We've had talks like this before. In an odd way, I trust Ziggy as much as anyone I've met in the business. He started his working life as a junior conductor on the Long Island Railroad; then a friend of his uncle's got him a job as a broker. He's never been to college, and yet he makes in a year what the average American family makes in ten. He never expected these riches, nor does he feel he really deserves them, but he isn't going to turn them down, either. "Make economic injustice work for you," he once told me. He says I'm close to the big time, I just have to stay at it. When I ask him how he can be so sure, he says he's been in the business long enough to know who the winners will be. This endears me to him, though I find it little comfort, for his plan seems to rest on my staying in the business for however long it takes to prove him right. I don't want to lay siege to the riches of Wall Street. I want to make a frontal assault.

Twenty minutes later, I find myself walking with Rachel and Sam and most of the other guests out to the pool deck. The pool is filled with icy blue water, and I make a note of the danger this will pose for Jane. At the edge of the deck I can see a long, sloped lawn that descends to the stables, beyond which lies an open field, and then the woods that were visible from the house. I scan the area for some sign of where Court's property ends, but find none. I feel as if I've veered off a road in Bedford and ended up in the English countryside, not that I've ever been to the English countryside. While everyone walks down to the horses, I head back inside to check on Jane.

Is there a sweeter sight than your napping one-and-a-half-year-old daughter? She sleeps on her tummy, her knees pulled up and her little ankles crossed, the dimpled, clean soles of her shoes facing up. She lies completely on top of the fleece blanket I covered her with maybe forty minutes earlier, and snores softly. I work the blanket out from under her, as I do on at least one of the several trips I make nightly to her crib to make sure she is still breathing. The blanket is warm from her heat, and I cover her with it. I've recently had to admit to myself that I harbor a growing paranoia about the safety and well-being of my daughter. She's a bit old for sudden infant death syndrome, but the possibility of leukemia and the other childhood horrors rumbles often through my dreams, as do even worse fates, usually involving abduction and abuse too awful to recount here, not that I can't find examples of such crimes weekly in the *New York Times*. My son, too, figures in these nightmares, and some nights, after checking on Jane, I stand at Sam's door and watch him sleep beneath his Dan Marino poster. Even after a tough day of fending off his nasty moods and hounding him to finish his homework and clean up his room—after all the daily, numbing chores of parenthood—I stand there and tears well in my eyes just to think of his innocence.

It's with such thoughts in my mind that I enter the main hall, as I've come to think of the large room that houses the party, and find Gretchen Barnes and her son, Buster. Gretchen wears jeans, a black blazer, a white turtleneck, and a grace that comes, I suppose, from knowing that you always look great.

Buster looks like the kind of kid you'd love till you actually had to raise him, with all the reining in of energy that would entail. He's a stocky kid with dark hair and green eyes. Buster's cheeks are ruddy from constant exertion. He moves back and forth from foot to foot and keeps opening and closing his right hand, as if he wants to grab or throw something. I have the urge to send him on a lap around the hall, before he bursts.

"Thank God," Gretchen says when she sees me. "We let ourselves in. Where is everyone?"

"Down at the stables," I hear myself say. It sounds pretentious as hell, but she wants to head down there, as Buster is eager to ride a horse, something at which Gretchen insists he's quite good. I wonder how this could be, given his upbringing in Manhattan. It's then that Buster and I are formally introduced. He shakes my hand and looks me in the eye, in the way that I always try to teach Sam.

They head to the stables and I to the bar, where I order a Virgin Mary, as I don't feel like drinking and this drink will make it seem to others as if I am. Not drinking at a desk event is highly suspicious behavior, more damning to one's career in many ways than losing money trading.

Several minutes later, Gretchen appears carrying a drink that could be a vodka tonic or a mineral water. She and I stand off in a back corner, not far from the hallway that leads to the room where Jane is napping. I want to be able to hear her when she wakes.

"So, Gretchen," I say, "how is it that I didn't know about Buster until last week?"

She shrugs. "I don't really tell people at work."

"Court knew."

"We run into him on the Upper West Side from time to time. He lives by us."

"But, Gretchen, having a child? I'd have thought—"

"Look, it's not like I was thinking, 'Hey, I've got to keep this secret from Barry.' "

"So tell me now."

"What's to tell? I got pregnant, I decided to keep the baby."

"You could have told me," I say.

"I could have, and I would have, if it had ever come up. Don't feel bad. I didn't tell many people."

She looks at me for a comment, but I don't know what to think. She's always had a self-possession that made me feel weak and unsure of myself. Even in college, when most of us had no idea what to become, Gretchen knew exactly what she wanted: Wall Street. Many at Dartmouth considered such a desire crass and base, but this seemed to me a double standard. Those who said they wanted to be painters or go into the theater were respected for their artistic ambitions, even if they never painted or even went to a play. Social work and teaching were considered noble, as were most career choices that allowed one to avoid anything that smacked of economic competition.

Gretchen was all action. She went about getting a job with the determination you might have expected from a middle-aged man with a wife and children to support. She spent hours studying the companies and preparing for interviews. She called alumni for advice. Her junior summer, she worked for Manufacturers Hanover. (Secretly I wanted to do what Gretchen was doing, but, like many of my classmates, I feared failure.) This was at the start of the Reagan bull market, and around the country there was fierce competition for Wall Street. When my classmates started getting rejection letters from the banks and posting them up on the walls outside their dorm rooms—an odd, public display of failure that, I learned, no true Wall Streeter would ever consider—Gretchen received callback interview after callback interview, and, eventually, a number of job offers. I took my backpack and went to Europe.

So I'm not surprised that, if Gretchen wanted a child, she has one. It's just odd that, with her ambition, she wanted one. Even now, it seems so impractical.

"I need to talk to you," Court says. At work this line means you are being called into the office. I feel a shiver ripple up my spine. I am sipping my third Virgin Mary in the main hall, wondering if there's something addictive in spiced tomato juice. Buster and Sam are back from riding, and are now running around on Court's great expanse of lawn. Across the room I can see Jane cruising the party with Rachel following.

I follow Court to a small library office. The walls are lined with built-in walnut bookshelves, themselves lined, surprisingly, with books. I spot a leather-bound version of the Harvard Classics, and another shelf with classics of twentieth-century American literature (*The Great Gatsby, For Whom the Bell Tolls, The Sound and the Fury*) dressed up in replicas of their original dust jackets. There's an art-book section, and another dedicated to economic standbys like *The General Theory* and *The Wealth of Nations.* On the upper shelves sit recently published hardcover fiction, the spines shiny and pristine. Finally, high and to the side I spy a picture of Court playing football for Michigan, his body midair and prone, catching a pass in front of an Ohio State defender.

Court sits behind a large antique campaign desk, and I take up position in the supplicant's chair.

"Your wife is quite accomplished on a horse," he says.

"She says the same about you."

"She's very charming. You're lucky to have her."

"She says that, too."

He sighs. "Things are about to change for you, Barry."

I nod.

"You're coming into your own. You're going to get opportunities."

I assume he is talking about the trading floor, but the first thing on his mind is a limited partnership. It's something the firm put together, a special investment opportunity for those with vice-president rank or above, and twenty-five thousand dollars. I have neither, though I only point out that I'm not a VP.

"You are now," he says.

I smile. I'm sure I now hold the distinction of being the poorest VP at the firm, which, I must admit, is better than not being a VP at all.

"Buster and your son seem to be hitting it off," he says. "They had a great time riding. We should do it again, without the crowd."

"I'd take it up with their mothers."

"Is Rachel enjoying herself?"

"She's loving it."

"And Gretchen? I saw you guys talking."

"Ask her."

He looks away for several seconds before he speaks again. "You have a rapport with people, Barry. You can talk to them. They like you."

I almost laugh. Rapport with people? Only in comparison with an iceman like Court Harvey. Rachel once said that I speak as if I were being charged by the word. I've long been aware that I am no natural at talking. I spent my formative years trying to achieve some glibness, revising conversations in my head that had taken place earlier, coming up with the right responses, but I still find it difficult to get the words right in real time.

Court talks on. He speaks of his position and the effect it has on his personal life. People in the business only see him as the head of worldwide government trading, he says, and he doesn't know anyone who isn't in the business.

"I have no other life," he admits.

"It's what you've chosen," I tell him. I wave my hand at the office and the house in general. "And it's treated you pretty well."

"I've always wanted a family, a wife and kids. These are the important things."

I nod. I've seen managers give family a lot of lip service on the Street, and then screw guys at bonus time for leaving early (after only eleven or twelve hours) to go home to their kids. I'm not going to fall for that here.

"Look, Barry," he says, "I need someone I can talk to about these things. I'd like to be able to go to you, as a friend."

"Sure," I reply. I can hardly say no. Okay, I tell myself. I can handle this. A social relationship with Court Harvey can only be good for my career.

"I know we're not that close now," he says, "but we come from similar beginnings. And I admire what you've done with your personal life. A lovely wife, two kids. I wish I'd done it like you're doing it. You're a family man, and I really admire that."

"Every guy on the desk but you has a family," I remind him.

"Yeah, Barry," he says. "But you're the one guy who really means it."

3. Whatever Hurts You the Most

The next morning, I take the kids into Mount Kisco for fresh bagels and some time out of the house. Rachel is still asleep when we return, so I hustle Sam and Jane out to the back deck. I sit in an Adirondack chair, my head still cloudy with fatigue, and my legs so heavy that they feel as if they've melted into the chair. Saturdays I run on the thrill of the weekend, but "clinical exhaustion" must be the term for what I feel on Sunday mornings. Sam heads down to the play set in the yard; Jane scoots around the deck in her plastic car. My eye is then drawn to the movements of a red-bellied woodpecker as it works the upper reaches of the beech tree to my left. Sunlight flickers through the leaves. It's warm, the sky cloudless, the humidity low enough to make it a deep, solid blue. It's a startlingly clear and pleasant day, one of the five or six we get every year.

On the arm of my chair I have the Sunday *New York Times,* a cup of coffee, and the portable phone, so I won't have to move if it rings. It does. I answer.

"Barry," says a voice.

"Speaking."

"How is the market?"

On Sunday? "Who is this?" I ask.

"It's Ben."

My heart skips. My brother.

"How did you find me?" I realize I'm standing.

"Wasn't hard. You're in the phone book."

"What do you want?" I ask.

"Barry, it's been what, eight years?"

"Five," I say.

"Five. We haven't spoken in five years, and all you can say is, 'What do you want?' "

He always had a way of working his voice, my brother, till he could make you feel whatever he wanted you to feel. This was how he was able to rip off my mother so many times. Again and again he betrayed her trust, knowing that she couldn't turn him down.

"You've got a reputation, you know," I say, wanting to believe that he won't ask me for money and knowing that he will.

"Six hundred bucks," he answers. "American."

"Ben," I answer. I wonder how long we have been on the phone. Thirty seconds? It's as if those five years haven't passed.

"Six hundred bucks, little brother, or some guys are going to break my legs."

"That's a lot of money."

"Come off it. I hear you're a big Wall Street guy now. I must say, I have a hard time picturing it. But, hey, shit happens. I know six hundred bucks is a lot of money, but I know you got it somewhere. And I'm in need. This is serious, Barry. I'm over fifty now. I can't go through this again."

"Through what again?"

"Getting my fucking legs broken. Man, you know what that is like? Till you pass out, the pain, well, you got no idea about the pain. I already got a metal plate and two screws in my leg. They use wood bats, you know, so it makes that sound, that wood-bat sound."

It's obvious to me that he's lying, that he's probably using a line from some shlocky Canadian television show. He's employed the mob before, and it has worked on my mother. I know of four separate occasions when she has given him money. I figure there must be more.

"Is that a baby I hear?" my brother asks.

"Ben," I say to change the subject, "if you're telling me the truth, how could you let this happen again? You know these guys are going to come after you."

He lets out a deep sigh and starts talking in his older-brother voice. "You've got such a normal life, Barry, you wouldn't understand. You don't know how lucky you are. I wanted a life like that, I really did. Maybe if I'd been born in the sixties and missed the war, like you. You had good timing, little brother. You got to admit that."

I admit it. Missing Vietnam *was* a stroke of good luck, not that anyone of my generation ever thinks about it.

"How's Mom?" he asks.

"Don't call her." After she's heard from him, she doesn't sleep for days. He's driven her to the point of insanity, and more than once.

"That's a helluva thing to say, telling me I can't call my own mother."

"Ben, just don't call her."

"You haven't said yes. Where else can I turn?"

"I'll give you the money," I say, "if you promise not to call Mom."

He's in Vancouver, and he has the Western Union instructions ready. I take them down, call, and send the money. They take my credit card. I figure my mother has paid enough.

Monday, six-fifty in the morning. We are slowed in traffic by the sewage-treatment plant on the West Side Highway. I look down to the river, where the remnants of piers rot in the inky water. I can never look at those tangles of old metal without thinking of war or some equally destructive force. Like time, I suppose. Meanwhile, the markets are still swooning. European stock exchanges are trading as if the Germans have again crossed the border into Poland. Financial panic is back, unabated by the weekend's respite. Our company stock will open today at half the price it fetched in January. This gets a mention on Bloomberg Radio.

"Great," says Mac. "Now even Bloomberg is dirting us."

"How 'bout this?" says Dino, his nose in the *Journal.* "What percentage of American households have net worths of more than a million dollars?"

"Net worth?" asks Mac. "Home equity, retirement accounts, annuities, everything?"

"Everything."

"Should I subtract out what certain people owe for commuting? Because I think you might make it, otherwise."

"Eat me," Dino says.

"Twenty-nine percent," Mac guesses.

I chuckle, because Mac is dead serious. To him, a million dollars isn't anything special. Every person he thinks about has that much, so he figures that almost a third of the families in America do.

"C'mon," Dino says.

"Forty percent?"

"Four percent. Chip, you live a secluded, deluded existence."

Mac shrugs his shoulders. "Yeah," he says, "but I'm good at it."

Soon I can hear the pounding of a machine sinking posts. We are stuck in traffic again, in what is becoming a routine part of our morning commute. I look up as Mac finally makes the right onto the side street that leads to our building. A construction worker suddenly appears in front of our car, his hand out in the universal signal to stop. Mac slams on the brakes.

"Fuck," says Dino, bracing his hand on the dashboard. "Watch it."

"What are you worried about?" says Mac. "You got an airbag."

A crane swings a huge metal strut past the front of Mac's BMW, then lifts it ten stories to three construction workers who stand atop the construction site. We all stretch our necks forward to watch.

"I can see the headline in the *Post,*" Dino says, " 'TRIPLE SQUISHING HOUR!! Three Traders Crushed on Their Way to Work!' "

"Have their best day of the year," adds Mac.

Mondays are always a busy day for bill traders, and today it's busier still, because of the panic and yet another tsunami of cash crashing down on the bill market. Nonetheless, I can't concentrate. I keep thinking about my brother, keep having conflicting impulses. It scares me to have him back in my life, even from a distance. At the same time, I want to see him. This is nothing new. I've never really been sure what to think about him. He's a lot older than I am, older than what most people think of as brotherly, and we don't have the same father. In fact, Ben doesn't even know who his father is. My mother served in World War II as a field nurse. She arrived in Europe a month after D-Day, and followed the front lines almost the whole way to Berlin, till she conceived my brother and the army sent her back to Detroit. Ben was born in May of the following year.

It couldn't have been easy to raise a young son as a single mother in the late forties. My mother did it, deflecting the raised eyebrows and whispers and general untouchableness of her position with a wall of silence that she never let down. Fifty years later, when it can't matter to anyone but me, she still refuses to speak of it.

My father came along when Ben was ten and already causing my mother to cry herself to sleep. Ben skipped class (in the fifth grade), threw eggs at passing cars, shoplifted candy. My father was freshly back from the army and Korea. He was certain that all Ben needed was what the boy had never had: a man in the house.

"I thought he was crazy," my mother once told me. "I was five years older than he was, and I had a son. But he was so certain, and optimistic, and that's contagious. I wanted to believe him when he told me everything would be all right. And, before your father, only the real rejects would go out with me. Or sons of my parents' friends, who pitied me, and I was tired of being pitied. Your father was really a wonderful man. Warm. And, before everything started to beat him down, he was a funny man. He used to make me laugh so hard I couldn't breathe."

Ben beat him down. There was a count of grand theft auto. Burglary. Shoplifting. And yet, at times, Ben showed so much promise. He pulled A's on most of his tests, and thus was constantly under suspicion for cheating, the only evidence against him being that he hadn't been to class. He started on the high-school baseball team as a sophomore, the only one of his class to make the team. That was the year I was born, Ben's last year at school.

"That last year," my mother said, "broke your father, because things finally seemed to be turning around. Ben was going to class, and he had friends. Well, he always had friends, people loved him. But he had friends from the ball team, good kids, and he seemed happy. And then you came along. Your father and I had been trying to have a baby for so long, and it never happened, and we just gave up. And then, *voilà,* for the first six months of that year, we couldn't have been happier."

Then, in June, Ben helped himself to our neighbor's Chevrolet. Ben always said he was just borrowing it, and the neighbor, a bachelor mechanic who often had let Ben work on the car, had told Ben he could borrow it, just not at the time that Ben took him up on it. They caught Ben crossing back into the U.S. from Canada. He was drunk. The authorities were not amused. He spent three months in a juvenile-detention center.

"We lost him after that," my mother said. Twice more that year, my father bailed him out of minor police trouble. The next year, near as I could tell, Ben discovered his preferred crime: forgery. My parents were his first mark. He cleaned them out of four thousand dollars. "Almost all the money we had saved," my mother said. "That was when your father took out the life insurance. A twenty-five-thousand-dollar policy.

"Your father, he was crushed, just crushed. He worked so hard for that four thousand dollars, and he had a plan and a schedule, and he just couldn't believe it was gone and that Ben—*Ben*—had taken it. He felt like he failed. He really took it personally."

My father worked for a small steel concern, peddling their products to the auto companies. His work took him to various plants across the southern part of the state, and, one night about six months after Ben had cleaned him out, he hit a telephone pole on Route 15, southeast of Flint. The police estimated he was driving seventy-five when it happened. The autopsy showed that he was drunk. There were no skid marks in front of the pole, and the police concluded that he had passed out or fallen asleep at the wheel. An accident.

The insurance company was not so sure. Perhaps being asked to pay off on a new policy made them suspicious. My mother had to hire a lawyer to get them to pay.

"I needed the money," she said, "but I thought they were probably right. Your father didn't drink, and he was supposed to be home that night. I think maybe he knew what he was doing."

I was less than a year old when he died. In later years, I've driven myself down the highway and thought of swerving off into a pole, or into oncoming traffic, but this is common. Who doesn't occasionally feel the urge to jump when standing on the edge of a cliff? I know I have. But actually to do it, to take that last, irrevocable step—I've never really been able to fathom it. Almost everything in life is, to some extent, recoverable, and thank God for that.

For all the turmoil surrounding stocks, only Monday turns out to be a busy day in the bond market. I suppose markets, like people, can get used to anything. By Thursday, after the futures close, it feels as though we've hit the summer doldrums of July and early August. I'm marking my book when Dan Connelly calls.

"You thought about what we talked about?" he asks.

"The garage band?"

"I'm serious," he says. "Can you talk?"

A legitimate question. Often I can't, though now I can.

"I've got to get out of this place," he says. "We've got this piece of software that should be God's gift to sales-force automation, except that we can't get the bugs out, the guys running the company are complete idiots, and I'm not sure there's enough cash left for the next payroll."

"So leave," I say.

"I want to. I just don't want to end up in this situation again, working for idiots who run my future into the ground. I was thinking you and I, together, might make something happen."

I tell him that we've had this conversation before, and that it's silly for him to think that I can save him. He is, after all, asking me to go into a business I know nothing about.

"I just need to do something, Barry. It's funny, but I can't figure out what happened to my career. One minute I think I'm on my way to tycoon-hood, and the next I've got a piece of a company that's going under water."

"Dan," I say, "you know you'll land on your feet. You can sell anything. There will always be hundreds of companies that want you."

"I'm thirty-five, and I'm nowhere," he says. "Think of Bill Gates at thirty-five."

"A lotta luck there. It's a crappy comparison. Fuck Bill Gates."

"Still . . ."

It's odd to hear him whine like this; he's a salesman, and thus usually an optimist, but now he even asks if I think he could get a job slinging bonds.

"I thought software was the place to be."

"Last month," he says. "I could sell bonds."

I tell him the truth: without an M.B.A., it would be hard to get him an interview. Still, I'd try if he really wanted it.

"Naw," he says, "I'm not that desperate. Yet."

Early the next morning, Court Harvey calls me into his office. I hate going into Court's office, but I walk in dutifully and take a seat. I realize I can still hear that machine sinking posts. Court and I haven't really spoken since the party.

"So," he asks, "how was your Sunday?"

It's Thursday. "Last Sunday?" I ask. I took Sam for some batting practice in the afternoon, then worked around the house. "About average, I'd say."

"I had Gretchen and Buster back out to the house. I almost called you."

I raise my eyebrows. Inside, I feel bothered that he feels it necessary to tell me this. Looking at Court from a slight angle, it seems as if his eyes have moved closer together, and slightly off-center. I imagine them wandering around his head, like a halibut's. I can't help wondering what it is about him that is so easy to dislike.

"I didn't want to bother you," he says.

I'm literally feeling hot under the collar. I give it a tug. Thinking of Gretchen alone at Court's house makes me squirm. "How was it?" I ask.

"Good," he says.

A long silence passes, and I realize that Court Harvey is even more pathetic at making small talk than I. The posthole machine ticks off the time like a metronome.

"Barry," he says at last, "I'm thinking of moving you to tens."

I bolt upright in my seat. I hadn't expected this. Tens! The ten-year seat is one of the most prestigious on the desk. High profile and high pay. Only the most senior traders trade ten-year notes. I've never heard of anyone making a jump from bills to tens. It's like going from water commissioner to the presidency.

"What about Colin Dancer?" I ask. Colin has been trading ten-year notes so long that many of the issues he once traded have already matured. He's an old timer, an ex–Syracuse football player, and he played high-school lacrosse with Ryan Hauptman, who now runs mortgage trading. When Court first came to the firm, he was Colin Dancer's assistant. Now Court is the boss. They sit some six inches apart on the desk, and it's common knowledge that for the past dozen years they've hated each other. Colin is the only guy on the desk who will tell Court to fuck off to his face. They get into public shouting matches from time to time. It's bold and, I think, stupid to confront Court, given that Court decides Colin's pay, which is assumed to be more than a million dollars a year. Maybe Colin figures Court will fuck him anyway—if that's what you can call making a million bucks a year.

"Colin?" Court says with a sigh. "He's done."

"Done? Colin's done?"

"We're going to talk tomorrow afternoon, and that will be that. It's not easy, you know. I used to work for Colin. He's never been able to get over that. It's been more than ten years, and it's still an issue. Well, we're ready for new blood, and you're it. Colin had a good run. He's got nothing to complain about."

I think Colin might complain, but I don't say so. "When will I start?" I ask.

"About a week or so. We'll let things blow over, and finalize a choice for bills. In the meantime, tell no one."

Bill traders make next to nothing for their firms, and next to nothing for themselves. The ten-year note, on the other hand, is the big time. I must be smiling, because Court says, "I told you things would be changing for you."

I walk back out to the floor, and pass Colin Dancer's desk on the way to my seat. He's hunched over in front of his screen, the fabric of his dress shirt stretched taut across his massive back. On his head there is a fitted Yankees cap, size 7¾, worn inside out and backward. This is his rally cap, which he puts on whenever he is long the market. Such are the antics to which government traders resort. I've always envied Colin for his position and pay, and for his luck, but now, knowing what I know, I feel a twinge of something I never before felt on the trading floor: pity.

About two that afternoon, a prospective recruit comes by, led in by Kathy Bradley. Kathy is one of five recruiters that the firm employs to cull through the mountain of résumés received from business-school classes and pick out talent that might make it on the trading floor. Once an M.B.A. has gotten his résumé noticed, he can expect to be interviewed on campus. If he passes that test, the firm will bring him to New York for the third degree on the trading floor. We are supposed to assess whether or not the kid will "fit." Wall Street firms chew up recruits from the business schools like so much hamburger meat. We actually call the new recruits Meat, after the minor-league pitcher in the movie *Bull Durham.*

This meat is from Harvard. The firm has flown him into town. Tonight someone will take him out to a fancy dinner, put him up in a nice hotel, and ship him back to Boston on the morning shuttle. All he has to do for this preferred treatment is to act interested and try to "fit." I remember the ache of this, of trying to smile at the right time, to be one of the boys, and of making sure not to smile at the wrong time, lest I not be taken seriously. So much seemed to ride on those dinners or few seconds spoken at some trader's shoulder, while he watched the screens and shouted obscenities at his brokers.

Today's meat is named Doug Cramer, and he "sits" with me first, which means that he must perch himself on a folding chair at my back and impress me while I try to make money in the markets. This won't be easy, because Doug Cramer is six foot four, broad, with close-cropped red hair, and that little folding chair makes him look ridiculous.

I check his résumé. He played football at the Naval Academy, then served five years in a nuclear submarine. He was a linebacker and a nuclear engineer. He has a master's degree in statistics, and scored in the 98th percentile on his GMATs. In eight short months, he founded a charity for abused children in Cambridge that has raised over two hundred thousand dollars. The year he went to the Naval Academy, the Texas Rangers drafted him in the ninth round. He speaks fluent Russian. He is, in short, your typical recruit. I go after him immediately.

"'Active participant in biking, golf, skiing, and sailing,'" I read from the last line of his résumé. "Tell me about your skiing. How many days did you ski last year?"

"About five."

"Five? You call that active?"

"Well."

"I had a dozen years during which I never skied less than a hundred. One year I hit one fifty."

He says nothing. I look back over my shoulder at him.

"You want to tell me about your biking?" I ask.

"I'd rather not," he says.

"What about this GMAT score? Seven hundred. Is that good?"

"It's the ninety-eighth percentile."

"Sure, for the nation. But, Doug, let me ask you something. What percentile do you think it is for traders here at the firm? In fact, let me speak frankly. For white guys trading on the Street, what percentile is it?"

"I . . . I don't know."

"Probably about, say, the sixtieth percentile. Just about everyone's over six fifty. So seven hundred is no big deal. And I thought Harvard doesn't consider GMATs. Why put it on?"

"I'm taking it off," he says.

He's doing well. He isn't defensive. Admits mistakes. Doesn't grovel.

"So," I ask, "what does the long bond yield, ballpark?" The "long bond" is the treasury's thirty-year benchmark issue, the issue Stevie Vollmer trades.

"About four eighty."

"How 'bout the two-year note?"

"About three ninety."

These answers are very close. The questions are simple, but I never cease to be surprised by the number of M.B.A.'s who come in looking for jobs, professing desire and interest, and yet have no idea where the market is. None. You'd think they'd at least check the paper.

"Okay," I say. "You pass. Turn your chair around and sit with Chip McCarty. He's a navy guy."

Mac hates sitting with recruits, probably because he doesn't have an M.B.A. or master's in statistics and he views everyone and everything as a threat. On the trading floor, this kind of paranoia is common and well founded: someone *is* always after your job. Mac will make small exceptions for navy guys. He must like Doug Cramer (or maybe he's just having a good day), because soon I hear him explaining to Doug the Chip McCarty Theory of Market Movement.

"At any given moment," Mac says, "the market will move in the direction that will hurt the most people. Probably you will have the same position as everyone else. That's how you can usually know what will happen next. Look at your position and figure out what hurts you the most."

Derivatives sit one row away from us, and after the three o'clock futures close, I wander over to chat with my buddy Stuart Konig. Stu trades interest-rate swaps. He and I go back to Wharton, where we met the first week of school at a Wharton Kids Club meeting. Before Wharton Stu was a Marine intelligence officer, and then a drug salesman, and he has grand schemes. For instance, he told me he wants to make a million dollars a year by his fourth year in the business. Well, we've started our fourth year, and I'm making less than a fifth of that. Stu is doing a little better.

"Big news," I say.

"What?" he asks. He's surfing the Web, a site devoted to Led Zeppelin. He closes the page and his spreadsheet of live, flickering bond yields and swap spreads comes to the fore.

"I could tell you, but I'd have to kill you."

He chuckles. He was stationed in Beirut after the U.S. Embassy was bombed. He is dark-skinned and swarthy, and he learned to speak fluent Arabic from his mother, and I doubt that these qualities were incidental to the Marines' sending him there. Stu and I are tight, but he'll never tell me anything about what he did in the Marines. Any secret I keep from him is a way of evening the score.

"You doing anything tonight?" he asks.

"Naw. You?"

"I haven't been out in ages," he says.

"Broker dinner?" I ask. Going out to dinner in New York is ridiculously expensive. Whenever we feel like a nice meal, we bring along a bond broker to pay for it.

"Why not?" he says.

"My guy, or yours?"

"You get one. I haven't been doing shit in the screens."

"Where do you want to go?"

"Sparks."

"I'll try," I say. Sparks is a steak restaurant loved by the Street and the mob. I've been three times, but could never figure out who was who.

I go back to my desk and call Rachel to tell her I won't be home till late. Then I hit my wire to Lance Bailey, one of my brokers, and tell him what he's doing for dinner.

At five-thirty, I'm standing outside our building in the fading light of early evening. I'm waiting for Stu to come down, and for the Lincoln Town Car ordered for us by Lance Bailey. In front of me traders and bankers are jostling along the curve. For each passing taxi a dozen arms rise, like buyers in a futures pit. If the cabbies could triple their rates at this time of day, guys would still pay it.

"Come here often?" asks a voice.

I turn. It's Gretchen, her eyes wide in the dim light, a smile of what I take as pleasant surprise on her face.

"Way too often," I say.

"Client dinner?"

"Broker dinner. You want to come? We'd love to have you."

"You want me to watch traders eat? I'll pass. But we should do something. We don't have to be such strangers."

"Sure," I say, as I always do to friends who make similar suggestions, knowing that we're all busy and tired and unlikely to make the time.

"I'm sorry I never told you about Buster," she says. "I should have said something."

"Don't worry about it," I tell her.

"Not here yet?" Stu asks, surprising me. He means the broker car. He introduces himself to Gretchen before I get a chance to do it myself.

"I've got to get going," Gretchen says to me. "Call me."

Stuart and I watch her walk away, and I have a memory of standing just like this in college, watching Gretchen take leave of me and feeling then, as I do now, a little wistful about it.

"Man," Stu says, "how do they ever get anything done in equities?"

Later, stuck in traffic on the FDR, I find myself thinking about my brother, remembering how he used to come around and talk with my mother. I was not allowed to listen to these conversations, but when they ended Ben would play catch with me or take me out for a root beer. It wasn't long till I idolized him. He always had some kind of older car that he'd worked on and turned into a prize possession, the kind of car that people stopped to look at, asking what was under the hood. He smoked cigarettes and was rail thin, but he moved with the supple grace of an athlete. He had an effect on people. As my mother said, he did not want for friends. He was, for me, the very definition of cool. Whenever he took me out, I'd hope that we'd run into one of my friends. I wanted to be seen with him.

All I Could Get

One day I spotted him when I walked out of school. He had a black Monte Carlo, and he let me ride in the front seat (our mother never would have allowed that), from where I could wave to my friends as we pulled out. We drove first to the apartment where my mother and I lived. I dropped my books at the door and got my savings passbook, as Ben instructed. We didn't have much time, he said; we had to do a few things and get me home before my mother arrived home from work. I knew not to question him. We were on a mission together, and I couldn't have been more thrilled. First we drove to the bank, where Ben gave me twenty-five dollars to put into my account. It was my college account. My mother had been saving money in my name for college, and the account had over three hundred dollars in it. Anytime a buck floated into my possession—a holiday gift, a bill found on the sidewalk, money made working in the neighborhood—my mother made me put it in that account.

Ben then drove south, to the Detroit River. It had been a few years since the race riots, but going into Detroit City proper carried with it, at least for me, a feeling of danger. Ben found a place to park by the water. We got out, leaned against the car. There was an organic odor to the waterfront, a dank smell of rotting wood and dying river life. I could hear water sloshing against the retaining wall in front of us. I lifted my gaze, so that I could take in Windsor, across the river, in Canada.

"I need you to do something for me," my brother said.

I was eight years old. He knew I'd do anything for him.

"Give this letter to Mom," he said, "but not until Friday." It was Tuesday. "And don't tell Mom you saw me."

He lit a cigarette and nodded toward Windsor, without saying anything.

We got back in the car and drove up to Oak Park. We stopped at the apartment, and I didn't want to get out of the car. I didn't want him to leave me, and I told him so.

"You can't understand, little bro. But trust me, there's no other way. Remember, wait three days to give Mom the letter, and don't tell her you saw me till then. Can you do that?"

The letter contained three words: "Gone to Canada." When my

savings account statement arrived at the end of the month, my mother was hardly surprised to find just twenty-five dollars in the account. "It would be best," she told me, "if you never thought about him again."

"Hey, you awake over there?" Stu asks.

I'm leaning my head back against the leather seat. I give him a brief rundown of my brother's reappearance in my life.

"I don't know," he says. "He found out you have money, so now he's back in contact. That's tough. It's hard to tell your brother to fuck off."

"What can I do?"

He thinks for a moment.

"You know, six hundred bucks, it's a pathetic amount to ask for. I mean, if he had any clue, he'd know you had a lot more than that. Think about it. It's weird, really. He finds you after all this time, and then asks for next to nothing."

"Maybe he only needed six hundred."

"Probably three hundred. But if he'd needed five thousand, what would you have done?"

"I don't have it. I just paid off some business-school loans. I'm trying to get through to bonus time."

"Whatever. My point is that you can probably afford to keep paying him. Just make sure you piss and moan a lot. Manage his expectations. Make him thankful. You don't want him to think it's easy for you."

We are hardly moving, stuck on the FDR because we couldn't get into Sparks. Bailey then struck out at Nobu, but, staying on the seafood theme, got us into a restaurant called Oceana. This means we have to fight our way to midtown on the East Side. I look out the window. There is a high-school baseball game being played on one of the fields that are squeezed between the highway and the East River. I watch as a pitcher winds up and throws, and the batter fouls the ball into the backstop. It's now so dark it's a miracle the batter can see the ball at all.

All I Could Get

"We support Sheila's sister, you know," Stu tells me. Sheila is his wife. "Real white trailer trash. I know this because we bought her the trailer." He chuckles.

"I didn't know Sheila had a sister."

"Families, you know. You make the money; they'll spend it."

4. Monkeys Can Think!

"'In a recent survey of seventy-eight animated films,'" Mac reads from the *Times,* "'sixty-seven characters smoked cigarettes or drank alcohol.'"

Dino swerves around a minivan, our tires squealing, as we approach the tolls on the Henry Hudson Bridge, heading in. Dino drives with trader mentality, always going as hard as possible, even when we're plenty early. I glance right. A light drizzle falls on the Hudson, and this obscures the view of the palisades of New Jersey.

"Don't you drink in front of your kids?" Dino asks.

"I drink because of my kids," Mac says.

I go back to reading the *Times* Metro section, dismayed by the suffering and depravity I find there. "A former Marine said he bludgeoned a 13-year-old boy because he wanted to know what it felt like to kill someone," begins the first story. "A 37-year-old man accused of stabbing his girlfriend to death last week stabbed himself to death as he was being discharged from the hospital into police custody," comes next. In the third story, a man is sentenced to thirty years in prison for murdering a woman over a parking space. And these are only the Connecticut stories.

Perhaps it's the newspaper or the rain or the low-slung sky, or just the idea of being stuck in that sweatshop of a trading floor, but I really don't feel like going to work, and this worries me. I took this job because I thought that being a trader would be extremely lucrative. I also hoped it would be exciting. I figured I'd be at the red-hot center of the financial world, helping to determine what interest rates—that is, the price of money—should be. Abstract, perhaps, to the common man, but vital to the country, and the world. Every day the newspapers would write about what happened at my place of work; they'd talk about it on television. Who but rock stars and professional athletes could say that?

But now, as I crawl out of the Infinity and take a look around the parking garage, I realize I never understood what a grind it would be, how I would end up spending the better part of my waking life staring—like some limp-brained invalid—at green numbers flickering on a screen.

Dino and Mac, meanwhile, are sparring over the commuting money. Neither seems willing to give up this bickering. They both use it to get up for the trading day, the way football players pound on each other for pregame warmup.

Upstairs the bond market prepares for the first leg of the government's quarterly refunding. The treasury plans to raise twenty-seven billion dollars. Twenty-seven billion dollars sounded like a lot of money to me when I started in the business, but in fact it's a paltry sum, just fifteen billion five-year notes and twelve billion new tens, without a single new thirty-year bond. Somehow, the government now has its act together to the degree that it just doesn't need that much money. This is great for the average citizen, but, like most things good for the public at large, it is bad for government-bond traders. We need ever more government bonds, and government bonds are the offspring of profligate spending: obsolete and unneeded bombers, excessive entitlements, two-hundred-dollar military hammers, newly paved roads to nowhere in underpopulated congressional districts. It's not that these things make bonds go up, just that they create supply, and we need ever more supply. What are we supposed to trade if the government stops bleeding red ink?

Today is the day of the five-year auction, which puts Chip McCarty at the center of attention and color into his cheeks. He spends most of the morning talking over the Hoot and Holler about how the new issue is trading and where he thinks the auction will come. "There's something to be learned from that guy," Dino once told me. "Say it and say it loud. I'm right and I'm proud. People will think you've got a view. In the end, no one really cares if you know what you're talking about."

After a public commentary longer than the Gettysburg Address, Tom Carlson stands up and waddles over to the space between Mac and me. "Could you repeat that?" he chides Mac.

Mac turns around, looks him up and down. "You putting on weight again, Tommy?" Mac asks.

No one ever calls him Tommy. Carlson, forever concerned about his weight, looks stricken. "I just lost twelve pounds," he whimpers. Mac ignores him. I watch as Carlson hesitates, perhaps wondering if he is invisible, before he waddles back to his desk.

When I turn back to my phone board, I see it flashing. I hit the button.

"Hey." It's Stuart Konig. He's in the next row, fifty feet away.

"Stu," I say.

"You busy?"

"Dead."

"A broker just gave me four tickets to *Side Man.* It's a play. Tomorrow night. Want to go, take the wives?"

"It's short notice," I say.

"Work on it tonight. Let me know in the morning. The broker wants to go, so if you don't I'll let him. Gotta hop."

The line goes dead.

Meanwhile, there are five-year notes flying all over the desk.

"Ditch, bid fifty WIs for Chase," says Fred Rose, a salesman.

"Five and a quarter!" Mac yells immediately. This is short for a yield of 405.25, which is the convention for quoting "when-issued" bonds. Any bond announced and about to be auctioned but not yet in existence is called the when-issued, or "WI" for short. That a bond doesn't actually exist does not stop us from trading it.

"Chip, bid thirty-seven fives for Bankers," yells a voice.

"Twelve bid," comes Mac's reply.

"Chip McCarty," says an English voice over the Hoot and Holler. "Offer one hundred of the U.S. Treasury five-year to Rothschild, please."

"Three-quarters."

"Please?" says Tom Carlson. "Who the fuck is that asshole?"

All afternoon I listen while the five-year notes go back and forth, till by the end of the day Mac has traded over six billion of them. It's a dream for a trader to get flow like this. We can often hear Mac making the spread between the bid and offer sides. Soon the desk begins to tease him, out of envy. Colin Dancer gets it going. He drops two towelettes on Mac's desk.

"To help you clean up from all that gravy," he says.

"Do you think maybe you could go to the bathroom, so someone else can have a chance?" Tom Carlson asks.

Even Court Harvey is smiling. It's a crooked, smirk-filled smile, but still a smile. At the end of the day he stands up and asks Mac what he made. The whole desk—Carlson, Dancer, Vollmer, myself—waits nearby for an answer.

"About five hundred," Mac says softly.

Five hundred, as in thousands of dollars. In one day of heavy trading, Mac—one guy—has managed to take from the market a half-million dollars. It's an awesome number, more than I usually make in a month.

"Yeah," Court Harvey mumbles, "sounds about right." He walks off to his office.

"What an asshole," Vollmer says, once he's seen Court Harvey close his door. So, then, here is the rub: lots of money has been made, but who deserves the credit and a decent share of the booty? To us, Mac's performance was inspired. To management, it is expected, a function of the firm's franchise that brings in all those buyers and sellers. The way the firm looks at it, if a guy loses money, he's a bad trader. If he makes money, it's due to the franchise. You could put a monkey in the seat and it would make money, and you don't need to pay a monkey much. Traders make jokes about monkeys as a form of protest. Tom Carlson has a *New York Times* headline taped to the front of his Sun workstation, right next to his diet program. It reads, "New Study Shows That Monkeys Can Think."

We all slap Mac on the back and hope some of his luck will rub off. Mac's cheeks are flushed, his eyes wet with a far-off, almost rapturous glow.

"Enjoy it," Colin Dancer says, "because you're still gonna get fucked at year end."

When I get home, I can hear Emmylou Harris's "Feeling Single, Seeing Double" as soon as I cut the engine. It's just after seven-thirty, and the weather has cleared. Above the house, I see stars and what looks like a planet (Mars, perhaps) against a navy background. It is, I think, a hint of the longer days to come.

Inside I find Rachel and the kids dancing in the living room. Sam bounces up and down while Jane stomps her feet and slowly spins around in circles, her head down to watch her steps. Every once in a while she flaps her arms with joy. This, I think, is why we're here: to be able to dance in our own house. When I was growing up, my mother made me listen to Bach because she'd read that it would help my ability to comprehend math. There was a worry in her that she would somehow leave me shortchanged, and so everything in our home seemed to focus on striving and accomplishment. I suppose it worked, though I'm happy that my kids are learning how to have a good time.

At dinner I tell Rachel about the theater tickets.

"How am I going to get a sitter on such short notice?"

We both know it will be impossible. We can't find a neighborhood sitter. Ours are mostly sixty-year-old grandmothers who want two weeks' advance notice and twelve bucks an hour, cash. They won't even take checks.

At the end of the meal, we send Sam upstairs to shower. Rachel turns to me and says, "It's not fair, Barry."

I notice her eyes, sunken and sad. She looks as tired as I feel. "What's not?" I ask.

"That here we are, with free theater tickets, and we can't even use them."

All I Could Get

"I don't know what you want me to do."

"I'm just saying it's not fair. We live here at the center of the theater universe, we have free tickets, and we can't go."

I hate it when she does this, complains about some problem and offers no solution. I don't understand why she brings it up. When I have a problem, I try to come up with a solution before I throw it at her.

"You know, I haven't heard from Ben in a while," I say, trying to move on.

"I guess six hundred dollars goes a long way in Canada these days, and don't always change the topic."

"I don't know what else to say about the tickets."

"How about saying, 'I'm really sorry that we can't go do this nice thing together'?"

"Didn't I say that?" I ask.

"Not really."

"I'm sorry we can't go," I say.

"You'll hear from your brother again. You're an easy mark."

"The question is, what do I do about it?"

"Keep paying him. Just not much."

"It's pathetic," I say. "He's fifty-one and still on the make."

"Get down? Bath?" Jane says. I check my watch. It's getting late. Jane has come to expect a certain routine out of Rachel and me, and we try not to let her down. I take her out of her high chair, carry her upstairs, and give her her nightly bath. She has several cups that she uses to pour water around while I sit on the tub ledge and scrub her with a washcloth. Afterward, I read her a story, give her a little milk, and put her to bed. It's eight-ten. At eight-thirty, Rachel and I say good night to Sam, who's reading in bed, and we're under our covers by quarter to nine.

I wake at 11:43, according to the scarlet numbers of my alarm clock. Rachel's light is still on, and when I reach for it, I wake her. She backs into me. Without saying a word she rolls my way and we begin to kiss. We move on, and make love. It is the first time in nine days. Between my work schedule and the kids, this is how we manage a sex life, stealing time out of time, sometimes almost forcing it to happen, lest we give in to fatigue and forget about living altogether.

69

The next day, the ten-year-note auction becomes the focus of the day, and thus Colin Dancer takes the spotlight. Unlike Chip McCarty, Colin speaks over the Hoot and Holler reluctantly. He mumbles, rushes important phrases, and generally employs the tone of a trader who is too busy to tell you what is going on and, frankly, doesn't really want you to know. Thus, the floor hangs on his every word. Managers from other departments solicit his advice. Outside of work most guys would jaywalk to avoid him, but everyone on the floor respects his abilities as a trader.

The market trades remarkably well for an auction day. Typically we expect some weakness, because of all the notes the government is selling. But today it doesn't back up. When Colin finally goes over the top, he says, "All right. This market trades short. We've seen good buying. The yield levels are low, but about as good as we've had recently, and if you ask me, the only thing holding this market in is today's auction. So I think you should be long, despite the supply. Once this auction gets out of the way, this market is trading up."

Immediately Court Harvey picks up his phone and starts his own rap over the Hoot and Holler.

"It may be worth noting," Court says, "that, out of the last twenty-four refundings, the market was down twenty-three times the day after the ten-year-note auction. So, if we do get a pop this afternoon, we're going to use it to make sales."

I've never seen Court so publicly contradict another trader. This is blatant humiliation, broadcast simultaneously to the firm's offices in Boston and Chicago, San Francisco and Dallas, Atlanta and Miami, London, Frankfurt, Tokyo, and Singapore, as well as the entire floor right here in New York. Colin Dancer doesn't take it sitting down.

"I'm the fucking ten-year-note trader here," he bellows for all of us on the desk to hear. "And I give the color on the ten-year auction. If you don't like what I have to say, tell me, but don't say it over the top."

"You don't have to yell," Court says.

"Yell! You are un-fucking-believable, Harvey. You might as well have gone over the top and said, 'Dancer sucks.' "

I glance over my shoulder. Court and Colin are now faced off at each other, standing maybe two feet apart. Up and down the row, guys all have their heads down with their hands over their headsets, but one look at the phone board proves that not one of them is on a line. Later, we'll all tell stories about this. The Dancer-Harvey feud was going on before any of us came to the firm, and it's something of a desk hobby to chart its escalation.

"You got a problem with me," Dancer is saying, "call me into the office."

"Hey, Colin," says Fred Rose, "can you offer fifty tens to Chase?"

This stops the argument. Both guys drop back into their seats and go back to trading. Dancer takes the Yankees cap from atop his Sun workstation, turns it inside out, and makes a show of putting it on backward.

Court pretends not to notice. He's too busy ripping his brokers. "Damnit, Ziggy," I hear him yell, "I am the buyer."

Gretchen calls me about twenty minutes later. The market is still going up, but quietly. I'm checking the weekend weather on the Internet.

"You seeing your girl after work?"

"What girl?"

"Going out with the guys?" she asks.

"What are you saying?"

"Do you ever go out with the guys, Barry?"

Which guys? I think. "Hardly ever," I say.

"What are you thinking? Any one of them could end up someday deciding your number. You can't be a hermit. You've got to go out with the boys."

"Thanks for the tutorial," I say, knowing she's right.

"There's more. Meet me for a drink after work."

"Depends on the carpool. Hang on."

I put her on hold and ask Mac if we might leave a little later for home.

"Can't do it," he says. "It's my wife's booze night. I gotta go home and look after the girls."

I tell Gretchen I can't meet her.

"Take a broker car," she says. "It's what they're for."

She picks a time and place to meet.

"Don't bring anyone," she adds, as if I had someone to bring.

About a quarter to two, the auction results roll across the tape, and market activity explodes. Most traders get short the market ahead of the auction, then bid in the auction to cover that short on the theory that bonds will be cheapest when the government sells twelve billion all at once. On the face of it, getting short is surreal: how can you sell something that you don't have? But in our world, it's as common as sweat. Once short, though, you need to buy back what you sold. You'd like to do that at a *lower* price than where you sold (sell high and buy low, and you make money), but, regardless, you still need to buy. If enough people share your problem, then you all reach for the same bonds, which trade higher, and your need to buy becomes desperate. Panic ensues, creating a buying frenzy, commonly called a short squeeze. That's what is happening now. The market is rising with a vengeance, and all across the Street traders are losing money. Nowhere is this more obvious than right behind me, where Court appears to be losing his mind.

"Goddamnit!" he screams at the top of his lungs. He throws his phone at his phone console. I hear it bounce and skitter around on his desk. I turn around to watch. His neck is the color of a radish. "Ziggy!" he shouts into his phone. "Ziggy!" But Brian Zigfeld, his broker, can't hear him through the busted phone, so Court slams it down on his computer keyboard. Plastics fly. A piece of the space bar lands all the way over on my desk.

Now the trading floor is in total silence. I look down the row. Carlson, Mac, and Vollmer are all staring. No one bothers to pretend he's on the phone. The only sound is the bond-pit squawk box from Chicago: "Lehman buys five hundred nines, nine bid. . . ."

That's when Colin Dancer, that ridiculous baseball cap still inside out on his head, turns to Court and says, "I told you this market was going up."

Court begins to tremble. I can hear the springs of his chair squeaking. I've never seen physical violence on the trading floor, but I have a feeling that I will see it now.

"In my office," Court says.

"Hey, I'm long a hundred and fifty tens here," Colin says. "I can't just walk off the desk."

"Sell me thirty-five. Have Stevie work the rest."

"Whatever," Colin says. He takes off his baseball cap, turns it right side out, and places it on his keyboard. With Court's back turned, he gives Vollmer a fist-to-fist salute, and then heads into the office.

We wait till the office blinds are drawn, then huddle in the middle of the row.

"He's fucking losing it," Vollmer says. "Did you see? He was shaking."

"How 'bout that keyboard? Look at it," says Carlson.

We look. There is a spot in the middle where the keys are all snaggle-toothed, and the space bar is missing.

"He's Captain Queeg," says Vollmer.

"What do you think he's going to do to Dancer?" Carlson asks.

"Colin's a big boy," says Vollmer. "I'd wonder more what he's going to do to Harvey."

"Hey," yells Richie Perlmutter, the salesman, "can somebody offer fifty tens?"

Vollmer puts a number on the trade as the rest of us scramble back to our desks.

"All I know," I hear Chip McCarty say when he sits down, "is that I feel sorry for any poor son-of-a-bitch who has to sit all day in that seat next to Court Harvey."

It takes an hour and fifteen minutes, with the market up another three-quarters of a point, for Colin to emerge from Court Harvey's office. Court stays inside. Colin takes the cap from his desk and hands it to Stevie Vollmer, and starts shaking hands.

"Stevie, it's been great," he says.

"You quit?" Vollmer asks, putting on the cap in solidarity.

"He fired me. Let me keep my stock, but he fired me."

"For having the right call on the market?"

Dancer laughs. He has plenty of money and a reputation on the Street. He'll have another job instantly, if he wants one.

"It's a stupidathon," Vollmer says.

Dancer moves down the row, and says goodbye to Mac, Carlson, and then me.

"Barry, it's been good knowing you." Colin is such a huge man that I feel small whenever he stands near me. "I'm sure I'll see you around."

I'm sure he won't, but I appreciate any Dancer attempt at social grace. He walks over to the sales force to say his farewells. It doesn't take long; no one over there likes him much. Back in the trading row, he looks around one last time, takes the photo of his kids and his H-P 12C calculator from his desk, and walks out. After seventeen years on the job, it's as simple as that.

I meet Gretchen at a bar called Logan's. It's three blocks from the firm, a place crowded with deliverymen, phone technicians, construction workers: the blue-collar side of Wall Street. There isn't a visible bourbon or single-malt scotch selection, or a cigar menu, nor does anyone here appear to have paid any attention to the last eight surgeons general. Beneath the ceiling, cigarette smoke dances and swirls like clouds in time-lapse photography. It isn't the kind of place people from the firm go; I wonder how Gretchen knows about it.

We chat for a moment about our kids. Gretchen orders a Rolling Rock, I a Dewar's.

"So," she says, "how well do you know Court Harvey, really?"

"Not that well."

"We've been seeing each other."

"And?"

"You know, Barry, it's probably never occurred to you what it's like to raise children alone. You have to be careful about your dates."

"Isn't Court nice to Buster?"

"Very nice. But that's not the point. The point is what I'm going to do about Court."

"Why do you have to do anything?"

"Because, well, it's hard to explain. See, if I go out with a man, he will basically fit into one of two categories. Call one fun and the other serious. The fun guys are for enjoyment, but I'll never let them meet

Buster or get into my real life in any way, because I know it will never be a long-term thing. The serious ones, well, they take more thought. More screening. Court falls into the serious-guy category, because he has met Buster and because he is so damn serious. But I don't know. He tries to ingratiate himself; he tries to joke with Buster. He's always opening doors for me and jumping up at the table, all that nice-manner stuff that I think I'd like in just about anyone else. But in Court, it makes me feel that something's off, like he's trying too hard. I mean, have you ever really looked at him when he smiles? It's like it hurts him. And I can't find one person, not one, who has a nice thing to say about him."

"He's a good trader."

"Yeah, they do say that. 'He's a machine,' everyone says. It's not much of a personal endorsement."

On the Street, a "machine" is someone who can work all the time, churn out a lot of money, or both.

"Why not declassify him to 'fun'?" I ask.

"Court? Forget it. Too old and too unattached. He won't go there. Fun guys are better-looking, and either very young, or very attached."

"Very attached?" I ask.

"Yes. Like married. I know it sounds terrible, but married men, they give you lots of room and you know it won't go anywhere. They just go out for fun themselves. They're undemanding. Most single guys want to be serious."

"Till they have to be," I say.

She chuckles. "You may be right about that."

"So—how many guys have cut muster in the serious category?" I ask.

"Two." She looks off at the smoky ceiling, and I get the feeling I'd better not ask about those two men.

"Sounds like you've had it with Court," I say.

"I have, but I admit that my judgment about men hasn't always been the best."

"What do you mean by that?"

"Well, look, I'm a single mother."

"There are legions of them," I say.

"True, and I could even argue it's for the best. In fact, it's the only thing I can argue. But the bottom line is that I got involved with someone I shouldn't have, and I decided to go ahead and have Buster in about three minutes. I had no idea what I was getting into. None. The most important decision of my entire life."

"But you're happy with the outcome, no?"

"I have to be. But I'm lucky, very lucky. Like the traders say, it's not only that you make out on a trade, it's that you take an acceptable level of risk."

"Traders keep on trading," I say.

"Yeah, well, I'm out of the child market."

She looks at her watch. We both decide we should be getting home.

Outside the bar there's a Lincoln Town Car at the curb, courtesy of Carlo Bonneti, one of my brokers. All of my brokers provide me with rides wherever I want to go. The economic logic of this perk is unarguable. The ride costs the broker about a hundred dollars, or the equivalent of a commission on a fifteen-to-twenty-million-dollar trade. By eight-thirty the next morning, I'll make sure that I've traded at least a hundred million with Carlo. I've heard our firm's managers gripe about this arrangement, because, in the end, any commission I pay comes out of the firm's revenue. "The less we pay in commission, the more we have to pay our people," Isaac Hunt, the head of our division, once said on a visit to our weekly traders' meeting. Hunt didn't mention that, of a hundred dollars of revenue saved, I only see five bucks, if that. Then the federal government and the city and state of New York take a cut. I'm left with two fifty, which I'll gladly forfeit for a ride home in a chauffeur-driven Lincoln Town Car.

I've perfected the art of sleeping in the back of broker cars, but on this night I keep thinking of my mom and brother, a subject that lately has been exacerbating my already normal state of sleep deprivation. Last weekend I asked her if she'd heard from Ben recently. She hadn't. She knows he's living in Vancouver, but other than that she doesn't know much, not even how he's making a living. Over the years he's been a truck driver, an auto mechanic, a carpenter, a bartender, a car salesman, a maître d', and, of course, a forger.

"Son," my mother told me, "I haven't talked to him for close to a year. He wrote me and asked for money. He said he needed it for a drug clinic. Again. Then he called me. He begged and cried on the phone. It was a thousand dollars. That's a lot of money for me. It comes right out of principal."

"I'll take care of you, Mom."

"That's not the point, Barry. I sent the money. Then I decided to fly out to Vancouver to see him. I didn't tell him. I went to the clinic where he was supposed to be, and they had never heard of him. I found him at the address where I'd sent the check. He looked so terrible, so old, thin. Anyway, there I was on his doorstep, and he didn't know who I was. He was drunk or high or something, but still. Eventually he invited me in. The place was dirty, sickening. It smelled. I wasn't there five minutes and he asked me for more money. That's when I snapped, Barry. I wanted to help him, but I knew it was impossible. I knew if I let it go on it would kill me. So—I stood up to him. I yelled at him. I told him he could never, never call or contact me again. You have children now. Can you imagine what that's like, saying that to your own flesh and blood? Can you?"

I couldn't, and I can't. Lean over and kiss your infant's head, take in that lovely smell of youth, which you made, and you know that you have given over your life, and you're glad for it. Forsaking that child is impossible.

"I had to let him go," my mother said.

I told her she did the right thing. It was the only thing I could say, but the idea was too horrible to think about deeply. You just have to do what it takes so that you never get to that point. You're there when they wake and when they go to sleep, for their meals and in the evenings to talk to them and read them books or help with their homework. You become a better person than you might otherwise be—you don't speed, or swear, or lose your temper at even the most infuriating things, you work hard at your job and around the house—just to lead by example.

My mother did not set a bad example. I'm proof of that. There are simply things a parent can't control. Sometimes I wake at night with a sense of dread that sends me to my kids' rooms, where I stand and watch them sleep and listen to them breathe. I try to find solace in these moments, as if, against what I know of the world, my vigilance can protect them.

5. He's Laughing at You

"This is amazing," Chip McCarty says from the front seat. "There's a special report in the *Journal* about schizophrenia, and I've got all the symptoms: mood swings, frequent bad judgment, lack of close friends, attacks of paranoia. It's all here."

"Sounds like your basic trader," Dino says.

I'm in my usual spot in the back seat, watching Westchester roll by. It's humid and hazy. A color-leaching mist coats the morning.

"Look at that," Mac says.

A coyote stands over a deer carcass in the large, scooped median of I-684. We pass the animal doing eighty, but there is no doubt it's a coyote. I used to see them all the time in Colorado.

"What was that?"

"A coyote," I say.

"Jesus," says Dino. "I'm not sure why I moved out of the city."

"So you could see animals feast on rotting flesh," said Mac.

"I get enough of that at work," Dino replies.

We come around a curve in the road—we're on the Hutch now—and suddenly there is a backhoe bobbing on the road in front of us. I can see the driver bouncing along in blue-jean overalls and a baseball cap. Dino tries to pull around, but a dark-green Porsche Boxster convertible that has been tailing us since Armonk gets to the left lane first. Dino slams on the brakes. I knock my head into the back of Mac's seat as we abruptly slow from eighty to twenty-five.

"Jesus," Mac complains. "Thank God I got disability insurance."

"And life," I chime in.

"Fucking guy," says Dino. We're now pinned behind the backhoe as twenty or so cars pass us on the left, rattling the Infinity. It's like being beaten on a trade.

"You are being schooled," ribs Mac.

Just then the backhoe driver turns around, pushes up the bill of his cap, and smiles.

"Look at that guy, not a care in the world," Mac says.

"He's got no credit risk, no managing director. What's he got to worry about?" Dino studies his rearview mirror. We swerve out into the left lane to a blare of car horns and squealing tires.

"That's right," answers Mac, as we pull by the tractor. "Look at him, he's laughing at you."

He's laughing at you. It's an expression applied to any person who, in any way, has gotten the upper hand. On Wall Street, you can be sure that if you fail someone will find it funny.

We drive on in silence. It isn't until we hit the Cross County that Dino brings up Colin Dancer.

"Is it true Dancer got the boot yesterday?" he asks Mac.

"Yep."

"What did he do?"

"He had the gall to say that the market was going up when Harvey was short. When the market did go up, Harvey fired him."

"I know guys with bad calls on the market get made managers all the time," Dino says, "but this could be the first time I've ever heard of a guy getting canned for having the *right* call."

"Are you listening, Barry?" Mac asks. "There's a lesson in this. Your call on the market doesn't mean squat."

"That's right," says Dino. "You've got to be connected."

"A relative at the firm," I say. "Long Island heritage. Fairfield U. Lacrosse." This is our inside joke. There are at least a dozen managers in our department who grew up together on Long Island, then played lacrosse at Fairfield University. They form a secret society within the firm. Dino says they have a secret handshake.

"Exactly," says Mac.

"Kinda makes you wonder about Dancer," Dino says. "He knew the handshake."

"And right now he's probably waking up," Mac says. "Out of habit. For a second he thinks he's overslept. Now he's realizing he doesn't have to get up. He thinks for a moment about all the money he's saved from getting paid a stick a year, and then about the three million of firm stock that's his to keep. Now he should be going back to sleep, but he can't. You want to know why?"

"Why?" asks Dino, taking the bait.

"Because he's laughing at you."

Court spends the morning trading ten-year notes. The market has traded up another half-point over night, and Court is now trading from the long side. It's odd seeing Colin Dancer's empty seat, the dark screen of his Sun monitor. It feels like a crime scene; I half expect building maintenance to come by and cordon the area off with yellow tape. All morning, salespeople call for Colin over the Hoot and Holler. Voices ask for him through his desktop intercom. "Ye-e-s," Court always responds, as if the caller is supposed to know that Colin has been sacked.

About eleven-thirty, Court tells Mac to listen up for ten-year flow, and walks off with his notepad to his office. Mac calls up Mickey O'Hara, one of Colin Dancer's brokers, and has him send up lunch. O'Hara works at Brokertec, the least busy and therefore least profitable brokerage. An hour later, sushi arrives, six big plastic platters of it, along with thirty miso soups and five platters of cooked appetizers.

"You know Mickey's sweating bullets," Mac says. We are in the midst of a feeding frenzy, fifteen government traders and salespeople, plus a few interlopers from derivatives and two young, skinny mortgage-back assistants known for scavenging food, all of us reaching over each other, grabbing tekka maki and California rolls with our bare hands. Most un-Japanese. "Colin used to take pity on O'Hara," Mac continues. "He'd throw him a couple easy trades a day.

Now O'Hara's sitting over there wondering how he's going to put food on the table."

"He did a nice job here," Tom Carlson says. He has positioned his stout body in front of the food trays, effectively boxing the rest of us out. He takes his time filling his plate, stacking it with chicken satay and chunks of raw tuna that he's taken from the sashimi platter, leaving behind little rectangles of rice, per his no carb diet. "He have kids, Mickey O'Hara?" Carlson asks.

"O'Hara? Six, I think."

"Seven," says Stevie Vollmer, who knows personal details about everyone. "Dancer felt bad for him. I think it was an Irish thing."

"Seven kids! Is he insane?"

"If he wasn't before the kids," Vollmer says, "he is now."

"All I know," Mac says, "is that he's an easy touch, and that's a good thing. Whoever ends up trading tens is going to have to take care of Mickey, because Mickey runs scared, and scared brokers keep the goodies coming. One day soon Brokertec is going to go out of business. We gotta milk it till then."

Just then Isaac Hunt, the head of the division, wanders into the government row. He doesn't look happy. Maybe it's seeing his government desk up to its elbows in raw fish. He once declared that broker lunches would no longer be allowed, but not even the head of the fixed-income division could stop the power of broker handouts. Isaac Hunt is a big man, six three and maybe 250 pounds. He played football at Holy Cross, a fact that is difficult to miss if you ever visit his office. His most noticeable feature, though, is that he is black, one of the three black men who work on the floor. Of the other two, one is Carlos, the Panamanian who runs the food cart. There is also a skinny guy with large, dark-rimmed glasses who sorts letters in the floor's small mailroom.

"Where's Court?" Isaac Hunt wants to know.

"In his office," answers Stevie Vollmer, the one trader on the desk who seems to have rapport with Hunt.

"Thank you, Steven," Hunt says. He turns and looks me up and down, as though I'm wearing blue jeans and a tank top, or maybe nothing at all. Then he strides off toward Court Harvey's office.

"I think he likes you," Mac says to Vollmer. "Steven."

"I bet him ten bucks every time Princeton plays Holy Cross in football. Cost me fifty bucks over the years," Vollmer says.

"You are fucking brilliant," says Mac. "You've got the big guy, the one who has ultimate say over your pay, in your pocket. And for just fifty bucks!!! Did you see the last supplement to the annual report? He's got forty million of company stock."

Vollmer smiles, tosses a California roll into the air, and catches it in his mouth. "Most guys come cheap," he says, chewing, "if you know how to buy."

"We're never going to get off the rock," Mac says. "The rock" is his name for Manhattan, which, as commuters, we view as convicts once viewed Alcatraz.

At present we are inching our way up the West Side Highway. I catch sight of a crane lifting a plane off the deck of the *Intrepid.*

"You ever think about the word 'money'?" Dino asks.

"All the time," says Mac. "Especially when I think about what you owe me."

"'Money.' It's such a nice word. Think of all the words that sound like 'money.' Money, honey, sunny, funny."

"Chummy," says Mac. "Pay me."

"Scummy," I add from the back seat.

"There he goes again," says Mac.

"Calumny," I say.

"Now he's making words up."

"Barry, doesn't it wear on you to always be so negative?" Dino asks.

"I'm an optimist," I say. "Just a realistic one."

"Why do you think Isaac Hunt spent all that time with Harvey today?" Mac asks.

"Got me."

"Probably in there telling Harvey the preliminary on what this year's Hooky Duke will be."

"Hooky Duke" is how traders refer to management's various explanations as to why we will be paid poorly: a guy trading the

Thai bhat lost fifty million dollars; equities had a bad year (again); a Japanese bank went under and some guy in London owned its debt; we had to take a write-off on our real-estate holdings; our investment bankers lost a big deal; investment banking made a lot of money and they are garnering a good share of the bonus pool. It cuts every which way; all you know is that it will cut against you. Not that, as traders, we should be surprised. On Wall Street, whole businesses are founded on deceptive language. So the bonds of weak companies are called "High Yield," rather than "junk bonds," ignoring the fact that there may be no yield at all. "Emerging Markets" denotes third-world nations that have been defaulting on debt and having currency crises for hundreds of years. Lucky for junk-bond companies and third-world debtors that memories in the markets are short. No one talks about the peso crisis of '94, let alone the great Mexican bond default back in the twenties. Prospects today aren't much better. The best economic hope most of the people in these countries have is to get a work visa to America. In the end, the United States may be one of the few countries ever to have "emerged."

I've fallen into a habit of looking in on the dining-table window before entering my house, just to get a view of home without me. I can't say, exactly, what it is I like so much about stepping out and spying on my own life. Perhaps it's that I'm a child of the television age. After spending a lifetime looking in on everyone else, why wouldn't I want to look in on myself?

It's Friday, the Sabbath, and when I glance in the window Rachel is right there, arranging the candles on the table just so, then standing back to look at her work. She has laid out the black tablecloth and the china we received at our wedding. There's a loaf of fresh bread and a newly opened bottle of Merlot from California, rather than Bulgaria, which was all we could afford—every other week—before Wall Street. It may seem trite, but I think that there is happiness to be had from being able to spend nine dollars on a bottle of wine, rather than four. It's silly to pretend that money doesn't matter.

Rachel bends down, and when she stands she has Jane in her arms, and I can see my daughter's round cheeks and ready giggle. She is a gorgeous little girl, healthy, full of life. Rachel looks to the wall where I know the clock hangs.

Whenever I think about it, I am amazed that Rachel and I ended up here, in suburban New York. We first met in Whitehorse, in the Yukon Territory. I had gone there to look for my brother. Rachel was playing in a country band. My first night in town, I walked out of the frozen night—it was four in the afternoon—and into a bar called the Inferno Lounge and there she was, singing a Jerry Jeff Walker song about being homesick in London. I managed to buy her a drink, and later she drove me around town looking for Ben, who, when I found him, ditched me as if I were a bill collector. Three years later, I spotted Rachel in the bar at Eastern Winds, a Chinese restaurant a block and a half from Aspen Mountain. She was sitting down the bar from me, and I kept staring at her, amazed at how much she looked like the girl I remembered from the Yukon. Unlike in Whitehorse, beautiful women are common in Aspen, and it seemed to me perfectly logical that I'd spot a Rachel look-alike. She caught me staring at her, and I saw recognition in her eyes. I moved down the bar. A week later, she called me, having looked my number up in the phone book. That she made the first call proved to her that I was aloof and arrogant. To me it proved that she had more guts than I. I called her plenty after that.

Now, still outside, I shuffle through the leaves toward the door. I haven't gotten around to raking leaves this year, nor did I do much last fall, and now the yard is inundated with them. That's a downside of my job: so many simple things fall by the wayside, get left behind, forgotten, or ignored, that when I finally notice them I'm standing knee-deep in the problem.

As soon as I walk inside, Rachel ushers me to the table, where we say the blessings over the candles, wine, and bread.

"We ran into Gretchen Barnes and Buster today at the Natural History Museum," Rachel tells me as she cuts Sam's chicken. Sam had the day off school, so Rachel called a broker car and took the kids to the city.

"Didn't she have to work?"

"That's what I asked. She said she can sneak out from time to time."

"Lucky," I say. Traders can't "sneak" out. Traders can barely get off the desk to go to the bathroom.

"I don't know if I'd call her lucky. I thought she was a little sad. What struck me was that there I was with the kids and you were at work, but that Gretchen has to do my role and yours. I don't know how she does it. Do you really think you could work your job and look after the kids?"

The answer is obviously not, which I don't have to say, because the phone rings. I go to the kitchen to answer it. "Hey, little bro," says my brother.

"Ben." It's all I can think to say.

"I'll cut out the crap, Barry, because I know you don't want to hear it, and, besides, you were always a smart kid. I need more money."

"Don't tell me you borrowed again from loan sharks."

"No," he says, "that's why I'm calling you. I don't want to do that."

"What do you need it for?"

"What kind of question is that? I need it for life," he says.

"How much?"

"A grand," he says.

"C'mon. It's too much money," I tell him.

"Five hundred American? For the family," he answers.

"What do I have to do now?" I say. "Support you? Pay a monthly big-brother tax? I've got a family of my own to support."

"Hey," he snaps, "fucking forget it. I didn't expect you to think of me as family."

Of course, he expects exactly that, and (I can't help myself) I feel bad about it.

"Go to the Western Union office tomorrow," I tell him.

"I knew I could count on you, Barry. You were always that kind of guy."

I'll send him $250. I want to lower his expectations and make it tough for him to ask for more the next time. It occurs to me that the way Court Harvey treats me at bonus time provides a useful example of how to deal with my brother.

All I Could Get

We are in the middle of dinner—Jane has just dumped her unwanted macaroni and cheese on the floor—when there is a Gestapo-like pounding at our door.

It's Steve Traxler, father of Tim, my son's best friend. I let him in. Steve's eyes bug out of their sockets and he's swiveling his head back and forth, as if he were expecting an ambush. Finally, he settles his gaze on Rachel, who is down on one knee, scooping up the macaroni and cheese.

"Have you seen Liz?"

"No. What's going on?"

"She's gone. I can't find her."

"Where's Tim?"

"Who?"

"Your son."

It takes a moment for this hint to register with him. I'm beginning to get frightened. He keeps pushing himself up onto his toes and swinging his arms in small circles by his sides. He has so much nervous energy that I get the feeling that at any minute he might break into jumping jacks. He's changed from his work clothes to jeans and a black T-shirt, over which he wears a fleece vest, despite the warm weather.

"I guess he's with Liz," he says.

"People don't just disappear," Rachel says. "Maybe she left a note."

"She took everything. All their clothes and stuff."

"Oh."

I suppose I should have more sympathy for him, but we're not really friends. He travels constantly for work, and one night he told me he had some action on the side. This was not something I wanted to know or contemplate, but it no doubt had a hand in the current situation. It's amazing how carelessly people can screw up their lives. I suggest we go outside.

He is shaking, and he walks into the driveway swerving slightly, like a man discovering that he is drunk. The loss of Liz seems to have affected his balance. She has family in Kentucky, and I figure he'll get a call—or at least a summons—from there.

I notice his car. It's a gray BMW, like Mac's, except that it's a smaller, less well-equipped version. What stands out now is that the entire left side of the car—front fender, both door panels, rear fender—is badly scraped and dented. I have the urge to ask him what happened, but I don't want him in my driveway any longer than is necessary.

"Listen, Barry, man," he says. He's still bouncing on his toes, and I'm practically about to start doing jumping jacks with him. "I'm, like, short on cash, and I gotta go out of town tomorrow on business, first thing."

"Don't you have an ATM card?"

He pauses, as if he doesn't understand what I am asking. Finally, he speaks: "Liz cleaned out that account. I can have money transferred in tomorrow, but it will take a day."

"How much do you need?"

"A hundred bucks?"

"I don't think I have that much here," I tell him. I have nothing on me, and I rarely carry that much. I leave him standing in our drive-way while I go inside and find ninety dollars in the stash I keep in my sock drawer. Back outside, I give him forty.

Once he has the money he doesn't waste much time getting into his car, which he has to do through the passenger-side door, on account of the damage on the other side. He doesn't say thank you. I go back inside, wondering what it means that I now have to pay people to get them to stay away from me.

I find Rachel trying to explain the basics of family dissolution to Sam. Shoulders slumped, head down, Sam is the picture of sadness, now that he realizes he's lost his best friend. I put my arm around him, and tell him that things will be okay. He's sniffling, just short of sobbing.

"Who am I going to play with?"

I mention half a dozen kids I know to be his friends.

"They don't live around here."

"Look, Sam, *I'll* still play with you, every day, when I get home from work."

"At seven-thirty?" He sighs with a world-weariness far too great for his age. "Face it, Dad. You're never home."

There isn't much to say. He sits there a moment, then slides off his chair and stomps upstairs for his nightly shower. It's the first time I can remember him doing this without being asked.

I have Rachel pour me another glass of wine.

"It's too bad for Sam that Tim is gone," Rachel says. We're sitting up in bed against the three rows of pillows she places by the headboard, books in our laps. The headboard is made of blond wood from somewhere in Asia. Given what's going on in the Asian financial markets, I can't help imagining armies of undernourished copper-colored men chopping down forests in Malaysia, just to raise a little cash. Rachel picked out the bed, including the special frame and box springs. The mattress is the third one we've tried. When I collapse on it at night I feel as if I am floating in a liquid that is unusually thick and buoyant, like mercury. Rachel is forever complaining about not being able to sleep, and that she needs this bed to get any rest at all. The bed cost us more than we got for the pickup truck we sold when we left Colorado.

"Aren't you going to say anything?" she asks.

"Kids are tough. He has other friends. Remember when we moved here and he was so upset about leaving his buddies behind? By the third day of school he was right in the groove."

"I know how he felt."

"What does that mean?"

"You know, we really don't have any friends here."

"We have Dan and Amy."

"Dan is your friend from way back. Amy is a real-estate broker. She's nice, but it's a generic nice. I always imagine her having to be nice all day long, and then not being able to turn it off. And you really don't see Dan much. The guys you see all the time are Chip and Dino, and never for fun."

"I get all the fun I can handle Monday through Friday."

"So you agree?"

"With what?"

"That you don't have time for friendship. If it wasn't something you had before you started, you don't have it now."

She's right, to some extent. I don't have time. Friendships are one of the things I've given up, while I get the money.

"There's Stu," I say.

"Small consolation. You only see him at work."

"I agree. I know I don't have time for friends. I'm too darn tired."

"Barry, I think we need to make more of an effort to make friends. It's important for us. We need some outside influence. It keeps things fresh, gives us something to talk about. And it will help me to feel more at home here. Right now, I feel like I'm living in a foreign country and I don't speak the language."

"Okay," I say. "I'm for it. How do we go about it?"

"I don't know," Rachel says. "It's hard to make friends around here. There are too many people."

Court Harvey calls me into his office the next week. I wonder what I've done wrong. As I walk down government gulch, I hear Mac yelling, "At the plus!! At the plus!!" into his headset. Vollmer is saying, "Work a hundred at eighteen." They're in their own little trading tunnels, where the rest of the world fades away and all that matters is the flicker of those little green numbers on the screen.

"How you doing?" Court asks when I enter his office. He smiles, and swings his feet off the desk, which I take as a sign of respect. I've had a few meetings where I did little but stare at his shoe soles.

"Fine," I say. How am I doing? I've always wondered why managers ask this question. What am I supposed to say? I'm tired of working all day and getting paid a third of what the guy next to me makes? I'm still pissed that you live like an Internet tycoon and I'm driving an Escort? My brother has started to put the pinch on me, and I'm really going to need to get paid this year?

"I've spoken with Isaac Hunt, and he agrees with me that you will do well trading tens."

I nod. I feel a tingling, almost a dizziness. This is for real. I am not in trouble. I am going to trade tens.

"So—congratulations. It's a fabulous opportunity. It's a high-profile seat. I'm thinking of making the move next week. Be ready to go on Monday. In the meantime, keep it quiet. I'll say something tomorrow. I think it's best that we let a little time pass."

Tomorrow is Thursday. Dancer was sacked a week ago. Maybe Court thinks his actions will appear less personal and calculated if it seems that he waits ten days to name a replacement.

"That's great," I say. "Of course, I assume that, with my new high-profile spot, there will be new expectations as to what I should make."

"Well, sure. At a firm like ours, that seat is worth a lot of money. Colin made twenty million bucks there last year," he says, in a tone that suggests that if Colin could make twenty million any monkey can.

"So—what should I aim for?" I figure the right answer is a million and a half dollars a month, at the start. In bills, that would be an average year.

"Just print the trades and do your best. Get your feet wet, control the risk. The money will come."

"And I assume that, when it does come, I will get some of it personally," I say. "If I'm going to make a big jump in profile and profit, I've got to make a big jump in pay." If I'm going to trade tens, I have to think like a ten-year trader. I cannot be quiet. I have to put Court on notice, demand that I be paid. I have to get the money.

Late Sunday afternoon, the phone rings. I'm thinking about the ten-year seat, trying to come up with some stock phrases for my market rap. On the third ring, Rachel yells from the kitchen for me to get the phone.

"Hello," I say. There is no sound on the line. Probably it's a phone solicitor, hoping for a woman. "Hello?" I say again.

"Barry?"

"Yes."

"It's Gretchen."

"What's up?" I ask. I walk to the back of the house and out to the deck. Sunlight is streaming at steep angles through the trees, lighting the misty air in the backyard.

"I just thought I'd call," she says. "We said, you know, that we should be better friends. I was wondering, well, do you want to get another drink after work?"

Her voice fades as she says this. I'm not sure if it's a proposition or not. I'm thirty-five years old, and I haven't been propositioned in a long time.

I agree, and we make plans to meet for a drink after work on Wednesday.

"Who was that?" Rachel asks when I return the phone to the kitchen.

"Stu. He wants to get a drink on Wednesday. Something's up he wants to talk about in person."

I could tell Rachel the truth, but it would take a lot of explaining, and I hate explaining. I always end up feeling like I'm lying, even when I'm not.

"Couldn't you guys just talk at work?" Rachel asks.

"We hardly ever talk at work," I say.

"Men," Rachel says. "You guys work together. You'd think you'd figure out how to communicate."

Monday morning, I pick up from my computer my picture of Rachel and Sam—it was taken atop Mount Moosilauke in New Hampshire before Jane was born—turn around, and walk the three steps to Colin Dancer's seat. I put the picture on his computer as an explorer might stake a claim to a new land. I am now the ten-year trader.

"Hey, Meat," says Stevie Vollmer, now just a few feet to my right. He holds out his hand and we shake. His hand is thick, but soft. He's not doing much yard work. "Congratulations," he says. "And good fucking luck."

Chip McCarty comes over. "I'm gonna need an extra five bucks a week for the carpool," he says.

"What for?"

"'Cause now you're the ten-year trader. And Dino never pays me. Jesus, I can't believe it. Who are you related to?"

"He looks like Blatts," Vollmer says. "But taller." Charles Blatts, the head of the firm.

"I should have known," said Mac. "It's still hard to believe. Even Barry is connected."

"Here," I say to Mac. I hand him a week's worth of commuting money, without any extra. I owe him for last week and this week, but he's gotten so used to my paying on time that I doubt he knows where he stands.

"Don't you owe me for last week, too?" he asks.

"I paid," I lie.

"You did?"

"Yeah, early last week."

"You sure?"

"Positive." It's odd how easily I can say this with conviction.

"Okay," he says, pocketing the money. "But I still think you should pay more, being related to Blatts and all."

I say nothing. I have no relation to Charles Blatts, or to anyone else at the firm other than Court Harvey, and that relationship is complicated. I have to admit, though, that Mac and Vollmer are right. Going from bills to the ten-year seat is an outrageous promotion, the kind typically reserved for close relatives of managing directors.

I spend the morning trying to get used to my new lines of vision. Sit in a seat long enough and you can see the price information almost without looking. But change locations and your eyes dart frantically from screen to screen, searching through the rows of green numbers for the information you need. My eyes do this for most of the day, as people call the desk for ten-year prices, often asking for Colin. Meanwhile, I take six aspirin, three Tylenol, and an Advil, and my head is still pounding.

"Baaar-reee," says a voice. Sophie Allen. She's a saleswoman, one of two who work in governments. She has long bleach-blond hair, and is pathologically thin. When she turns her head you can see all sorts of cords in her neck, if her hair isn't in the way. From time to time I've heard salesmen complain about her flatulence. Sophie has been at the firm forever; she got her start as Charles Blatts's secretary, back when he ran the money-markets division. There was also a rumor that she was his lover, though I've never believed it. She covers the handful of funds whose managers are women.

"Can you offer Barron's Funds two hundred and fifty million tens?"

At that very moment, the futures pits in Chicago turn sellers. Within a second, our market is sure to follow.

"Sixteen," yells Court Harvey, just as I say, "fifteen-plus."

"You can sell them at sixteen," Sophie says.

"DONE!" yells Court. "I sold those," he says to me as tens trade down at fourteen.

I don't know what to do. I'm the ten-year trader. That was supposed to be my trade. It's a clear winner. In fact, it's the kind of juicy trade that comes along less often than good weather. Within fifteen seconds, Court is buying his ten-years back at twelve and twelve-plus. He's making more than a quarter of a million dollars on the trade. I seethe as I watch him punch the various broker-phone buttons. "Pay it, tens. PAY IT! Damnit, Ziggy, get me in the trade." I find myself staring at his neck, which is blotchy red with excitement; a vein bulges out blue from his crimson forehead, a river on a map of dry and arid land. "Fifty," he yells, meaning he wants to buy fifty million. "A hundred," he says.

Once Court has bought what he needs, he stands up and walks off the desk without saying a word. Stevie Vollmer leans his head in the tiny sight line between my desk and his, his face framed by computer monitors. "Bossman steal your gravy? You fucked up. Fucked up, big-time. You better get better at boxing him out."

"How do I box him out?" I feel a bead of sweat run down my ribs. My face burns, and I'm hot with rage and embarrassment. Assume the firm will pay me five percent of my trading revenue: Court has just taken over twelve thousand dollars out of my pocket. It's as if I've been physically mugged.

"Tell him you need the sale, then give him some. That trade, you could have gotten away with giving him fifty. Make him bargain for more. But if you don't stand up to him, he will squash you like a cockroach."

"It's extortion," I say. "It's outrageous."

Vollmer chuckles. "It's his nature. Management is all about taking from your employees and giving to yourself. Court's a master at it."

Chip McCarty comes over and sits in Court Harvey's vacated seat. "You can't let him do that, Barry," he says gravely. "It's bad for you and it's bad for us. We can't let him walk over us like that."

Vollmer stands up. “That’s what I was saying.”

Mac nods his head toward Court’s office. “He had to run back there, Barry, because he couldn’t laugh at you on the desk.”

“He’s the head guy,” I say. “He gets paid no matter what. It’s not like he’s got to fuck his own guys out of two hundred and fifty grand.”

“Court Harvey?” Vollmer says. “He’d fuck his own mother for two hundred and fifty grand.”

6. One Best Person

Summer hits. The beautiful people flee to Fire Island and Martha's Vineyard. The rest of us are stuck with the heat. On my commute I watch pedestrians move like zombies up the sidewalk, their faces all grimace and sweat and resignation. Even the animals can find little relief. One afternoon a squirrel collapses on our deck, belly-up, and that night I shovel its carcass into the woods.

I find it difficult to dress in the morning, as we have no air conditioning. Our bedroom won't accommodate a window unit. We got a quote of nine grand to put in central air, which was out of the question, though strapping on a tie in this kind of heat and humidity is nothing short of masochistic. I take to carrying my tie and jacket to the Park and Ride, tying the former in the cool interior of Mac's BMW or Dino's Infinity, but only once we've reached Manhattan. The jacket I never put on. I simply carry it up to the trading floor, where I hang it in the closet, then lug it back down to the garage at the end of the day, like the useless prop that it is.

Today our commute north runs up against a Ku Klux Klan rally at City Hall. Like any City Hall event, the rally is a tourniquet on the traffic veins and arteries of lower Manhattan. We've been listening to news of the rally for the last three weeks, as the Klan had to sue the city in federal court for a permit to march. The city refused the permit, on the grounds that it is illegal for marchers to wear masks. When the Klansmen agreed to expose their faces, the permit was issued. All the publicity has brought a lot of people out. According to Bloomberg Radio, there were ten anti-Klan protesters for every Klansman.

"There's no room for hatred in New York," says a protester on the radio.

"Oh, yeah?" Dino responds. "You haven't been on the West Side Highway."

Dino cuts hard to the right. Horns blare.

Meanwhile, the radio moves on to the weather report. "Today, hot, hazy, humid, highs in the upper nineties. Tonight, hot, humid, highs in the upper eighties. Tomorrow, hot, hazy, humid, highs in the upper nineties to the one hundreds."

"Jesus," Mac says, "we might as well be in Jakarta."

I happen to have the *Times* opened to the weather page. Jakarta is cooler than New York. So are Kuala Lumpur, Khartoum, and Saigon. In fact, the only international cities hotter on this day than New York are Riyadh and New Delhi.

Dino pounds on the horn.

"What is with you?" Mac says. "Calm down."

"How can I calm down now that Schwartz is the ten-year trader?"

"Vollmer and I figure he knows somebody. You don't go from the bill seat to a seat like that without knowing somebody."

"In the biblical sense," Dino says.

"Do you guys ever stop?" I ask.

Dino has to jam on the brakes at an intersection when the car ahead of him fails to race through a yellow light. A young black man walks by in shorts and no shirt. He carries a BAN THE KLAN placard.

I look right, and there's Gretchen in a Yellow cab. Court Harvey sits next to her. I feel a pang of jealousy. When we met for drinks two weeks ago, Gretchen said that things with Court were over. She kept touching my hands, and those touches carried something electric. I didn't reciprocate, fearing where it might lead, and curious about that destination, too.

"Hey," Dino says, "there's that girl from equities."

"Holy shit," says Mac. "Harvey's in there with her. You think that asshole is shtupping the girl from equities?"

"Why not?" Dino says. "He's shtupping everyone else."

That night, I play catch with Sam while Rachel cooks hamburgers on our gas grill. Sam and I have fallen into a nice rhythm this summer, playing catch whenever I can get home early enough to do so, about once a week. He has quick hands and good feet, which are useful qualities in baseball and life. The fifteen minutes he and I get in after a day of work do wonders for me. My job removes me from my wife and children for such long hours that I often feel I'm losing that familiarity that is the essence and comfort of family. Baseball helps to bring it back, and it allows me to play the role of the father I never had.

Rachel calls us to our back deck, where we will eat outside. Jane is there, playing in her beloved plastic car. It is, as I've said, a warm night, but here, forty-five miles north of the city, among the trees, it's probably ten degrees cooler than Manhattan, and pleasant enough. I put Jane in her high chair, and we sit down to dinner.

It's a simple and not quite common enough domestic moment, and I try to capture it in my mind, make it the kind of memory that finds purchase there forever. Sam is practically dislocating his jaw trying to get his mouth around his ketchup-, mustard-, and relish-soaked burger. Jane picks up the pieces of meat Rachel has placed on her high-chair tray, puts them on her yellow plastic spoon, and then shoves the spoon at her mouth, with a hit ratio of about 50 percent. Rachel leans back in her chair, her long hair draped behind her, and takes a swig of an Amstel. Above us birds flit about in the day's last light, and I can hear a squirrel rummaging about in the pachysandra just off the edge of the deck. I sip my beer. Here is a family, I think, like any other. Nothing special, yet special.

"Hey, Mom," Sam says, "when's Tim coming back?"

Sam's friend Tim. We know now that Tim isn't coming back. Liz Traxler has called Rachel. Liz is, as we suspected, in Kentucky, seeking divorce. Her grounds are that Steve is a crack-cocaine addict. Much of the "business" travel he's been doing was to rehab clinics, but once he was released he rarely stayed off the drug for a week. Liz told Rachel that it wasn't till the week she left that she discovered that Steve had inhaled all the money, and that he'd even borrowed against their retirement account. They missed four months of mortgage payments, and the bank is foreclosing. Their credit cards no longer offer credit. Liz's Volkswagen Passat was repossessed one day while she and Tim were eating at a Wendy's. Now Liz is back in Kentucky, trying to get work as a schoolteacher for the coming year. I remember marveling once at how the Traxlers spent money. I can't help wondering how a guy like that could get messed up with crack cocaine. He must have gone out of his way. I've never even seen any.

Sam still wants an answer. Rachel looks to me.

"Tim probably isn't coming back," I say. "He and his mom moved to Kentucky, and that's where he's probably going to stay."

"Why? He's supposed to live here. Why can't he come back?"

"Well, sometimes things like this happen. He really doesn't have a place to live here anymore. His mom and dad split up. It's a mess, Sam. I don't know what else to say."

When I go in to check on Sam at bedtime, he tugs at my shirt, pulling me down to my knees at his bedside. "Are you and Mom ever going to split up?" he asks.

"No."

"How do you know?"

"I know."

He stares at me then, realizing, perhaps for the first time, that he has something to lose.

The next night, a Wednesday, I meet Gretchen for a drink. We've been getting together for drinks every other Wednesday or so, after my traders' meetings. We're developing something close to the friendship we had fifteen years ago. Tonight we meet on the Upper West Side, in a moderately crowded bar not far from Gretchen's apartment.

"I saw you yesterday with Court," I tell her. I'm a little upset about this. Jealous. "In a taxi," I add.

"I broke it off, for about the third time. I've really had to spell it out for him."

"What did you say?"

"I said no. It's not something Court hears all that often, I imagine. Except maybe from women."

"But I bet you have to tell a lot of guys no," I say.

She shrugs.

"A couple a month," I suggest.

She leans back and laughs, one hand on the bar to keep herself from toppling off the stool. "Hardly. I'm a single mother who works all the time. I don't see a couple guys a month."

"You used to send them away in droves, in college," I remind her.

"College was fun," she admits. She looks at me as if she has something more to say, but stops. I find myself staring into those eyes of hers, dark and very big. A moment later we have somehow leaned our heads close together, and I am suddenly aware of the smell of her perfume and the feel of her breath against my cheek. We kiss, and not exactly innocently. I feel an electricity run through my lips that I haven't felt in years.

"You sent a few away yourself," she says, finally.

"Not really," I reply, when I manage to exhale. All these years, we have never kissed like that.

"You probably don't even know," she tells me.

Friday night, having finally gotten both kids to sleep, I stand in the kitchen and sip at a scotch. I find myself thinking of Gretchen with blatant physical lust. Today I was taking a ninety-second break by the vending machine, trying to decide between the pretzels or the granola bars in lieu of lunch, when I heard a click of heels on the stretch of parquet floor by the reception area and I knew it was Gretchen. I stepped out from behind the machines and there she was, in a tight-fitting black shirt, black slacks, black shoes with an enormous platform and heel. There was a string of pearls around her neck. Casual-dress day on the equity floor. When she saw me her face brightened and she veered over to the vending machines. For a moment it seemed as if she would hug me, but then she caught herself and said hi with a giggle so unlike the Gretchen I've known on the trading floor that I must have looked startled, for she blushed, looked down at her shoes, and said, "Sorry."

After the kiss on Wednesday night, I was afraid to linger. I made an excuse to get back to the desk.

I've never been unfaithful to Rachel. I down my scotch, bound the stairs two at a time, and slide into bed. Rachel is asleep on her side. I run my hand up her thigh, gently, in an attempt to wake her. She pushes my hand away.

"Barry, what is it?"

"The Sabbath," I say. By Jewish law, a husband is to satisfy his wife on the Sabbath. We are fairly unobservant Jews, but I do try to uphold this one law.

"I'm too tired. We just did it . . . the night before last."

True, at my urging.

"Please," I plead. I don't know what else to say. Something in my voice makes Rachel turn around and face me. It's hard to decide what expression she's wearing. Bewilderment, perhaps, or fear. "Please," I say again.

She sighs. "Okay, Barry, okay."

I leave the house Monday morning confused. Where did the weekend go? I can remember nothing, except Friday night, when I forced my wife to make love to me so, I soon realized, I could pretend she was a different woman. It turned into a wild and athletic night, until finally we collapsed on the damp sheets. Rachel reached back to hold me to her, and that's how we woke the next morning, to the sound of Jane singing in her crib.

Now, at quarter to six in the morning, the heat is heavy and wet. The air that comes out of the Escort's vents—the air conditioning is broken—is as hot as the exhaust from a bus. My wheels make a sucking sound on the asphalt, and the sun is not yet visible on the horizon.

Even at work, nine floors above the street, the heat takes its toll. Tom Carlson, our two-year-note trader, stands up and says, "I can't believe how fucking hot it is here."

He's right. On hot summer days the air conditioning is not up to the task of cooling a room crammed with bodies and computer screens. Each is its own little hearth. Stevie Vollmer even uses his to heat the Pop-Tarts he buys cold every morning from the vending machine. "Trader gourmet," he calls it.

Carlson has the worst seat for the heat, and the worst body. There are no vents near him, and he is short and fat and subject to overheating on normal days. On hot ones I glance over and see him sweating through his blue end-on-end shirts. The fabric is blue with white thread sewn though the exterior, and, despite how easily these shirts show perspiration, Carlson wears one at least every other day. Carlson employs a small fan atop his Sun monitor, and another beneath his desk (where it is called a ball fan), but these seem to have little effect. Early in the morning half-moons of sweat grow beneath his arms. By mid-afternoon I notice dampness on his back and below what I think of as his breasts. He carries that kind of weight. He has thin, dark hair that he combs west to east across his bald pate. He has other physical difficulties. His eyes are going bad. Sometimes he complains of blurred vision. I'll look down the row and see him covering one of his eyes with his hand, his head tilted back, like an old man.

By ten to three they're mentioning the heat on CNBC. It's 103 outside and maybe eighty on the floor. We've had a second brown-out already, there are reports of seventeen heat-related deaths in the last twenty-four hours, and the mayor's office has asked that nonessential personnel go home. Our desk is fully staffed, though Court is in the office. Just ahead of the three o'clock futures close, Carlson starts to act out. He is a more expressive trader than most, especially when things are going badly. He has a habit of grunting and then slamming his palm down on his desk in rapid succession. Argh! Slam! We all imitate this maneuver when Carlson isn't around, and this afternoon Carlson is doing it so often that he becomes a parody of himself. Argh, slam! Argh, slam! Argh, slam!

"They are killing the two-year!!" he yells, to no one. "Murdering the fucking pig."

Argh, slam!!

"Tom, bid fifty twos for Chase," says Fred Rose, the salesman.

"Twenty-seven," Carlson says. Argh, slam!!

"Done."

"Motherfuckers," Carlson says, his eyes wide. "They know my position. They know my fucking position!"

"What are you talking about?" Mac says. "How could they know your position?"

"They know it. I know they know it. They get it off the Web, or something."

"No one can know your position, except the rest of us on the desk, who have to listen to you moan about it."

Court Harvey comes back to the desk, and this stops the discussion. Futures close, and we all go to work marking our books. As the ten-year-note trader I mark the ten-year area; Mac marks fives, Vollmer thirty-years, and Carlson twos. On this day, Carlson marks at 99-27+. It is a ridiculously high mark. He might argue more convincingly that he is six feet tall.

"Tom," Court yells, "what the hell are you doing?"

It is one minute after three. Carlson is very long the two-year note and it is trading poorly. He's been long the two-year note all day. Now, by marking them too high, he is trying to make his P&L look better than it is. It's a short-term fix—he'll have to sell those twos eventually—but maybe it helps him to sleep better at night. For most of us, marking bonds to market makes us face reality on a daily basis. Bond trading is tough that way. You tally up your profit and loss, and every night when you go home you have to face the music, or, like Carlson, resort to denial.

"You can't do that," Court says.

Carlson ignores him. Court walks over and gives a forearm shiver to the back of Carlson's chair.

"Listen," Court says, loud enough for all of us to hear, "you are supposed to mark your issues where they trade, not where you'd like them to trade. I can't help it if you're in a bad trade, but I've had it with your whining and complaining. You can't sweat your way out of this one." Court turns and yells at Duane, the clerk, who is posting the marks on the board. "Hey. We're marking twos at twenty-seven, damnit."

I can't look at the humiliation, so I turn my head to the right. Vollmer is staring right at me. "Captain Queeg strikes again," he whispers.

That night I go out to dinner with Court Harvey, my revulsion at the idea tempered by what it might do for my career.

Court picks a restaurant on Ninth Avenue in the Twenties, a schizophrenic neighborhood of early-morning transvestite prostitutes and nighttime restaurants for the young and beautiful. We walk in and find people standing five deep at the bar. I immediately feel old, as though I've walked into a high school. Needing a purpose, I walk to the bar, which turns out to be made of dark wood—walnut or mahogany—and stocked with every possible flavor and hue of bourbon, vodka, and scotch. I spy a bottle of Oban and order a glass. It is only Monday night, and I'm as dehydrated as a man lost in the Kalahari. I feel I better have one.

I sip my scotch while Court limps over to the hostess stand and negotiates for a table. This can't be tough; it's so early that none of the trendy people at the bar have any interest in eating. There's hardly a guy in a suit, and the women tend to wear dresses that show a lot of shoulder and leg. Everyone is tan. I can't help wondering, who are these people? How do they all happen to be out on a Monday night? How do they find the time to be outside and get a tan? Where do they get the money to order nine-dollar drinks? How come they don't have to wear dark, conservative work clothes? Why don't they have to eat early, so they can go home early, so they can get up in the wee hours of the morning and get to work? Where, in short, did I go wrong?

I need a second scotch by the time we sit down at a small table in the back of the dining room.

"How's it going?" Court asks.

There's that question again. "Fine," I say.

He praises my adjustment to the ten-year seat. This makes me nervous. Court is stingy with praise. Usually he says nothing, which is how most guys like it. "Worst thing," Chip McCarty once said, "is when he praises you. Remember Dave Kolinski? Harvey actually said he was doing a great job in a traders' meeting. Hearing that was like reading Kolinski's obituary. We all knew he was going to get fucked, and, sure enough, he did."

"I know you'll do great in the seat," Court says. "It wasn't easy for me to put you there. I had some real resistance, especially from the sales force. They said you didn't have the experience. But I told them to keep an open mind. Colin had been doing that job for so long that no one could imagine a younger guy doing it."

Colin Dancer is thirty-eight.

"Who in sales was opposed?" I ask.

"Let's not go into that."

His story is so self-serving that it almost certainly has to be false. It occurs to me that mastering self-serving stories is a valuable talent on Wall Street. As for the sales force, I'm sure it hates Colin Dancer and is glad to see him gone, not that I have any fans in sales, either. Court knows this; he knows that he can claim he's my protector and actually sound plausible.

We order. I choose the steak. Before Wall Street I rarely ate red meat, but at my first Street dinner I understood that ordering something like chicken or Egyptian couscous would seem weak. Seafood is generally acceptable, especially if it is raw. This menu offers nothing raw, though it does have fish sticks at a little more than twenty bucks a plate. As with practically everything else in New York, you can get comfort food—if you're willing to pay.

"So—how's your wife?" Court asks.

"Fine."

"Rachel, right?"

"Right." I'm three years at the firm, and he now knows her name. Dan Connelly once told me that he and Amy have at least one business social engagement a month. Three years at the firm, and I've never known the wives to be invited to a dinner. Were it not for Court's party, he might never have learned Rachel's name.

"How did you meet her?" he asks.

"In Canada. It's where she's from."

"Toronto?"

"No, British Columbia."

"What were you doing there?"

"I met her in the Yukon. I was visiting my brother."

"That's amazing," Court says, "how fate works. If you hadn't been there, and then she at the same time, well . . ." His voice trails off. "Do you believe that for every person there's one best person?"

"One best person?" I drain my scotch, let its embers roll down my throat. I'm not really up for a philosophical discussion. Especially not with Court Harvey.

"You know how people say they are meant for each other?" he asks. "Even though there are five billion people on the planet?"

"So you think there are probably several choices? One-in-a-million gives you five thousand possible mates." Bond traders do this kind of calculation with ease.

"No," he says, "that's just it. I mean, I don't. In my mind I would have to admit that there probably are, but really I don't believe it. I believe there's one right person. If that."

"You're a romantic, Court. I never would have guessed it."

The scotch is going to my head. I make a mental note to keep my mouth shut.

"I'm thinking that Gretchen is that person for me," he says.

I stifle a laugh. This is a truly unoriginal thought. It's as if he's trying to plagiarize a love affair. Court may be a size player on the trading floor, but he's pathetic at life.

"I'm pursuing things along those lines," he tells me, "but Gretchen doesn't seem to understand."

I guess not. "That's tough," I say.

"She says she doesn't want to rush things."

"She's got Buster to think about. That makes a woman go slow. You can't force it."

"I'm thirty-seven," he says. "And I'm not where I want to be in my life. Almost every man my age has a wife, a family, the start of a legacy. With Gretchen, I just don't understand why it's not going better. It should be so right."

"You can't force it," I say again. "I'd ease off. Love is not a market you can muscle."

The food arrives, and that cuts the conversation. I glance over at Court as the waiter lays down his steak and find that he is staring back at me, as if I've crossed him.

The broker car drops me at the Park and Ride at nine-thirty. Eight and a half hours, I think, and I'll be back here again. As I walk to the Escort, I notice that the pavement has a gritty feel; there's still fine gravel left over from when it was dropped here during the winter. Now we're into summer and the sky shows strands of fading sunlight. The seasons come and go, and I barely notice.

Our neighborhood is dark, covered by enormous trees whose leaves are now fully out. I park in our driveway and notice that the windows to Rachel's car are open, so I stop to roll them up. It's an odd sensation, rolling up those windows in the dark. I try to imagine all that happened today in this car. It's as if I can feel my family most keenly in its absence.

It's quiet in the house. A light in the living room leads me there, where Rachel is asleep on the couch in her housecoat. Even in sleep she looks pained or worried—there's a slight V in the middle of her forehead—and so I get down on my knees and whisper to her that we should go upstairs to bed. Then I whisper it again, and again, till finally she mumbles, "I'm too tired."

"C'mon," I say. "I'll help you."

She sighs and drifts off to sleep. I give her a nudge.

"I can't," she mumbles. She puts her arm around my neck.

I slide my left arm behind her back, and my right beneath her knees. "I'll carry you," I say.

"Don't be ridiculous." It's still a groggy voice; she hasn't yet opened her eyes. It's like talking to someone who's been hypnotized.

I brace myself for the weight. Rachel is thin, but no waif. I take a deep breath and lift. At first I almost don't get her off the couch, but then I'm standing, and she feels light.

She opens her eyes, smiles at me, and then nuzzles into my chest. I carry her up the stairs to bed.

Doug Cramer appears on the desk the following Monday. It's been almost two months since I grilled him about his GMAT score. Apparently he's taken a summer-associate job with the firm and been assigned to our desk. Court hasn't mentioned it, which means nothing. Last year's summer associate worked on the desk three weeks before Court introduced him at our weekly traders' meeting.

We put Cramer right to work. Mac and I each chip in twenty bucks and tell Cramer to go down to the cafeteria for bacon-egg-and-cheese sandwiches.

"Where's the cafeteria?"

"Fourth floor," Mac says. "If you learn one thing this summer, I want you to learn your way around the fourth floor."

Mac is right. Forget all the preparation of business-school finance: getting food is the summer associate's most important job. We are stuck on the desk. If we don't want cold food off of Carlos's food cart, we need someone to go downstairs. This is especially true at lunch. In the old days, the firm delivered lunch, gratis. The traders just had to order it when they arrived that morning. Those kinds of perks went the way of ticker tape.

While Cramer is downstairs, we ogle the summer associate assigned to sales. There is an unwritten rule that female summer associates always go to sales. This one is a tall redhead, not beautiful exactly, but attractive in an exotic way, as redheads often are. She has a thin face, but with a strong chin and jaw, and freckles you can see at thirty feet. She carries herself with a quiet confidence unusual in someone so young. She is by far the most attractive woman who has ever worked in governments.

"Buyer," Mac whispers. He's come over and plopped down in Court's seat. "Offered side bid for size."

"She's good-looking," I agree. Her eyes, I notice, are metallic blue.

"She's Cramer's sister," Stevie Vollmer says.

"Challenge," I reply. They are both redheads, and tall, but Cramer has a much wider build and a slight overbite. They don't even look like distant cousins.

"Okay," Vollmer says, "I made that up. Do you think my wife would mind if I slept with her?"

"Probably not," Mac answers, "but the girl would."

The trading day has begun in earnest by the time Cramer returns with twenty-seven bacon-egg-and-cheese sandwiches in two heavy-duty shopping bags. Vollmer takes three sandwiches, leaving two atop his PC to stay warm.

Court Harvey comes back on the desk when the futures pits open. He begins to buy ten-year notes, while selling ten-year futures and bond futures. Unlike the rest of us, who enter all of our trades directly into our computers, Court writes everything down on specially lined paper called trade sheets, as traders did back in the Jurassic period, before they had computers.

By eight-forty-five, Court has over five pages of filled trade sheets, and he realizes he is no longer sure what his position is. He calls Cramer over.

Cramer snaps to attention. He's been sitting in my old seat, answering phones. (We still haven't found a new bill trader.) Answering phones will be his second-most-important task of the summer. He'll be paid fifteen hundred a week.

"I need to know how many ten-years I'm long or short," Court says. He hands over his trade sheets and tells Cramer to count bond futures as one and a half ten-year notes, and ten-year futures as three-quarters of a ten-year. It's work any competent sixth-grade math student could handle, though it's clear that Court wants the answer in a hurry. Of course, had Court entered these trades into his Sun workstation like the rest of us, he'd already have his answer.

Cramer sits down at my old desk. It takes him about three minutes.

"You're long a little over seventeen tens," he says.

"What?" Court challenges. The market has been falling all morning. Court doesn't want to be long. Seventeen tens? It's probably cost him a hundred grand. He grabs the pages out of Cramer's hands. One tears. "That's not right," Court bellows, loud enough for everyone on our side of the floor to hear. I stare intently at my broker screens. Cramer is standing two feet to my left.

"Don't they teach you how to add at Harvard?" Court says, his voice still loud enough to turn someone's head in foreign exchange, two rows down. "Go sit down."

Cramer retreats to my old seat. I turn around to look at him. His neck and ears are flushed, till they practically match the color of his hair. He's been on the job about ninety minutes.

Court sets out to do the work himself. He finishes and goes back to trading. Close to an hour later, he turns to me and says, "Tell Doug he was right."

"What?"

"The new guy. He was right. About my position."

I stand up and walk over to Cramer, who is studying his phone board with a finger raised, as if daring a light to flash twice. His ears are still flushed red with humiliation. I lean close and whisper, "Court says you were right. Welcome to the desk."

7. Top Dollar

"Can I ask you something?" Gretchen asks me.

"Sure." We are sitting in the dimly lighted bar at the Millenium Hotel, on Church Street. The bar is on the third floor, out of the way, an unlikely spot to see someone from the firm. Not that we should really have to worry about being seen, but Gretchen draws attention.

"Did you find me attractive in college?" she asks.

I look at her. "C'mon."

"Seriously," she says. She's blushing.

"Gretchen, you are a beautiful woman. You were beautiful then. You must know that."

"So why didn't you ever make a pass at me, ask me out?"

"I . . . I, well, first, I had a girlfriend, and then, well, I thought you didn't want me to. We were good friends. I didn't think you . . ."

I was young and stupid, is what I should say.

"I remember once," she says while she curls a few strands of her hair behind her ear—her fingernails are painted a dark, cedar red—"I practically begged you to ask me out."

"You never," I say.

"I had a crush on you."

I doubt this. At least, I doubt this was true in college. I sip my scotch, feel my face glow. Her eyes are enormous and dark, truly remarkable.

"You're flirting with me," I say.

"Well, you've learned something over the years." She places a hand very lightly on my knee. I consciously take a breath.

"I don't know, Gretchen. I'm not sure I can . . ." I wave my hand, as if I might find in the air what it is I can't do.

"Lean close to me."

That I can do. I again smell her perfume, mixed with a musky odor. Even Gretchen Barnes sweats it out on the trading floor. There is a silver chain around her neck, a small bull dangling from the end of it. Her skin is very smooth and clear. I like being this close.

We kiss again, longer this time. "Listen," she says. "Why don't you ask me out now?"

"Gretchen, I want to. I really do. It's just that—"

"Nothing outside us will change. No change of permanent allegiances, no divorces, none of that."

The glow in my face has turned into a full-scale fire. And the rest of the room has gone blank; in fact, right now it feels as if Gretchen and I are the only two people on the planet.

"You're speechless?" she asks.

"Flattered," I say. "I mean, you must have your choice of guys." Bid without, as Vollmer would say.

"Every guy I go out with is either a creep, like Court, or he wants to get married. Or both. Who needs it? I'm not sure I want to get married. Ever. I've got a couple girlfriends, it's all they talk about, but I have a child, so that whole biological-clock thing is moot with me. And I have a great career. Why would I want to change any of that?"

"Loneliness?" I say.

"Yes, that's the best reason. But I've seen some of my friends suffer to avoid loneliness. The cure for loneliness can be worse than the disease. Besides, I've got Buster, which I know isn't really what you're talking about, but we've got things right, I think, and I don't want to mess that up."

I think that Gretchen may be the most practical person I've ever met. It's as if she's tallied up her emotional capital and decided to deploy it where it will get the best return.

"I mean, Barry," she asks, "don't you want to ask me out?"

"Yes," I admit. I've always wanted to ask her out. Right now my heart is thumping in my chest. I'm feeling other stirrings as well.

"I like you, Barry. I know this will sound selfish, but aren't I entitled to a little fun? Is there anything so wrong about that? Ever since Buster came along, my life has been a study in selflessness."

It's odd, but I think of my mother. She was once a single mother; she must have been in need of some fun. No doubt she was entitled to it. Probably that's how she met my father.

"Nothing bad will come of it," she says. "I know you have a family, but, in a way, that makes it better. What we do together is for the here and now, and then we'll go our separate ways. That's all I'm saying."

I can't say I will call. I can't say anything.

The next morning is hazy and warm. I am sitting in the back of the Infinity, thinking about Gretchen, when my attention is drawn to a story on the radio about an old couple, concentration-camp survivors, living on Social Security. They have been found dead in their Lower East Side apartment. There are no signs of burglary. The man was found beneath the room's one large window. It was shut and difficult to open, its wooden frame swollen with humidity. The police surmise that the man had been unable to open the window, and the couple was overcome by the heat.

I wonder if New York is a place where senseless death is unusually common, or just a place where such deaths get reported.

"Disgusting," Dino is saying. "Baked fogies. Think of the smell."

"Cold all winter, an oven all summer. I hate to admit it," Mac says, "but this place may have the worst weather on earth."

Dino says, "Last week you said that anyone who wanted to make it in the world came to New York."

"But not for the weather."

That afternoon I'm summoned to Isaac Hunt's office. I sit down, take in the framed Holy Cross pennant and a photo of a very young Isaac Hunt in a mud-stained uniform, helmet off, arm around a coach. Isaac Hunt's exterior window looks out over the river to

Hoboken. It's not only bright today, but also windy. Little whitecaps tumble about in the Hudson. I'm left to sit here for five minutes—an eternity in the middle of the day, when the market is open—till Isaac Hunt strides into the room and throws himself into his high-backed leather chair. "Tell me what happened today," he says.

What happened today is why I've been summoned to the office. Richie Perlmutter, one of our salesmen, had an account that wanted to buy 450 million thirty-year bonds from Stevie Vollmer. In long bonds, this is an enormous trade. Upon hearing the inquiry, Court Harvey went into the market and bought for himself, before Vollmer had a chance to do the same, a move known as "front-running." In short, Court made a lot of money for his trading ledger by taking it out of Vollmer's. Front-running is blatantly against desk rules, perpetrated by the very man who is supposed to enforce them. Vollmer turned cherry red, stood up, and bellowed with rage. That first sound, a howl that sounded like a cross between "ore" and "are," was deep, guttural, preverbal. Soon he and Court were yelling back and forth like the old days, when Colin Dancer was on the desk. It occurred to me then that Vollmer would take on Dancer's role of not-so-loyal opposition. Isaac Hunt happened to be walking by, and now he is collecting evidence from the witnesses. I keep my testimony short.

"There seems to be some discontent in the ranks of the government desk," he says.

I chuckle. I can't help it.

"You agree?"

"Of course I agree," I say, "but Court Harvey has always been fair with me. He gave me the ten-year seat." With my chuckle, I've gone far enough. I'm far too weak to bad-mouth my boss.

"I suggested that," Isaac says. "He was going to go outside the firm. I wanted to bring someone up from within. I suggested he give you a shot."

We both know that Isaac Hunt gives orders, not suggestions. *You owe me, not him.* This is the message.

"Court has always had a bad temper," he continues. "I've spoken with him about this. Many times, many, many times. It does no good to lose your temper. It's a weakness."

Spoken like a manager. It's easy to stay calm when you do not have to deal with the second-by-second pressure of the market. It's easy to stay calm when you have tens of millions of dollars in the bank. When you're that rich, what is there, really, to get upset about?

"Let me ask you, Barry, how do you think the government desk could be better run?"

In over three years at the firm, I've never been asked a question like this. "You want *my* opinion on how to run the government desk?"

"Yes."

The business is changing, I tell him. The sales force is becoming superfluous. Now there's only profit in superior trading knowledge, coupled with low transaction costs. We have both, and need to use them. Hunt and I get into specifics then, go back and forth on accounts and salespeople and the trading desk. He asks a lot of questions. Outside his window I notice that the light is fading from the sky. When I finally emerge from his office it's close to seven-fifteen, and Mac and Dino have gone home without me.

"Watch your back," Dino says the next evening on the commute. Chip McCarty is out "drinking with friends." ("Since when do you have friends?" Dino asked when Mac announced his plans this morning.) I ride shotgun, which gives me a whole new perspective on the commute. There's an orange glow over the city to our left. Ahead I can see hundreds of cars inching up the FDR, their headlights glowing as daylight fades. I look at those headlights and think I should feel something profound, all this humanity on the move, but the metaphors of exodus and flight are simply silly against the ugly reality of thousands of working stiffs fighting their various ways home, cutting and slicing for that imagined advantage that might save them a minute or two. It's a Darwinian battle against time, and there are no winners.

"Who's carrying the knife?" I ask.

"Dumb question. Everyone. Start with Hunt. You think he spent all that time with you yesterday because he's concerned for your career? No, he wants something from you. He has some need for you, and when he doesn't, see if he gives you five seconds."

"I'm no threat to him."

"Barry, I'm trying to teach you something here. He does not care about you. Let me repeat that: he does not care about you. He is totally indifferent. All he cares about is that the division makes money so he can make his eight sticks a year and pretend that he is a man of importance. Can you believe this guy?"

Ahead of us a windowless van has turned into our lane, forcing Dino to move left and slam on his brakes.

"Probably forty illegal Chinese in the back of that thing, looking for a lawsuit," Dino says. "I tell you, this job is starting to get to me. You do it long enough, you think everybody is out to fuck you. Which they are. I just don't want to have to think about it, you know? I'm not sure how much longer I can hang on."

"What would you do if you quit?"

"If I have enough money?" he asks.

"If that's possible," I say.

"I'd be a carpenter," Dino says.

"A carpenter? Hammer and nails? Why?"

"I like working with my hands. I like building things. I used to do this kind of work. Put me through college, and I felt good about it. I was building somebody's home, you know, the place where they would live, raise their kids. Christ was a carpenter, you know."

"Yeah," I say, "and look where it got him."

"And look where bond trading has gotten us, Barry. It's quarter to seven at night. We probably won't be home for an hour. You probably left your house before six this morning. How do you feel?"

"Like dog snot."

"Exactly. And when you look back on your day, can you point to something and say, 'Hey, I made that, I made a difference in somebody's life'? All that effort, but what in the grand scheme of things have you really done?"

"We've done something," I say. "We're part of something big. The American financial markets, they fund all sorts of activity that makes the country strong and prosperous. I'd argue that, one way or the other, all the opportunity of America really gets funneled through these markets."

"Jesus, you sound like a goddamn I-bank brochure."

"It's true," I say. I do sound like a brochure. Sometimes the brochures are right.

"Maybe, in a big, abstract way," Dino says. "Look, last night Stace and I are watching the Discovery Channel, and we see this pack of lions take out a wildebeest that got sick and couldn't move too well. I mean, the thing was sick. It should have been on injured reserve. It wasn't a fair fight, but these lions jumped on the thing, and next thing you know, the wildebeest is down on its side, kicking its legs, and then it's getting eaten by half a dozen lions. Now, you could say it's good to cull the herd, but in the end, those lions were just being lions, getting their own, and they couldn't have given a fuck about the health of the herd, the circle of life, the greater good, and all the rest of that crap."

"So what's your point?"

"Don't think you're so noble. You're just getting yours."

God, I hope I am.

Several moments pass. "Carpenters don't make much money," I say.

"I know. That's why I'm a bond trader. It's hard to make a lot of money *and* go to heaven."

"You sold out," I say.

"Damn right, but at least I got top dollar."

It's dark when I pull into my driveway, though the downstairs of the house glows with a yellow light. I walk toward the door, then stop and try to picture what I would notice of this house were it unknown to me.

It's a modest home, grimy white and in need of paint, with black shutters and a gray-shingled roof. Ancient trees tower over the property, oak and beech and even one walnut that probably got their starts back when this land was still claimed by the British. There's a large maple by our bedroom window. A boy's bike lies sprawled by the side door. The air is very, very quiet, just the slight rustle of a breeze and the sound of a revving car engine, fading.

Quietly, and slowly as a stalking cat, I approach the side window, then look in at our dinner table. It's set for three, along with a high chair. There's a pitcher of water and a salad bowl, two unlit candles, and what's left of a bottle of wine we opened last night.

I continue around the back of the house, where I climb onto the back porch and look into the family room. Sam is sitting on his knees on the carpet, a full array of toy cars carefully laid out in front of him. He seems to be playing a game of demolition derby. His little sister is beside him with two cars of her own. She studies him, and then copies his every move. Rachel sits on the couch, bare feet up on the coffee table. She is watching the television and balancing a glass of wine on her jeans. Her hair is tied back into a ponytail that is draped over her left shoulder. She looks relaxed, and quite beautiful. A stranger looking in on this room would, I think, be quite jealous of the man of the house. Well, I want to say to Rachel, here's the life we made. Here it is.

Of course, I'm not in the picture. And I know that Rachel is not really just watching TV, nor are the kids just playing on the carpet. What they're really doing, at seven-forty-three at night, is waiting for me to come home for dinner.

By the time Rachel and I get Sam into bed that night, I'm ready to turn in myself, but Rachel insists that we settle on the couch to watch a little TV together. Her idea is that we so rarely see each other alone that we have to take an hour or so after the kids go to sleep or our lives will dissolve into nothing but work and child care. "We should at least make an attempt to spend *some* time together," she says.

We check the *TV Guide* and find that the Yankees are the only thing worth watching. The Yankees have been the best show on television for several summers. Rachel is a big fan, something she learned from Sam. I, of course, remain a Tiger fan, which leaves me, like all Tiger fans, slightly bitter and wistful for the glory of 1968.

So Rachel and I are settled in on the couch. Rachel is dozing. Knoblauch bats in the fourth. I am thinking about Gretchen, what to do about her. On the one hand, I've made a vow to Rachel, and I intend to live up to that vow. And I can barely stay awake for my wife; how would I handle a mistress? On the other hand, if I'm going to have an affair, Gretchen is the perfect choice, someone whom I've known for a long time, a friend, someone committed elsewhere, someone I can trust. Someone with extravagant, heartbreaking beauty. I've been tempted by other women before, and almost acted twice. I never did, and the temptation and desire never went away. Now I think about it all the time. When I was a single man I rarely dated only one woman at a time, and I became convinced that love for one woman was not diminished by having sex with another. Marriage, of course, changed all this, and having children upped the ante even more. Suddenly infidelity could have an effect on three lives, and precisely the three lives I care most about. I think about Sam and his routines—school, sports, the elaborate internal world he seems to have built around his fleet of toy trucks—or about Jane and how her eyes open wide and her face brightens when I walk in the door in the evenings. And then there's Rachel, whose voice still chirps with happiness when I call and she realizes it's me. I know I've spent a lot of effort and love to build what I have, and I want to have it. And, I can't help myself, I want Gretchen, too.

The portable phone rings. I answer, figuring it's Tokyo or some old friend who has no idea that I have no life and that nine-thirty at night is a terribly late hour to call.

"Hey, little bro," says Ben. I'm suddenly wide awake. "You know," he says, "I wanted to call and thank you for that extra wheat you've been sending. It's been a big help."

He asks me about our mother, and about Rachel, even about Sam and Jane, whom he seems to know about. He is almost avuncular. I start to believe that he has called just to communicate, as I'm sure brothers often do, and then he hits me up.

He says he has lymphoma, a type of cancer. At least, that's what the doctor at the Canadian Health Service says. Ben wants to get a second opinion down in Seattle, and he even set up the appointment, but he's short on money and, being a Canadian resident, he has to pay up front for the visit and the tests he will need.

"How much?"

"Seven fifty."

"C'mon," I say.

"What can I say, Barry? I need it."

"Do you work?"

"When I can. I'm not like you, you know, with a fancy education and all. I've got to take what I can get."

"I can see that. But what is that? What do you do?"

"I'm a carpenter," he says. "I'm good at it, too."

"What bothers me," I say, "is that you lie to me. It's obvious."

"I'm not lying. I'm really sick."

I don't know whether to believe him. I figure that anytime he wants money he starts lying.

"Why did you go to the doctor in the first place?" I ask.

"Because I felt bad. Inside. I had pain."

"Pain," I repeat. I don't really believe him. I ask a few questions. His answers are vague, his memory is poor. I decide to send him a hundred dollars. Lower his expectations. Keep him away for a while.

Rachel wakes in the fifth inning. "I dreamt I heard the phone ring," she says. "Did someone call?"

"No," I say.

8. Eat the Cheese

On Sunday evening, late in August, Rachel and I sit on our back porch, sipping scotch. It's a wonderful night, the air warm and dotted with the tapping of a woodpecker. Jane is playing nearby at her toy kitchen, and Sam is out in the neighborhood riding his bike. School starts in a week.

"Another summer," I say, remembering how I used to feel as a kid, when the start of a school year portended great change. In a way, I feel like that now. For one thing, the fall season is the last chance you have to put money in your ledger before bonuses are decided in December. It is perhaps the most important season in a year of bond trading. And I feel good about how things are going. Our lives are ticking along. Rachel and I are living the life we planned.

"Sad, isn't it," Rachel says. She has her arms spread wide on the Adirondack chair. Those arms are cedar-color against the white expanse of the armrest. My arms are still the color of chalk.

I ask what's sad.

"Another year lost in a place we really don't want to be. And it's all for money. We do so much we don't really want to do, just for money."

"Everyone does."

"But wouldn't it be great if we didn't have to worry about it? We could just chuck all this, just do what we want?"

"But we can't," I say.

"I know we can't, but, God, I'm tired of thinking about money."

She gets up to start dinner, and I head out into the neighborhood to find Sam. In my neighbors' backyards I see cookouts and men trimming hedges and cutting lawns. At some houses dogs come running up, barking to defend their territory. I wave to a few people, if our eyes meet, but I'm around so little that I don't really know any of my neighbors.

I find Sam's bike lying among the trees and fallen leaves of a strip of woods that leads down to the Croton Reservoir. Once I walk fifty feet down the hill I am past the houses, and the oak and beech and maple look, I'm sure, as they have for thousands of years. I see Sam. He's sitting atop an enormous rock, a slab of granite four feet high and maybe six by six across its top. He's facing the reservoir, which I can see through the trees. The sun reflects off the water. The glare is blinding.

Sam turns when he hears me walking through the dead leaves.

"Hey, Dad," he says, and turns back to the water. There's a fallen tree by the rock, and I use it to climb up next to him.

"Whatcha doing?" I ask. I sit next to him, our legs flat out on the rock, our arms reached behind us to buttress our weight.

"Just looking," he says.

"At what?"

"The water. Look at how bright it is. Like it's on fire."

"You come here a lot?" I ask.

"I guess. Tim and I used to, then play war or something. Now I just like to come by myself. It's a good place to think."

"What do you think about?"

"I don't know. Stuff. Sometimes I like being alone. It's, like, when you're alone you can think about all kinds of things, except that you're almost never alone, you know?"

I tell him I know exactly what he means.

"Last week, I saw a white deer. He walked right by, over there. He was all white, with a few brown hairs right on the top of his back. It was freaky."

"An albino?" I ask.

"What's that?"

I explain, and he nods. We look at the water, its surface scalloped this way and that by the shifting wind. The reflected sunlight is still almost blinding.

"Mom's making dinner," I say.

"Dad," he asks, "what do you think I'll be when I grow up?"

It's a question I wonder about every day.

"I don't know," I say. "I suppose it depends on what you want to be."

"Do you think I'll end up working at Wal-Mart, like you?"

I smile. "I work on Wall Street, not at Wal-Mart."

"Well, do you like it?"

"Some parts I like, some I don't."

"Can't you find a job where you like all the parts?"

"I wish I could. Most people can't." I slide forward, then jump off the rock. "We've got to go home for dinner," I tell him, "but first I'm going to let you in on a secret. Your parents don't have everything figured out."

He nods, as if he's known this all along.

Athletes speak of being "in the zone," a place where they can do nothing wrong. Traders have a place like that, too, and I find mine at the beginning of the week. By the end of the day Wednesday, I'm up $535,000 for three days. I feel at one with the world; being right so often is good for the soul.

"Make any wheat today?" Vollmer asks, as we stand up to go to our Wednesday traders' meeting.

"Short all day," I say, which was the right trade. "You?"

"I was short for about thirty seconds, then I got hit, and it's been a shit show ever since. But you're on a roll. Next time you get short, let me know."

I like traders' meetings. They're relaxing. We sit in a windowless conference room, without computer screens or squawk boxes. After a day on the trading floor, there is nothing better than sensory deprivation.

"So," Court says toward the end, once we've talked about several problem accounts and a new sales-credit schedule, "there's been some talk about year end. It's still a long way off, and no firm numbers have been determined. It's shaping up to be a fairly tough year. The worldwide volatility in equity markets has hurt, as have the difficulties in corporate bonds, and the slowdown in both equity and debt issuance. Our London office is having a terrible year, there's no other way to put it. There are several disaster situations within our division, and one right in global governments. I can't go into the specifics, so please don't ask. Now, our desk here in New York is doing reasonably well, but we will not be unscathed by what's happening in the rest of the department, division, or firm."

"Two years ago, when London set records, we didn't see any of that money," says Stevie Vollmer. "This year, we may well set records here in New York. Why should we get hurt now?"

"We're all one firm," Court says, "with one P&L."

Later, when Mac, Dino, and I are riding the elevator down to the garage, Mac lets his feelings out about Vollmer, which is unusual. Mac rarely has a word about anyone. "Vollmer is an idiot," he says. "Talking at a traders' meeting."

"But he was right," I say.

"Of course he was right, but you never question the Hooky Duke. Never. That comment today, I bet it costs him fifty grand."

"He questioned the Hooky Duke?" Dino says. "At least fifty. He'll go in and Harvey will say, 'Tough year, Stevie. Eat the cheese.' "

"Eat the cheese?" I ask.

"Yeah, eat the cheese."

"What's that mean?"

The elevator opens, and we head out into the garage.

"If you have to ask," Dino says, "I can't explain it to you."

September slips into October, and suddenly the light is fading fast. Morning mist makes the lights of oncoming traffic look like balls of white fuzz. The commute home up the FDR—that five-miles-per-hour game of brinkmanship—takes place in the dark. Some days, if I don't remember to look out the window at work, I don't see daylight at all.

All I Could Get

On a Tuesday, I get a call from Jennifer Springs, the head recruiter, who begs me to go down to Wharton the next night for the fall M.B.A. recruiting drive. When I started at the firm, I eagerly volunteered for these trips, in which swarms of bankers and traders descend on a room of desperate business-school students (desperate meaning jobless), eat and drink to excess, and then pass out on the last Metroliner back to New York. I had once been one of those desperate M.B.A.'s, and I felt superior as a firm representative. I also assumed that volunteering would help at bonus time. After all, Jennifer Springs said that one's participation in recruiting events was "noticed." This might have been true, but not by anyone who mattered. Eventually, I quit the charade. Certainly Jennifer Springs had no say in my pay, and Court Harvey didn't give a damn about recruiting, so what was the point?

"Jennifer," I now say, "I live forty-five miles north of the city. I get home so late from these things. It takes too much out of me."

"We're really short, Barry. How 'bout if I put you up in the city? What do you say?"

I'm about to say that I'd rather watch my leg burn than go to Philadelphia and chat with a room full of M.B.A.'s, but then I get an idea. Maybe it's time to call Gretchen.

"Where in the city?" I ask Jennifer, fairly certain of the answer.

"How 'bout the Millenium? You can practically roll out of bed and get to your desk."

"Done," I say, and so, the next night, I'm standing in the University of Pennsylvania Museum, among ancient Chinese sculptures, wall-hung tapestries, and shadowy lighting. I sip at a Heineken, talk to a first-year M.B.A. about the bond market, and think of Gretchen. Months have gone by, and I have not called her. I haven't figured out how to work it into my life, until tonight.

"So," the M.B.A. says, with an odd country lilt. You don't hear much twang at recruiting events. Most recruits wring it out of their systems before they talk to recruiters. "Do you think I could visit you on the trading floor in New York?"

I look at him. He's a short kid with bad skin and a bad suit. He's from outside Tulsa. He graduated from the University of Oklahoma at twenty, got a Ph.D. at twenty-five from Berkeley, then spent a year as an assistant at the particle accelerator in Texas. When Congress shut it down, he packed up his bags and headed for business school, which shows that he's unusually practical for a particle physicist.

But visit me in New York? This geek may well be brilliant—he might even be, as he claims, very good on a horse—but if I bring him to the trading floor, I have to take ownership for him. He becomes my geek, my cowboy. I'm in no mood to defend anybody. I try to think of a polite way to say no.

"Not a good idea," I finally say. There are five or six students standing behind the physicist, all trying to weasel their way into our conversation. I turn the geek down loudly, so as to discourage the others.

A cell phone rings. The geek pulls a Motorola flip phone out of his pocket, and hangs up on the caller. "Why not?" he asks me.

"Tell you what," I say. "Let me make a call on that thing."

I don't own a cell phone, mostly because I want there to be times when no one can contact me. Now I pull Gretchen's number from my wallet, along with one of my business cards, which I hand to the kid in exchange for the phone. He cradles the card in his hand as though it were fragile.

Gretchen answers on the second ring. She says hello in a deep, throaty way. I may have woken her. I turn away from the M.B.A.'s, and find myself talking at a stone Buddha of some unknown dynasty.

"Gretchen," I say, "it's Barry. I know it's been a while. Can you meet me tonight? I'm staying at the Millenium Hotel, room 1426."

She lets out a deep breath. "I'd given up."

"Can't talk. I'll be there after eleven," I say.

"So will I," she says. I take a look at the Buddha. He looks as content as can be.

The cowboy/geek is beaming when I hand him back the phone. I excuse myself, avoid the waiting students, and head for the bar.

Later, I hear a knock and open the door to my hotel room. Gretchen stands before me, wearing black boots, jeans, and a black leather jacket. I step aside and she brushes past me, a faint smell of a new perfume in her wake. I pause to take it in, then follow her to the middle of the room. We kiss. This time there is no need to stop. Soon we are doing what I've dreamed of doing, on and off, for almost half my life.

At first, I want to make the night last. It's wonderful to give in to an attraction we've both held so long. I feel young again, as I did in college, when all paths were open to me in a way they never would be again. I know all paths are not open to me now, but still, I'm in no hurry for this night to end.

Gretchen dresses and leaves a little after one. She wants to get some sleep and be home to wake Buster before she heads off to work. I try to sleep, but can't. I am left to channel surf in the wasteland of late-night New York television. The TV is still playing when I am jarred from sleep by the wake-up call at six.

Forty-five minutes later, I walk out onto the street. Taxis are racing up Church Street. The sky is gray. An army of subway commuters marches from the Fulton Street station to the courtyard of the World Trade Center, from where these soldiers will take up positions in the Trade Center and the World Financial Center across the West Side Highway. As I wait to cross Church, steam and last summer's heat rise from the subway grate. No, I tell myself, nothing has really changed.

The next Sunday, Dan and Amy Connelly come over for an afternoon cookout. It's a cool, raw day. Fog floats among the homes of our neighborhood and condenses on the windshields of cars. It hasn't really rained, but the street is wet. The Connellys arrive in a new Land Rover, a massive English racing-green vehicle with bush guards over the lights and windows along the corner of the roof. "For spotting giraffes," Dan says.

They have warned us that they have some news, and I knew from the sound of Dan's voice that there has been some turnaround in his career. He and Amy are practically giggling when they arrive. Sam sprints out the side door and tries to tackle Dan before he can climb down from the driver's seat. There's always a football game when Dan comes over. He has no children, but he's perfectly suited for them.

"Hey, L.T.," he says to Sam. "Easy. Let me get to the field."

Amy and Rachel hug hello.

"So—what's this news?" Rachel asks. She looks to Amy, and then Dan.

"We got bought," Dan says. "Signed the deal this week."

"That's great," I say. "How much?"

"Four . . . seventy-five."

"Thousand? Million?" He's told me that he hoped the company would go for a hundred million, but he doubted it. He still has 1 percent.

"Million," he says.

"C'mon," Sam says, "let's play."

"Wait a second. Am I hearing you right?" I whisper to Dan. "Did you just make four and three-quarter million dollars?"

"Uh-huh."

Almost five million bucks. Dan Connelly got rich while I work seventy-hour weeks and can barely put any money away. I am the guy with the Ivy League degrees. I'm the guy working on Wall Street, and Wall Street is supposed to pay more than anyplace else. I have to wear a suit and shave every day, while he dresses in khakis and a golf shirt, if he goes to the office at all. I sneak in a couple weeks of vacation every year, while he and Amy travel at least once a month, and last summer they took twenty-five days together in Europe. I seem to be making all of the sacrifices and none of the money.

Dan and I high-five. "You son-of-a-bitch," I say. I'm happy for him, and pissed off, too. I'm being left behind.

Later, after our game of football with Sam, Dan and I stand on the deck as I flip hamburgers. Our beers stand with the potted plants on the deck railing.

"Dan, I can't believe you hit the jackpot. You thought you were going under."

"Yeah, and this is only the beginning. There's so much money flying around right now, you wouldn't believe it. My contract says I've got six months more, and then I'll be on to the next venture. Our head software engineer already approached me. He's got an idea and he wants me to come along. We figured we needed five million bucks to really get the thing up and running. Two weeks ago, he and I went looking for venture capital. Now we've got three firms trying to give us twenty million apiece."

"I guess I should have jumped at your offer last spring," I say.

"I can't believe how things have changed since then," he says. He takes a swig of beer. "I'll definitely keep you in mind."

A silence wafts over us. It's pretty clear that Dan doesn't need me.

"So," he says, "how's work?"

I call Gretchen on Monday, and suggest a night like last week.

"Done," she says. She gives me the name of a hotel, and I call and make a reservation. It's that simple.

Bonus talks soon become the subject of the carpool. "You walk in," Dino says one day, "and they poke you in the eye. Then they turn your head and they poke you in the other eye. Then they check your head to see if you've got a third eye, 'cause they don't want you to get off easy."

"I wish they'd do away with the talk," Mac says. "It's so painful listening to Court Harvey make up reasons why he gets to be rich and I don't. They ought to just post the numbers on a bulletin board, next to your Social Security number, like they did with grades in college. It's not like you can say anything in your meeting, anyway."

"Who says you're not rich?" Dino says. "You're driving the ultimate driving machine. You live in a Bedford mansion. You send your kids to private school. Where I grew up, that's rich."

Dino's right, of course. Where anyone grew up, Mac is rich, but that's not really the point. It's the paradox of Wall Street, maybe of life everywhere, that success creates an ever-deepening need. I wish I could go back to the time when seventy grand a year seemed like plenty of money, so that now I could be content with three times that, but whenever I start to think that way I picture Dino and Mac and Court Harvey, and even Isaac Hunt, and I feel like a chump. I know that there will always be someone richer than I am, and that it will always piss me off.

Bonus day is cold, with pouring rain. "Just in case you weren't depressed enough," Dino says as we fight our way through the construction. The cement barriers contain the rain, so that we are driving through several inches of standing water. "They ought to have crisis counselors on the floor today, like they do at those schools after the kids shoot them up."

Court calls me in first. I take this as a good sign. The year before, I went last, and it wasn't a good year. At least, not for me.

"How's things going?" he asks.

I smile. Every several seconds, a sheet of rain slaps against the window that looks out over the construction site. I catch my reflection. It's ten-thirty in the morning, but dark enough that the window is a mirror. I wear a crooked half-smile, like a man who has smelled something too embarrassing to acknowledge.

"I've been wanting to talk to you," he says. He's leaning back in his chair, arms full on the armrests, a picture of proprietorship. Still, something strikes me as off. His eyes, perhaps. They seem deeper-set. I can see his crow's feet from across the desk.

"Well, it's that time of year," I say.

"Things are going really badly with Gretchen," he says. "She doesn't want to see me."

"Hmmm."

"I don't get it," he goes on. "I did everything I could."

"Well, Court, sometimes that's how it goes with women."

"Have you talked to her?"

"No," I lie.

"Would you?"

"What do you want me to say, Court?"

"Talk to her. You know her, Barry, and people like you. She likes you. She told me. Plead my case. At least, find out why she won't see me."

"Didn't she give you any hints?"

"She said we had different interests, but I don't really think that's true. And, besides, I'm willing to expand my interests. Isn't that the point of relationships? For example, she likes the theater. Do you know I've been to six plays in the last two weeks? I've seen all the big shows. I've got this theater thing down. I'm conversant, but I can't get her to talk to me."

I look at Court's face, so pale, with those narrow-set blue eyes. I can see how a woman might find him frightening.

"It's a lot of pressure you probably put on her," I say. "No one likes that."

"It's what's right."

I watch a couple sheets of rain slap the window.

"I know what you're thinking," Court says, "that I'm trying to muscle this trade, but I'm not. I know it's meant to be, and I can wait for her to come around. I have a lot more patience than you think, Barry. I'm not asking you to do anything special, but you have Gretchen's ear. Please use it." He pauses. "I did just put you in the ten-year seat."

I take a breath. "What?"

"I did just put you in the ten-year seat."

I don't know what to say. His insinuation—that I've been given a special opportunity so I can help him score with Gretchen—shocks me. I'm not naïve. I know that Court had the major hand in my ascension, and that he was motivated, in part, by his belief that I could help with Gretchen. I just hadn't thought that he consciously understood it that way, that he could plan it all with such purpose.

"What do I do?" he asks.

"Do you really want my advice?" I ask.

He says that he does.

"Forget Gretchen. Too much baggage, too complicated, and not willing. Why waste your time on her? Look at you. You're relatively young, single, rich, straight, a man, and in New York City. There's a short squeeze for guys like you."

This is not what he wants to hear. His jaw is set hard. Over the rain I think I might be hearing him grind his teeth. I remember the conversation we had some months before about Court believing in one right person. He isn't going to let go of Gretchen easily.

"You want your number?" he asks at last.

"Sure, I guess."

"Look, Barry, I got talking points here, but I'm not going to bother with them. London, equity volatility, you know the drill. The point is, I paid you more than I really should have. I hope you enjoy it, but, let me tell you, money is not everything."

"I've heard that said," I answer—usually from rich guys like Court Harvey. This is, I realize, the most bizarre bonus talk in history.

"Four hundred," he says. "Some of it's stock, as you know. Make lots of wheat in tens and you'll do even better next year."

I almost leap out of my chair and start jumping up and down like a pitcher who has just gotten the last out in the World Series. Four hundred thousand dollars. Last year I made $180,000. In my wildest dreams, I hoped for $260,000. Now I want to grab Court's phone and call Rachel. Instead, I say nothing. I know I am supposed to act with either indifference or disdain.

"Aren't you happy?" he asks.

Of course I'm happy, but I can never really show it. And I also know that Court has paid me a lot less than he once paid Colin Dancer.

"You know, Court," I say, "it will help me pay off some debts, but I don't want to be a cut-rate ten-year-note trader. I bet I made well less than half what you would have had to pay Colin Dancer."

"That's one reason why Colin doesn't work here anymore," Court says.

Back on the desk, Vollmer hisses at me, "Hey, Meat. You were in there a long time. Didn't you take the Vaseline?"

"Forgot," I say.

"How was it?"

"How is it ever?"

"A stupidathon." He shakes his head. "That son-of-a-bitch."

I call Rachel.

"Well?" she asks.

"Rachel," I tell her, "all of our dreams are about to come true."

I don't trade much the rest of the day. Like Midas, I spend my time counting up my riches. Out of the four hundred I have to subtract the eighty I've already received in salary, plus the thirty in restricted stock that I won't see for five years, if at all. That leaves $290,000. I figure that, after I pay federal, state, and local taxes, plus Social Security and Medicare, I'll be left with a check of $150,000. I can pay off the last of my student loans, buy a new car, and invest the rest. I study my scratch paper, and a feeling of triumph comes over me. I want to raise my arms in victory.

9. The Garage of Conspicuous Consumption

"Look at this," Dino says, as we sail through the construction area. Miraculously, three straight lines appear, rather than the serpentine track and cement-barrier-induced lane splits of the last nine months.

"This is just a Christmas present," Mac says. "You mark my words. Those guys'll need work in the new year. They'll have this torn up again by the middle of January."

It has been a quiet ride in, the morning after bonus talks. All the anticipation, the anxiety, the hope. It all has faded against the ugly reality that we are now fourteen months from collecting our next number. No matter the outcome, there is something depressing about the bonus system. You work all year, then walk into a room and in several minutes have a price put on that year. It's as if the managers are saying, "We bought you, and here's what we paid." And because it's tough to leave trading at the office—you think about it at night, in the shower, and (God help me) when you're putting your kids down to sleep or having a family meal—what they bought is more than just your labor.

"So," Mac says as we descend the garage ramps, "it was about how you guys expected, less than you hoped for last summer but a little better than you thought you might get last week?"

"Exactly," Dino says. "Shit."

We are in the garage now, on the lowest level. Dino swings the Infinity into the front row, the one closest to the elevator. On most days, at least half the spaces in this row are empty when we arrive, to be filled in the coming hours by managing directors from around the firm. Today, though, there isn't a clear spot. Instead, there's one shiny and large Mercedes and BMW after another, along with a couple Lincoln and Land Rover sport-utility vehicles. Most have personalized license plates, an even mix of New York, New Jersey, and Connecticut. I know the managing directors didn't go out en masse and buy new cars with sacks full of bonus money, but it seems that way. Suddenly four hundred thousand dollars a year feels like real chump change.

"Look at these cars," says Mac. "Is there a managing-director meeting this morning?"

"They're celebrating with the Swedish-massage team on the twelfth floor," Dino says. Top management has its offices on twelve. Dino parks in the second row, between a Lexus and a Porsche. The Porsche's license plate reads, BUY BUY BUY, the Lexus's, MR BOND. On the other side of the Lexus is an MG with the plate GOJANEGO.

"It's getting tougher and tougher to find a place to park," Dino says, "in the garage of conspicuous consumption."

Upstairs, I can barely bring myself to look at the screens. Another year of this till the next bonus. I decide to think back to last night, when the thrill of it was still with me. I was elated. I couldn't get over the chunk of money that was coming. I kept picturing it, wads of hundred-dollar bills sitting on the dining-room table, as in a gangster movie. In actuality, the table held a bottle of Heitz Cellars identical to the one we'd received from Lance Bailey the previous Christmas. (All of my brokers engage in a bidding war of generosity at Christmas.) The wine was fantastic, and obviously expensive, but I caught myself before I asked what it cost. I didn't need to know. I wasn't in business school anymore, when I wouldn't even buy Sam a drink from a convenience store because a buck nineteen for a cranberry juice didn't fit into our budget.

Rachel and I hurried to put the kids to bed. I rushed Jane through her bath and sang her favorite songs in the darkness of her room while she drank from her milk bottle and dozed in my arms. Rachel helped Sam lay his clothes out for the next morning and pack up his book bag, and a little after eight-thirty we were both back downstairs, sitting on the couch, sipping wine by the light of two candles Rachel had placed on the coffee table.

In the flickering light of that room, Rachel looked different. Younger, I suppose. She wore a thin cashmere sweater and black jeans. She rested her bare feet on the coffee table, by the candles.

"It's really a lot of money," she said.

"It's a start," I replied, half joking.

"If we start making money like that, we'll live pretty nice. There won't be much we can't do."

"Oh yeah? And what is it that you want to 'do'?"

"Travel. I've always wanted to go to Italy. We could walk through Florence, Rome, all the places we really ought to see. And we don't always have to go so far. We just need to get out of here more often, even if it's just to Boston or Vermont for a weekend. That's what money could really do for us: give us some variety."

I thought of all the places I'd been in Europe, with a backpack, and how great it would be to go back and see them again with Rachel.

"It sounds wonderful," I said.

"Well, then, we have to do it. Not having money was always the excuse for why we couldn't do things. We don't have that excuse anymore."

"Okay," I said, "Boston this weekend?"

"Let's find someone to look after the kids and then go alone. It could take a little time."

She slid over to my side of the couch, and I put my hand on the small of her back, then worked my way up beneath her sweater. She purred in a way that I knew meant that what I was doing was good, and that I should keep doing it. Live with someone long enough and you pick up on all sorts of unspoken cues. Soon I've tossed the sweater to the floor, and Rachel has peeled off her pants and worked mine down to my ankles, where I can't seem to shake them free and soon stop trying. It's the first time since we married that I can remember making love with Rachel outside our bed. It's like a getaway itself.

We're on the downhill side to Christmas and New Year's. A lot of the world is already on vacation, but Wall Street stays open for trading, albeit at a greatly reduced pace. Court is out. ("To avoid assassination after giving out numbers," says Stevie Vollmer.) Chip McCarty becomes the temporary head of the desk, a role he's assumed ever since Colin Dancer was sacked. Tom Carlson has more experience than Mac, but no one makes mention of this. Carlson is just too short and disheveled even to be considered.

"Barry? Hard to say," I hear Mac say to Stevie Vollmer, who is standing by Mac's desk. It's lunchtime. I'm staring at the broker screens. Not a single bond is flashing.

"What?" I ask.

"Come over here," Mac says.

Vollmer, Mac, and I stand in a circle. We constitute the government desk on this day. Stan Glover is trading strips, but he sits in his own world at the end of the row. Court still hasn't hired a bill trader, and, with Carlson out, we have Duane Rizzo sitting in the seat. Duane normally works on the floor below, checking that all the trades we enter into our computers are entered correctly. He is called a "checkout" guy. In the old days, checkout guys were routinely made traders, the way minor-league ballplayers are brought up to the major leagues. Now, though, the firm tends to hire M.B.A.'s like Doug Cramer, leaving the Duanes of the world with a difficult and thankless job that has far less upside than Duane's boss lets on when hiring checkout guys out of college. I feel bad for Duane that he's the vacation bill trader; it's cruel to give him a taste of the big time and then send him downstairs. Court will never give him the full-time job. It will go to some new M.B.A., provided somebody's nephew doesn't get the job, and I doubt that Duane has any well-placed uncles at the firm.

"Court Harvey is out of control," Chip McCarty says. Vollmer stares at me, daring me to disagree.

"He's got a problem with his temper," I say, "if that's what you mean."

"Hey, Meat," Vollmer says, "that may be the biggest understatement I've ever heard."

"Here's the problem, as I see it," says Mac. "Court Harvey is supposed to be our leader, a guy we can look up to. In the navy, they taught me to have respect for my own position. I was supposed to be someone who the enlisted men could look up to."

"A fucking gentleman," Vollmer says.

"Well, Court Harvey is not someone anyone can look up to. He loses his temper, steals our good trades, takes all our bonus money. There's no leadership, no vision for the business. Look at a guy like Ryan Hauptman. He's created a massive business over there in mortgages, and his traders not only like him, they respect him. That's what we need."

I know that Ryan Hauptman's traders respect him because he pays them so well, which, in short, is how a manager earns his traders' respect. Everything here has a price. Mac and Vollmer would probably put up with Court's temper tantrums if he paid them more. In any case, they're suggesting open rebellion, something I've never contemplated. For all his failings, to me Court is the boss. Not because I like it that way, but because I've never imagined anyone else in the job.

"So what are you going to do?" I ask.

"We're going to go around Court."

"Go around?"

"To Isaac Hunt."

"Carlson's in," Mac says. "And Stevie, and Stan. And me. We'd like you, too. I know Harvey's some kind of boyhood friend of yours, but he fucks you over just like he fucks everyone over. We've all seen it."

Vollmer nods at me, then I see his eyes focus in the distance. I turn to see Ryan Hauptman and Isaac Hunt walk past the government row, as if on cue. They are deep in conversation. Hauptman is doing the talking. He's small and thin, built like a jockey, with hollow cheeks and hair so black that I have sometimes wondered if it isn't dyed. Hunt, big man that he is, leans his ear to listen, his gait uneven from walking almost doubled over. If I didn't know better, I'd pick him for the underling. It occurs to me that even the most powerful men are always working it, always laying the groundwork to get farther ahead, aiming for some spot so far out in front that they won't be vulnerable, if such a place exists. I used to assume Court was there.

I think for a moment of what Court would do if he were to find out about Gretchen and me—if he were even to suspect it.

"What do I have to do?" I ask Mac.

"Keep quiet till Isaac Hunt calls for you. Then tell him you think Court Harvey has to go."

"To be replaced by who? You?"

Mac nods. He's the obvious replacement.

"Can I still get a ride with you in the morning if you become the head guy?" I ask Mac. I intend this to be a joke, a way of saying I am with them.

"The fee might go up," he says.

Vollmer slaps me on the back, now that I'm one of the frat brothers. "Attaboy, Meat."

That night I meet Dan Connelly for a quick drink after work. We plan to head for our homes by six-thirty. We haven't seen each other since our football Sunday, and we rarely go so long without getting together.

"How'd you make out at year end?" he asks. He's wearing a black turtleneck and three days of stubble. It seems that this is the new high-tech style, to look as if you trained for the job in your high-school smoking lounge.

"I did okay," I say. Dan's paycheck from his firm's getting bought will be twelve times as much as mine. I think back to high school, when I thought I was the one with all the potential. I'm not even sure where I went wrong.

"You don't sound happy," Dan says.

I look around. We're in a midtown bar with lots of indirect lighting and mirrors, a room that's all reflection, tough to get one's bearings in.

"I don't know that I am."

"Jesus, Barry, lighten up. What did they pay you?"

I tell him.

"That's a lot of fuckin' money."

"I know," I say, thinking, "It's chump change compared to what you got."

Two brunettes saunter by our table, both of them impossibly tall and thin, but with an odd lack of shape to their bodies. Model types. Their heels click so loudly that they cause every head to turn in their wake. I wouldn't exactly call these women pretty, just exotic, like some undiscovered, elongated breed of gazelle.

"You probably make more than the two of them put together," Dan says.

"I'm probably smarter than the two of them put together."

He laughs. "Like that matters."

"Seriously," I say, "it should matter."

"It matters for something, but you can't go through life bitter because people without your brains have more money than you. It's always going to happen."

"I know, but it offends my sense of justice."

"I bet your sense of justice isn't nearly so offended when that bank of yours brings in some young engineering genius out of college at fifty a year to build your spreadsheets."

"Then I'm thankful for luck."

He raises his glass. "Amen to that."

Our waiter comes by. He has short brown hair, except on the top of his head, which is dyed white and moussed up into little spikes. I try to remember when, exactly, young men started dyeing their hair.

Dan and I order another round.

"Amy and I are trying to get pregnant," he tells me.

"Easier for her than you," I say.

"We've had to go to a fertility doctor."

"Really? Something wrong?"

"We don't know. We've been at it a while, and now she's on these drugs. Still no luck."

"Well, Danno, I—I don't know what to say."

"You see, Barry, money can't buy everything. A cliché, but true."

"It bought you a fertility doctor," I remind him.

"You always were a cynical bastard."

"I'm sorry, man. I know this is serious. Good luck, really."

"Thanks. There's not much to do but wait to see what happens. But my point about money is this: just because you don't have what you want, don't sell yourself short. Remember when you told me you wanted to 'win'?"

I nod. I remember.

"You've got a family and you've got some money. From what I can tell, you're doing well. I think you are actually on your way."

I know he's trying to be nice, but I can't even look at him. I just can't get around how much money he has. I feel some awful concoction bubbling up inside of me, till my cheeks tingle and my ears feel hot. It takes everything I have to hold it in. It's a brew made of one part jealousy, one part anger at my failure, and one part rage at the sympathy it elicits.

Ben calls the next night.

"Okay, I'm not going to bullshit you," he says. "I've got cancer. It's a growth by my lungs, underneath in there. I've got to have surgery to get it out. I'd like to have the surgery in the States, but it costs a lot of money. So I'm having it in Vancouver. Thing is, I can't work. I'm going to be laid up for a long time with this thing, and I'm going to need care that the government is not going to pay for. I need money, Barry. That's what it amounts to."

"That's what it always amounts to," I say. Cancer? He must be getting desperate to expect me to fall for that. I doubt there's even a small chance he's telling the truth.

"I know. Go ahead, little brother, lay it on me. I'm a layabout and a lout. I'm fucking lazy. I'm a drug addict. Tell me something I don't know, Barry. I mean, so what? So fucking what? It's my life. I am not ready to die. I need help."

I take a deep breath. "I don't know whether to believe you."

"Look," he says, "come visit, then. My operation is scheduled for January 12. It would be great to have some family around."

"Family? We haven't seen each other in six years."

"We're still family. I'm asking you to come and see for yourself. What do you say?"

"I'll look into it," I say. "But, for now, I've got to go."

"Could you send me a couple hundred bucks in the meantime?" I hear him ask as I put down the phone.

The next Monday I find myself in Hanover, New Hampshire, at Gretchen's invitation. She and I, plus a twenty-seven-year-old investment-banker vice-president with a receding hairline, make the trip to give a presentation to Dartmouth undergraduates as to why they should sell their souls to Wall Street. It's finals week, with Christmas imminent, and yet, judging from the two hundred seniors (out of a thousand at the school) who show up to watch the I-banker give a slide show, I'd say that there are plenty eager to make the deal.

The presentation takes place after the last flight out, so we all eat dinner at the Hanover Inn. Afterward, the I-banker goes to "work the phones," while Gretchen and I take a walk around campus. It's a frigid night, the air clear and fresh, the snow pack squeaky in the cold; somewhere, someone is burning wood. Students hustle by us carrying book-laden backpacks. Baker Hall, the library built as a replica of Independence Hall in Philadelphia, is lit up like a cathedral to higher education. I hope that Sam and Jane are lucky enough to come here. I am reminded of what a Dartmouth alumnus once said to me, back when I was applying to the school: college is wasted on undergraduates.

"Do you remember that day we climbed to the top of Baker Hall?" I ask Gretchen.

"Sure. You put your arm around me," Gretchen says, "and I thought something would happen between us. *Something.* A kiss, maybe. But no."

We stop and look up at the tower. Gretchen and I hiked up there together one day late in the spring, during finals week. We stood together looking over the miles and miles of green and rolling mountains, and I put my arm over her shoulder. She slid an arm around my waist. For several moments, maybe a minute, we stood there together, and I was simply too scared and timid to take it any further. It was all I could do to stand there with my arm around her. Like most young men, I lived in awe and fear of beautiful women, especially if they were self-possessed.

"I—"

"Don't try to explain," she says.

We enter the library and walk through the entrance hall, warm, with a radiator clanking loudly as it heats. Where I remember the card catalogue being, students now sit at trading-floor-like rows of computer terminals. Ah, I think, progress. We make our way to the tower.

The sign at the entrance to the tower says "Closed," but the door itself isn't locked, and so I follow Gretchen inside and begin the climb. It occurs to me that back during my Dartmouth days I never would have ignored such a closure, but now I'm a flight above the ground before I give it any thought.

The stairwell is lighted with widely spaced bare light bulbs, each covered in a blanket of dust. There's something highly arousing in walking up these shadowy stairs, following Gretchen as if we're climbing up to a bedroom. With each step the anticipation gets greater, and greater, and there are a lot of steps, spinning us upward. After perhaps ten minutes, we reach the top and push through the door into the New Hampshire night. I immediately feel the sweat freeze on my forehead. Before us is a canopy of stars, and below a wide ocean of darkness dotted by the lights of small Vermont and New Hampshire hamlets, plus the greater glow of White River Junction and West Leb to the south.

"It's nice," Gretchen says, slipping a hand inside my open overcoat. "Listen."

There is the faint whistle of a wind.

"It's so quiet," she says.

I pull her toward me and we kiss and hold each other till it no longer feels cold. Then we slip back inside the tower door. Soon we are making love on the landing, atop the combined blankets of our overcoats.

Afterward, I chuckle at the absurdity of it all. Here we are, two thirty-five-year-olds with our own hotel rooms in the nicest spot in town, and we're humping like freshmen.

"What's so funny?" Gretchen asks.

"I'm thinking that my bed in the Hanover Inn might be more comfortable."

"Don't knock this," she says. "This is something you won't forget."

We're silent then, and I wonder about Gretchen, wonder what her life will be like in five years, or in ten, when Buster heads off to college and she is truly alone. Does she worry about this? Does she wonder who will share her days, who will take care of her? Wouldn't it be ironic if a woman of her beauty and appeal spent most of her life without companionship?

We soon get cold. We dress and go back outside to the observation deck, and talk beneath the stars. I ask Gretchen how long she plans to keep working on the floor, and her answer surprises me. "Forever," she says. Like Chip McCarty, she sees herself as the head of the desk, and then the head of the department. She has big plans: she even has her eye on the operating committee. "They need a woman," she says, "and I'd be good. But you know what's unfair, Barry? All the nasty things that will get said. If I were a man, I'd be respected for making division head. It would be, you know, a sexy thing. As a woman, they'll call me a cold-hearted bitch."

"What do you care what other people think?"

"It matters. In this business, you need people on your side. You really do, at every step."

"What about Buster? How do you find time for him? I mean, my kids barely know what I look like."

"I find ways to see him during the week, and all day on the weekends. I have a really great live-in nanny who gets him to where he needs to be. I bet I do better than most single moms, who have to work at jobs a lot worse than mine and can't afford help. Sure, I wish he had a father. I know that's important, but there's just so much I can do about it."

"You could get married," I say.

"I don't know. I don't have many good examples. My folks, they've been married thirty-seven years and I figure they both really regret it, though neither will admit it. I wonder how they ever got together, or why they stayed that way. It breaks my heart, really. They've been carrying this burden around for years, and now they both have health problems, and they have to look after each other."

"At least they've got each other," I say.

"I think it makes them resent each other that much more. I go over there with Buster, I feel like I'm letting two prisoners out of their cells for an hour of sunshine. I'll tell you the truth, Barry. I want to believe in true love and all that, but maybe love between a man and a woman is fleeting. The whole idea of marriage, it just scares me to death."

Christmas almost passes me by unnoticed, but for the day off. Then New Year's Eve is upon us. Mac takes the day off, so Dino and I drive in together.

"Mac has something up his sleeve," Dino says. Traffic is extremely light. We're cruising at about ninety-five miles per hour down I-684. I can barely read the dash from all the vibrations.

"What do you mean?" I ask.

"He's gunning for desk head. I'm sure you know that. He thinks Court Harvey is vulnerable. And he's got a point. No one will feel sorry for that son-of-a-bitch when he's gone. But there's something else. Mac's talking to someone. I think he's got a bid away."

Dino means that Mac has found himself a trading job with a competitor. This is the time-honored way to get paid more money. You get a bid away, for, say, 50 percent more than what your firm is paying you. Then you tell your managers, "I got an offer for sixty percent more, do you want to match it?" Usually, they do, if for no other reason than to keep the other firm from "winning." I have to admire Mac's planning. He knows that if his plot against Court Harvey fails he'll need a place to go.

"What about you, Dino?" I ask. "Where's your bid?"

"Right now there seems to be an oversupply of short Italians who trade toxic-waste bank debt. But—I do have a Plan B."

"What are you going to do? Carpentry?"

He pulls a takeout menu from his visor. It's from a deli called Corsetti and Sons.

"Your father opened a deli in Yonkers?" I ask.

"Not my father. My father is dead. I did it with Stacy's brothers. They're running it. Stace and I are the money, except that I gotta work there tonight."

"Work there?"

"Big night, New Year's. We sell lots of beer and, more important, munchies and noisemakers and crap, the high-margin stuff."

"You're going to work behind a deli counter tonight?"

"Yep."

So—here's a guy making in one year what the average American makes in twelve, and he still has a second job.

"Why do you call it Corsetti and Sons?" I ask. "You don't have any kids."

"Look, no one wants to eat from a deli of childless Italians. Italians are supposed to have big families."

"What happened to you?"

"Hey, I grew up in a big family, so I learned. Besides, I'm only thirty-two. If life were like a hockey game, it would be the opening of the second period. Too early to pull the goalie."

Despite the speed we are traveling, he's tapping out a drum rhythm on the steering wheel with both hands.

"What about carpentry?" I ask.

"Plan C. Get it? Besides, I can't do that and work my voodoo in the bond market. The deli doesn't take much time, and I get cases of beer for next to nothing."

We cross under the I-287 overpass and make the first curve on the Hutch. The Infinity's wheels squeal in protest. I feel the car shudder. "You know, Dino, it's going to be dead today. There's no rush. Could you slow down?"

"What for?" he asks.

Dino phones at one. "We're looking for a two-oh-one departure," he says. The market is set to close at two, and I'll still have to mark my book.

"Do my best," I tell him. "We're short-staffed over here."

"Look, have you been reading the news? There's about ten thousand crazies out there who want to blow up Manhattan to bring in the new year."

It's true. Terrorist threats are way up this year. This morning, on the way into the garage, the attendants stopped our car and checked our license against the parking sticker on the front bumper, while two German shepherds sniffed at our fenders and trunk.

"How 'bout two-fifteen? That's still close to ten hours before midnight."

"Look," Dino says, "some maniac is going to blow the place up. What if he doesn't wear a watch? What if it's set to Baghdad Terrorist Time? Get your coat. I want to get the hell off the rock early."

I promise to do my best.

10. When Will You Know?

The next week, an Arctic air blast arrives from Canada, bringing first a three-inch snow that closes Sam's school early one day and all day the next, and then a frigid gale that coats Westchester in ice and chill. High temperatures barely reach the double digits—twelve one day, ten the next—and the wind chill hovers around thirty below. When I leave my house in the morning, I can hear the trees creak. My Escort starts with a groan, and the belts whine and screech when I touch the gas pedal. When Mac or Dino drops me off at the Park and Ride in the evenings, I scurry from the warm Infinity or BMW to my frozen car and sit there while the engine warms and the wind rattles the windows. The radio keeps a tally of the dead: four by the third day of the front.

"A guy I know died yesterday," Mac says one morning. I'm sitting in the back of the BMW, next to his pinstriped suit jacket, which has a banana tucked into the breast pocket. He's been on a banana kick lately. Even in this weather, he doesn't wear an overcoat.

"Freeze to death?" Dino asks.

"No, he had a heart attack. Three kids and a wife. He was only forty-two years old."

"So what are you worried about?" Dino says. "You've got six years."

"Not at the rate I'm going."

"True, but you got that term policy, right? You've got to accentuate the positive. You're worth more dead than alive."

"That's what I told my wife," Mac says. "I thought I saw her smile."

It's 6:47 at night according to the emerald numbers on the alarm clock beside the bed. Through a crack in the blinds I can see the glow of an artificial light. It's January, and we're ninety minutes past sunset. The wind whines just outside the window.

Gretchen sighs. She is lying in my arms, a leg resting over mine.

"Something wrong?"

"Not at all," she says. She chuckles. "It's just that I needed that."

I ask myself the question: did I need that? Could I not get that at home?

"Remember that talk we had in Hanover about marriage?" she asks. "I just want to say that you made the right choice with Rachel."

"That's a hell of a thing to say." Lately, though, I've come to the same conclusion. I'm really only here because I haven't found a way to stop. It was something I felt I had to do, and, now that I have, I wish I hadn't. As with a lot of things in my life. I've taken to dealing with my betrayal of Rachel by trying not to think about it. Why, I wonder, when I have exactly what I want, do I want something else, only until I get it?

"Don't ever tell her about this," Gretchen says in the darkness.

"Do I look suicidal?"

"Men sometimes feel the need to fess up. I don't know why."

I decide there's something profoundly not intimate about Gretchen, as if she's protecting herself and judging me all the time, even during the act itself. She is telling me not to make a mess. Gretchen is a singularly practical woman, in control of her life and emotions. It's a pity, really, that she went into sales. She could have been a great trader.

She reaches for the phone, and hands it to me. "Call us a couple broker cars," she says.

I gladly do as I am told.

My family and I finally escape the cold front by taking a ski trip to Colorado. It's the second time we've gone back since our move to New York. Rachel and the kids leave from La Guardia on Friday morning (Mickey O'Hara provides the Lincoln Town Car that picks them up and deposits them at the terminal), and Lance Bailey sends a car to take me to Newark at the end of the day. I am always amazed by the wonders of airplane travel. At two in the afternoon I'm hunkered down in front of my broker screens in the stale air and murky light of the trading floor, and tonight I will be two thousand miles away and eight thousand feet above sea level, where stars elbow each other for space in the sky, and the air is light and clean.

This comes with a price. I take a forty-five-dollar cab ride to the condominium complex where we are spending $375 a night. Tax adds 30 percent. This is a discount, January rate. We once lived frugally in this town, never reporting more than twenty-seven thousand dollars to the IRS between Rachel and me. There were several thousand dollars more that came to us in the way of tips, money that meant the difference between destitution and being able to heat our home and keep a Toyota pickup on the road. So call it thirty thousand dollars. Now it feels as if I might drop that in a single week. In addition to the condo, I spend enough on lift tickets to buy a used Chevette. Dinner at the most casual restaurant usually runs us at least a hundred bucks. Sam skis in kids' ski school for free—we are not without connections—but Jane's day care comes to almost five hundred for the week. One night I add it all up and realize we might spend six grand on one week of skiing.

"It's outrageous," Rachel says, sitting at a corner table at the Woody Creek Tavern. Above her is the mounted head of a buffalo. Sam is shooting pool with two kids, one of whom belongs to Kyle McClure, the famous movie actor, who's drinking Flying Dog drafts (a local brew) at the bar. Jane chases the three boys around the table. "We lived here on nothing, but it's so expensive to visit."

"Tell me about it."

"I'm just worried that we won't get back. It would be terrible if we gave up this lifestyle to make some money and then couldn't make enough to be able to get back to it."

"Which lifestyle are you referring to? The one that had us struggling to pay the electric bill? Remember holding the pickup's fender together with duct tape after you hit that deer?"

"We got by, Barry. You skied a hundred days a year. We went hiking in the mountains all summer and it didn't cost a dime. We had a life together then."

"We have a life together now."

"Together? You work all the time. Your children barely know what you look like. Sam, especially, needs you around more."

"I do my best. I'm not the first man who would like to spend more time with his family, but can't because of work."

"Last week I tallied up the hours you were away from home. It came to seventy-four."

Without Gretchen it would have been seventy-one. Still a long week.

"Are you mad at me for working hard?" I ask. We've had this conversation before. On the one hand, she is happy about our new lifestyle. Two weeks ago we ordered a new Ford Explorer; last week she spent fifteen hundred dollars on new clothes. On the other hand, I get little credit for working. I'm somehow supposed to make the money *and* be around the house.

"It's just that I'm not sure it's worth it," she says.

"Not worth it? We're finally getting somewhere. Do you realize how much money we're making now? This vacation will be paid for by this time next week. When, by the way, we'll have the new Ford Explorer that you wanted. And that takes into account taxes. For the first time in my life, I can breathe easy about money. Doesn't that feel great? And this is only the beginning."

Sam lets out a shout. He's managed to sink a ball, though the table is still covered with them.

"Rachel," I say, "I don't know what you want from me. I went to business school, got this job, am making the money. I just don't know how I could have done better. How could I have done better?"

"Barry, you've done great, really. I know you think I don't appreciate what you've done, but I do. I think the problem is that it takes a toll on all of us for you to do well at your job. It beats the hell out of you, and we never see you. Yes, the pay is great, and, yes, I like spending some of the money, but do you really have to work like you do just so we can buy a new car? I don't think so. I see lots of people driving new cars who make a lot less than you. I think you're killing yourself at this job for a lot more than a few new shiny things. You want to get rich, and maybe you can, but I'm saying that I'm not sure it's really worth it."

I have my right hand on the table, and she grabs it.

"I think we should probably look at moving back here," she says. "There must be something you could do that would allow us to live comfortably and be together."

"It's always been our plan to move back."

"I mean now."

"That's crazy," I say. "We're finally making big money. Four hundred is big money." Well, I think, maybe not big. I don't know what to think about money. I just know that I don't want to go back to holding my life together with duct tape.

"It's big money," she says, "but at some point you've got to say, 'So what?'"

"So what? All this work and sacrifice, and I'm supposed to say, 'So what?'"

"Yes, Barry, sooner or later. I am willing to give up the money to have you. Don't you see, the longer you stay, the more you'll become like all the other Wall Street guys. It's happening. I can see it happening. The deal we made was that we would come back as soon as we could. This is important, because I can see now that we are changing, and that frightens me. I know it's hard to let all that hard work go, and to pass up all that money, but every year it will get harder and harder, and then another year will be gone. Don't you see the trap?"

"I'm not like everyone else," I say, wondering, for the first time, if I really believe this.

"That's why we're having this talk. You've got to come up with a plan to get out."

"I think I have a plan, Rachel. It's just that we're really close to where we've been aiming, but all the money comes at the back end. I don't want to get out before it arrives."

"It's a dangerous game, Barry. It may never arrive. And, listen, you've got to decide what matters to you, because you're sacrificing your time for this, time with me and time with your children, time that's gone forever."

"I'm doing this for you and the kids."

"Funny, isn't it?"

She smiles at me, and I smile back. She's right. It's a silly game, but I still have to play it.

There are other times during the week, better times, when Rachel and I get away together, when we have the kind of romance that vacations are made for. We walk arm-in-arm down the Hyman Avenue Mall, breathing in the mountain air, and I can feel that, at least here, the world is right, till I begin to wonder about myself. Why am I not happier? Am I not wholly content with this woman on my arm, who is beautiful and kind, with whom I have said I want to spend the rest of my days?

I find it easy this week to block Gretchen from my mind, as if there is nothing between us. I've always been able to compartmentalize myself in this way, so that the separate parts of my life don't mix, even in my mind. This is an essential skill for a trader, for whom emotion is a weakness, something to be exploited in others. Still, I realize that being two people is not the best way to make a life with my wife or raise my children. Also, it's exhausting.

I like the person I am on vacation. Rachel and I spend time reminiscing and laughing, skiing together. It feels almost as if we're dating. One night, once the kids are asleep, she pushes me down on the bed and makes a show of undressing me, then ties one of my wrists to the headboard with a pillowcase—she's never done anything like this before—and when she crawls on top of me I want her as badly as I ever have. We stay up late, and wake early for more of the same. It is, for a few nights, as it was when we first fell in love.

Five days later—it feels like five hours—Rachel, Sam, Jane, and I wait in the Aspen airport, trying to get home. It's been snowing all day, and our flight has been canceled. The snow has stopped, but a low layer of clouds still hangs in the valley. All about us, people languish on chairs, surrounded by their carry-ons. Airport Hades.

"There's nothing worse than not being able to get home when you really don't want to go home," Rachel says.

Up at the counter, a man is yelling, "When do you think you might know?" His voice is pure New York, all mangled vowels and rounded consonants.

The trip will be less expensive than I had thought, because Steve Reeson, an old neighbor of mine turned real-estate dealmaker, gave me a check for two thousand dollars as a referral fee. Last year I gave Dan Connelly one of Steve's business cards, and this year Dan and Amy bought a house in Aspen that neither bothered to mention to me. It's odd how business school and Wall Street have changed my life. I've lost touch with my best friends, though suddenly I am able to make money off them.

"Barry, we've got to move back here," Rachel says.

It's the third time this week that we've had this conversation. Rachel wants to move back immediately. I do not want to be poor again. I tell Rachel that I am on the verge of making a lot of money—hell, I'm already making a lot of money—and I'm not going to walk away just as the Golden Goose is starting to produce.

"You know, Barry, you've got nothing left to prove there. I know you think you do, but you don't. You made the grade, proved you can be a Wall Street guy. But, God, don't become one. The more you make, the more you think you need. Look at us. We make ten times what we used to, and somehow it's not enough."

Actually, it's closer to thirteen times more. The truth is that I'd like to leave but I'm too scared of being poor. I just can't go back to that. Rachel and I can't go back to that. We wouldn't survive it.

"Well," I say to Rachel, "the answer is not to make less. When the time comes, we'll make the move. But it has to make sense. What could I do out here where I could make even a quarter of what I make in New York, where I can set us up for life? It makes sense to hunker down, work, and put money away. When we get to the right point, we'll move."

"When? I want to know when that will be."

"I've told you, I can't answer that now. Please stop badgering me."

"I'm not badgering you. I'm communicating. And very soon you're going to have to answer that question."

Our flight finally lands at La Guardia a little after two-thirty, without two pieces of our luggage. I snatch twenty minutes of sleep in the back of the broker car on the ride from the airport. At home I crawl into bed with fifty minutes till I have to get ready for work. The pressure to make use of these minutes is too much, and I don't even doze. I think about my job, and whether I can leave all those years of work and school behind. I wonder if I, like most people, am being most loyal to my biggest mistake.

My first evening back, I go out for a "quick beer" with Tom Carlson at his urgent insistence. I'm so tired that my shoulders ache, and I just want to go home, but Carlson promises it won't take long, and he even orders me a car paid for by his broker. I always feel a bit guilty around Tom. When I first came to the firm, he trained me, and we drank together often as he introduced me to the various bond brokers. But that was years ago, when I knew nothing and did not understand that a close friendship with him would likely hurt my image on the desk. When that understanding came, I acted on it. I felt bad for Carlson, and relieved at how quickly he picked up on my hints.

Now we sit at a window table that overlooks the black, roiling Hudson. A commuter ferry churns toward Hoboken, which stands in front of a sky alight at the horizon in winter pink.

Carlson orders a Ketel One and soda and a Griffin cigar. I go for an Oban and a Griffin. Everything about Carlson is sloppy and disheveled until he has a cigar in his hand, when a strict punctilio overtakes him. He cuts the end off the cigar just so, then carefully twirls it while lighting, his cheeks working in perfectly rhythmic puffs. The whole act is almost musical.

He asks about Rachel, Sam, and Jane, and I am impressed and touched that he remembers their names. He congratulates me on how fast I've moved up—I sense jealousy—and then, with another puff of his cigar, tells me why he needs to see me. "I want your support, Barry. There's a shake-up coming. Court is not going to last. You just can't treat people like he does and get away with it. Chip is going to go for that spot, but I have more experience, and the truth is, I'd be a better manager. Don't get me wrong, Chip is a great trader. But that's not the same as a great manager. I trained you, so you know me, know the kind of man I am. I'm not flashy like Chip McCarty, but I am more solid. Chip is all about Chip, and the desk just can't afford that. I'll be for everybody—including you. What do you say? I'd like to know that you are behind me."

"Jeez, Tom, I don't know what say I will have in the matter." I puff on my cigar, buying time. Carlson may have a point. If he could keep his cool and stop his griping, he would probably be a better manager. Also, he's made more money every year for thirteen years, which is a pretty good record. When I think about it, it's clear that he's the most underrated trader on the desk. Being underrated is not a good thing. In fact, Carlson is a bit like a corporate bond that's cheap but always trades cheap, the kind of issue that Isaac Hunt ordered off the company books. I know there is no way that Isaac Hunt will pick Tom Carlson over Chip McCarty, and so neither can I. Backing lost causes is for the young, the stupid, and the unambitious.

"You'll be asked. Can I count on you?" Carlson asks.

I don't know what to say. I'm cornered. It's like being hit up by a beggar on the subway. I resort to a lie.

"If it comes to that, Tom," I say, "then you can."

The next day, I am summoned to Isaac Hunt's office to discuss Court Harvey, who is on vacation. When I enter Hunt's office, he doesn't stand, as he normally does. Rather, he gives his head a little nod back, the way you might acknowledge someone across a crowded and noisy room. Dark, sunken circles underline his eyes, and he looks pale. I never thought of a black man as pale before, but, then again, I'm thirty-five years old and don't know a single black man well. This strikes me as odd. I've lived in Detroit, Philadelphia, New York. How come I don't know any blacks?

"How was your week off?" Isaac asks.

"Great. I didn't take any time at Christmas or New Year's, so I really needed the break." In other words, I really don't take much vacation.

"Barry, I want to talk to you about your desk. There is obvious dissatisfaction with the way it is run now. I'll be frank. Most of the people who work for Court do not hide that they hate him. That alone does not prejudice me against him. He has done well for us in the past. He's always delivered good numbers. But I have seen his behavior and I'm at a loss to explain it. What do you make of it?"

"Of Court's behavior?"

"Yes, of his temper."

"I don't know. Something sets him off and he becomes a different person."

"Do you think he's fair?"

"Fair?"

"Yes, fair."

"That's too relative a term. This business is based on a subjective bonus process. So no one thinks his boss is fair."

He smiles. "Well put. When we spoke earlier, you had some interesting ideas about how the desk might be better run. Let's go over some of those again."

And so we do. The business trends are clear. The cheapness of computing power and the speed and ease of communications are eroding our traditional advantages. We have to change the business or lose it. We need to differentiate better between our customers, and make markets less aggressively for those who rarely make us money. We have to be more comfortable letting bonds trade at other firms, and more willing to risk our own money in the market when our trading expertise and low trading costs give us an advantage. Isaac takes notes and grunts occasionally.

"Let me ask you one more thing," he says. "If I were to replace Court Harvey, who would you choose to run the desk?"

"Replace Court?"

"You know why you are here."

"Chip McCarty is the most obvious successor," I say, "and I'm sure Tom Carlson and Stevie Vollmer want the job." As these words roll off my tongue, I get an idea. Why not me? Isaac Hunt is looking for leadership, and I get the feeling he isn't happy with what he's found. "But," I go on, "I'm the best candidate for the job."

"You? You're still wet behind the ears." He laughs.

He's testing me. I can tell that he likes that I'm making this play: from low-man bill trader to head of the desk in less than a year. It's preposterous. The color is coming back into his face.

"Look," I say. "Naming the most senior trader to management is a haphazard way to approach the business, especially when such big changes are afoot. It makes no more sense than naming the best trader. Look at Court. He's a great trader. Better that he trades than manages. Chip McCarty is a great trader, but I don't think he'll be a great manager. Keep him trading, and making money for the firm. Tom Carlson? Very consistent, but not a leader. Vollmer? Like McCarty. I've got ideas and a vision for this desk. Give me your support and I'll gain the support of the inner circle of traders, who will be the desk's future. I'll make the changes that will ensure the long-term profitability of the business."

Hunt just stares at me, and though I'm not a salesman, I know I'm close to closing this deal. I just need to throw in one more thing, and that thing is Chip McCarty. It's not that I want to sell out a friend, but it's clear that this is an entrance test. Just as wannabe gangbangers go out and cause mayhem to be accepted, I must show that I can play the game hard, that I'm tough enough to succeed. I've known this moment was coming. Rachel has told me time is running out, and for her and Sam and Jane, I must act now. I may not get another chance like this one.

"Well, Barry—" Hunt begins.

"Look," I say, cutting him off. "I'm the guy. Chip McCarty has another job lined up. He's waiting to see how this situation turns out. You want more loyalty than that."

"Chip? Do you have proof?"

"I don't have hard proof, but I ride to work with him every day. I know his habits. He spent several weeks in December meeting with someone. There was a two-week period during which he only rode home on Monday and Friday."

Well, I've now taken shots at Court Harvey, Chip McCarty, Stevie Vollmer, and Tom Carlson. It's easy to rationalize the betrayal. They would certainly do the same thing to me, if they thought of me as a threat. I'm here to make things better for my family, and, besides, I doubt that Isaac Hunt can throw me the job. I *am* wet behind the ears. But I want to lay the groundwork for the near future.

"That's all very interesting," Isaac says at last. "I haven't made any decisions, but I always enjoy talking to you, Barry."

That night, Mac, Dino, and I run into Gretchen as we're exiting the security turnstiles. I'm still feeling queasy about my meeting with Hunt, and I've been thinking all afternoon that I need to break it off with Gretchen, that I ought to make at least that step toward redemption.

"Barry," Gretchen asks, "can I get you a minute?"

Mac and Dino walk off toward the parking-garage elevator to wait for me.

"I need your help with Court," she says.

"Huh?"

"He won't leave me alone. Will you tell him that I am no longer interested, and to grow up? He started calling me every day. Every day!! Sometimes the phone rings, I pick it up, and there is no one there. So, last week, I got Caller ID, and guess what? It's him. Then, last night, I ran into him on *my* street, in front of *my* building. He's on vacation this week. It's creepy, Barry. What is wrong with him?"

"Just ignore him. He's like a little boy. He doesn't know how to act."

"God, I'll say. I don't want to cause a scene, but he has to leave me alone."

"How have you been otherwise? How's Buster?"

"Fine and fine. I know you just got back to town. How about next week?"

"We'll talk," I say, pushing off the unpleasantness into the future, as though it were a debt payment.

I find Mac and Dino by the elevators. "Be careful," Mac says to me. "Divorce can be expensive in this profession."

"I still can't believe Court was sleeping with her," Dino says. "There ought to be a law against that."

"I'm not worrying about it," Mac says as we step onto the elevator. "Nothing Court Harvey does is ever going to worry me again."

11. What Does This Mean for Me?

Bonuses are three days in the bank when I come home to find a new burnt-orange Ford Explorer parked in a pool of light beneath the motion-sensitive spotlight Rachel installed above our driveway. Otherwise, it's a dark and still night, flecked with snow flurries in languorous descent.

As I walk up to the Explorer, the door opens and Sam pops out. "Hey, Dad," he says. "Check this out." He starts talking as fast as only children can. Here's how the seats fold, here's where to find the cup holders, the reading lights, the pockets for toys and books and maps for long trips. He opens the rear door, then closes it and opens only the window, by standing in his untied sneakers on the rear bumper. Snowflakes catch in his sandy hair, and suddenly I have one of those memories of being a kid and getting excited about a car my mother bought, a Maverick purchased used from the father of a friend of mine and brought home on a dark and cold Michigan night. The car had what to me was an odd and exotic smell—my friend's father was a smoker—and I literally jumped up and down for a ride. God, I wish I could get excited like that again.

Much later, with the kids asleep, Rachel and I lie in bed beneath our down comforter. The flurries have turned to a steady snowfall. We listen, which is an exercise in noticing how everything sounds muffled, how the cars pass by our house in a hush, how even the neighbor's dog barks softly on a night such as this.

"I had the most maddening thing happen today," Rachel says.

I ask what it was.

"I went grocery shopping. I get up to the checkout and I've got about a hundred and fifty bucks' worth of food, plus Janie. There's a line, and it probably takes twenty minutes to get to the cashier, by which point I've already had it, because I've had to fight with Jane not to pull all of the candy out of the display that they must put there just to torment mothers. Anyway, I'm down at the end, bagging my own groceries, and the girl finally gets the total, so I slide my credit card through the machine and it comes back unreadable. Now, I just bought gas before I came to the store, so I know there's nothing wrong with the card. I ask the cashier to enter the number manually, and she says she can't do that. I ask, Why not? There's no reason, Barry. I spent over an hour in that goddamn store and I had to walk out with nothing. Jane starts bawling her head off because we're leaving without the food, and the people in the line behind me are all looking at me like I just got caught shoplifting. I was so angry and there was nothing I could do, and I just lost it. Janie's crying and I'm crying and sobbing and carrying her outside in the snow to our car. I mean, I know it sounds silly, but I knew then that I'm just not cut out for this. The insolence of that cashier! I hate this place."

Lying next to her, I can feel that her body has stiffened. Her anger is physical.

"I'm sorry," I said.

"It's not your fault. But don't you hate it, too? It's not like this the other places we've lived, except maybe Philadelphia."

"You've just got to roll with it," I say. "But I know working on the trading floor has changed me, made me less patient. Someone says, 'Barry, bid forty-three.' I say, 'The plus.' And that's it, forty-three million dollars of ten-year notes change hands. You start to expect the whole world to be like that. So—I had an experience kind of like what happened to you. Late one afternoon last week, I went off the desk to hit the New World Coffee that just opened in the basement of our building. This was a big deal, Rachel, going off the desk. I really needed the air, and the coffee. So I get there, and there are two guys ahead of me. I check my watch. I mean, that's something right there—ever since I started working on the trading floor, I time how long it takes whenever I get in a line. Anyway, the girl behind the counter would shout out orders and then stand there and wait while some guy with a ring through his nose sweated it out at the milk steamer. She didn't help him when he got backed up. She didn't ring up customers who were waiting. She didn't move on to the next customer. By the time I get to the front of the line, eight minutes have gone by. *Eight minutes!* To make two coffee drinks! Throw in the escalator ride down and up from the lower level, plus security and the elevator ride back to the trading floor, and I realized I'm going to end up spending fifteen minutes just to get a cup of coffee. I'm burning up, I'm so angry. I actually feel myself sweating. I give her my order and I'm ready to wring her neck. I could picture myself reaching out and strangling that little pencil neck of hers, just because she was so goddamned inefficient. I got a craving to do physical harm."

"You see, that's not good, Barry."

"Well, I didn't do it."

"Still," Rachel says, "you talk about rolling with it, but I've noticed a change in you. Like when you drive. You're a maniac now. When we lived in Colorado, you used to drive so slow that I almost couldn't stand it. Now you're flying around like there's a fire, pissing people off, gunning it through yellow lights. You're much less patient than you used to be."

"Well, in Colorado I had two points on my license, and it made my insurance go up by a hundred and fifty bucks a year, for three years. And we couldn't afford that. I was scared to get another ticket. Here I don't have time, so—"

"It's not a good change," Rachel says. "It's not a good change in me. God, this place has taught me to hate other people."

Just then the phone rings. I roll to the nightstand and answer it.

"Bahwee," says the voice. It's Yoshi, our trader in Tokyo. "Is Yoshi. Greenspan speaking in Australia. Market down over point. I being asked bid one sixty-four six-one-eight Feb '06, and offer weight ten-year. For Japanese Post Office."

This gibberish means that the Japanese Post Office wants to sell 164 million of the 6⅛ percent treasury bonds due to mature in February of 2006, and buy a risk-equivalent amount of ten-year notes. Yoshi has called me because he doesn't want to do the trade. We once had traders in Tokyo—Americans mostly, but also Brits and Japanese—who executed these trades themselves, but they lost so much money that Court Harvey has instructed Yoshi to call New York for help whenever a big trade comes in. I get a call a week. On this night I have Yoshi walk me through where the market is and where he thinks this bond is, and then, naked and lying in my bed with my eyes closed so as to picture myself at my trade station, I put a number on the trade. Yoshi puts me on hold. The room is silent, except for the Asiatic buzz in my phone receiver and a sigh from Rachel. I picture the snow falling outside, like sand in a timer. It takes at least a minute for Yoshi to come back on the line.

"They get better price from someone else. They say we miss trade three times in row. They say other dealer better. They say we are *worst* dealer. No call again."

"Well, Yoshi, I'm sorry, but the level was decent, considering the circumstances. If you find out where the bonds traded, please let me know by e-mail."

I hang up. "Those motherfuckers," I say.

"What?" asks Rachel.

"You don't want to know." I set the phone in its rack, and roll back toward Rachel. "Now, where were we?"

"Let's get some sleep," she says. I agree, and soon I hear the steady breathing of Rachel's sleep. For me, sleep won't come. I find myself wanting to wake her and rekindle the conversation we lost to the Japanese Post Office. It's been so long since we just hung around and talked.

"We miss another trade with the Japanese Post Office last night?" Court Harvey asks me when I sit down the next morning. I've just come back from the end of the row, where I took a quick look out the window. It's barely light enough to see the men working on the construction site. Now I glance at the clock. It's 7:03. In Tokyo they're still eating dinner. Only Stevie Vollmer and I are on the desk. I haven't even had a chance to log on to my computers.

"Yes," I say.

"We can't keep missing with them."

"Look," I tell him. "That was my first miss. I get a call in the wee hours of the night, Greenspan's just threatened to tighten, and the market is wildly different from the close. I'm lying in bed. I put the right price on the trade, given all that. I wasn't sitting at a trade station."

"The Japanese Post Office is the biggest account over there."

"Then get a trader over there who can handle their size."

Court stares me down with his narrow eyes; I see color come into his cheeks, his lips tremble. I've never spoken back to him before. Maybe it's the early hour, or the coup I know is coming. Maybe it's Gretchen. I feel emboldened.

"I make those decisions," he says, his voice rising. "I decide who trades what. The bill seat is still open, you know. In fact, why don't you go sit there. You're trading bills today."

Behind Court Harvey, I see Stevie Vollmer stand up. Derek Lane, the salesman, ducks his head behind a screen in the salesman row. Making me go back to bills would be humiliation in its purest form, public and lasting. All day long people would come by and ask what had happened.

"I am the ten-year trader," I say, feeling my blood rise. "And I will not be bullied by anyone. Not by the Japanese, and not by you. You owe me an apology."

"An apology? Get in my office right now." His face and neck are deep cranberry-red.

"No." I say this as if his request were ridiculous, which it is.

"What do you mean, no?"

"I mean no. It's not a difficult concept. You got something to say to me, you say it here," I say. I feel as pumped as when I played high-school football.

"Hey, Court, why don't you leave him alone?" This is Chip McCarty. He stopped at the New World Coffee on his way up to the floor, and is just now arriving. He sets the New World Coffee bag on his desk and takes off his suit jacket, which he put on in the garage solely for the purpose of buying his morning coffee.

"*You* get in my office," Court says.

"Sure," Mac says. "Let me hang up my jacket." No one moves while he walks over to the closet, disappears, and then returns, rolling up his shirtsleeves. When he and Court go into the office, Court closes the blinds.

"Attaboy, Meat," Stevie Vollmer says. He stands and rests a meaty forearm across the top of a computer screen, careful not to crush the Pop-Tarts he's heating there. "That's how you hold your ground. You don't have to take that shit from anyone."

I must admit, it feels great to get Vollmer's approval. I'm starting to feel like one of the boys. I give Vollmer a nod, then look out across the trading floor. Everyone has arrived now. I can see hundreds of head tops, each held close to a computer screen, as if by a magnet. Then, pulled by the same force, I sink into my seat and go to work.

"I figure eight more years," Stuart Konig says that night at dinner in the large back room of a restaurant called Angelo and Maxie's. At Wharton we made an agreement to get together every month, realizing even then that friendship on the Street must be worked at. Despite these good intentions, it's been three and a half months since our last dinner. All around us are tables crammed with Wall Street guys in shirtsleeves, most of them drinking and laughing at the hilarity of everything shouted at their tables, each of these voices combining into a futures-pit-like roar. Surprisingly, all the noise gives the room an intimate feel. I lean close to Stuart to hear him. "If I can just last eight more years," he says. "This job takes it out of you. I mean, in the Marines I did some things that were supposed to test the limits of human endurance, but this, this job is a grind."

"Rachel wants out now," I tell him.

"Tell her she has to wait. You're the ten-year guy. You've got an opportunity to make your killing. Show no mercy. Take no prisoners."

"Isn't it funny," I say, "that a schoolteacher works ten years to earn what I earn in one, and that I'm still pissed off by how little I'm paid."

"In the Marines, I had a little special group, twenty-five men. I was responsible for them, and they looked after me. Took care of my stuff, took care of all the little things, so I could concentrate on the major tasks at hand. I mean, they even pitched my tent at night. I'd come up and there my bed would be, made. Everything. Any one of them would have laid down his life for me, and I was responsible for them. Very serious stuff. It wasn't about money, it was about duty, honor, country, proving yourself, you know? Seeing what you could really do. For almost the whole time, I felt I was doing something meaningful, and I never made over twenty-two thousand dollars a year."

"So now you feel like you sold out?"

"Hell, no. I bought in. I'm taking what's mine."

"Yours?" I ask.

"Mine. Mine 'cause I'm taking it. That's the logic of it, Barry. A schoolteacher or a Marine is not entitled to make much money, because he doesn't take it."

"There's not much for him to take," I say.

"What do you mean by that?"

"Just that a schoolteacher can't make much money."

"Only because he chose to be a teacher," he says, working his hands to make his point. Stuart sports a five o'clock shadow, but otherwise his face is bright and unlined. "What are you going to tell me next?" he says. "That the American dream is dead? Bullshit. It's the same as it ever was. I'm in this book group, and we just read *The Grapes of Wrath.* You read it, like in high school or something? Good book, but it misses the point. The point is not that we're all Tom Joad. The point is not to be Tom Joad."

"So you think you can get your eight million in eight more years?" It sounds like a lot to me, but I want to believe.

"Maybe. It's possible."

"So—you've got your eight sticks. Then what?"

"Travel. Take the family and see the world. Get back to my guitar. Give some money away. I'll do all that self-actualizing stuff you learned about in Psych 101."

"Maybe you won't leave."

"I will, just not till I've made what I've come here to make."

"It seems like lots of guys who make that kind of wheat don't leave."

"I'll leave," Stuart says. "Those guys don't leave because they've got nothing better to do. It's exactly who they are. For them, trading is self-actualizing, the poor sons-of-bitches."

I make it home at eleven-thirty. About midnight, the phone rings.

"Ah, for Christ's sake," Rachel says. She rolls over, away from me and the phone.

It's Yoshi.

"Japanese Post Office want bid one sixty-four six-one-eight Feb '06 and offer weight ten-year," he says. This is exactly the same inquiry as the previous night. I point this out to Yoshi, who assures me that the post office did not sell the bonds the night before, even though they said they did. For accounts, this kind of blatant lying is so common that they obviously don't consider it wrong. Still, I want to buy their bonds, because I am short the bonds by virtue of selling them today to Mickey O'Hara. I sold to him because I knew the Japanese Post Office was a seller, so I might as well be short. The fact that the post office is calling Yoshi back suggests that the bid I gave them last night was the best one they received.

"Yoshi," I say, "I thought we were the worst dealer."

He puts me on hold. Again, there is that buzz, and then Yoshi comes back.

"They say other dealer *more* worst," he says.

I put a price on the trade, one less aggressive than the night before. I buy the bonds. I take a moment to tally up what I've made for my ledger—about fifty grand—and go to sleep.

I wake at four to the screech of my alarm, then lie in bed and contemplate whether to go on the run I had planned. On the plus side is the exercise, which can set me right for the day. On the negative side are the snow, the cold, the dark, and the deer. I wonder at the implications for the rest of us that an animal so profoundly stupid can be so successful in Westchester. One morning last week, after my flashlight died, I almost ran right into one. I was two steps away when I saw it and started, and then it started with a big cloud of steam coming from its snout and scampered off, its hooves clattering on the icy asphalt.

I am just about to get out of bed when Rachel puts a hand on my shoulder.

"Are you out again tonight?"

"Yes, but not late."

"Don't get up yet." She pulls me to her; I won't be going running. After we make love, we lie together so long that I miss Mac and Dino at the Park and Ride, and show up for work an hour late, having taken the train. I've never done this before.

"Where were you?" Court asks.

"Doing a trade with the Japanese Post Office," I say, without looking up.

The next Wednesday, it rains. Not a light drizzle but the steady downpour of an April shower. Except that it's still the first week of February, and there's a foot of snow on the ground. The Park and Ride lies covered in a half-foot of slush, which I have to stomp through in my loafers on the way to Dino's Infinity. When I sit down in the car, I notice that there is slush packed into the cuffs of my pants. Mac arrives prepared, wearing an overcoat and mukluks. He carries a leather briefcase in one hand and his loafers in another. It's odd that Mac is wearing an overcoat and boots, for the luxury of a heated garage usually means that he never has to do so. The briefcase is odder still. What could he possibly be carrying in that briefcase? It's stiff and shiny, obviously new.

Dino pounces immediately. "What the fuck is up with the briefcase, Slick?"

"It's a good place to carry a banana."

Dino pulls out of the lot, and I can feel the slush hitting the bottom of the car. "I know you don't have a position report in there," he says. "I hope you don't have a weapon. If you're going to go postal, please make sure to do it on your side of the floor."

"Or on twelve," I say. Charles Blatts and Bob Frear and the other firm bigwigs have their offices on the twelfth floor.

"God, he's bitter and cynical," Dino says.

"I'm cynical and bitter," Mac says, "but I've been at the firm for eleven years. What's your excuse?"

"I learned it from you," I say.

Little is said for the rest of the ride, which takes twenty minutes longer than normal. In the parking garage, puddles of rainwater form around the newly arrived cars. We step over the little rivers that flow across the cement to a central metal-grated drain. At the elevators I can hear a whirring, but no elevator arrives. A fluorescent light flickers and buzzes. Dino puts on his tie.

"Listen, guys," Mac says, "I'm leaving the firm today."

"I knew it!" Dino shouts.

"What?" I exclaim. "What about your coup?"

"No go, Barry. I was in with Isaac Hunt yesterday, and he's just not ready to let Court go. Somebody has to get rid of Court Harvey, but it's not going to be me. I'm not going to work anymore under Court, and I told Hunt that. Besides, this other offer is a good one."

"Where?"

He looks at his loafers, as if maybe he shouldn't tell us. As if maybe it matters.

"First Boston," he says at last.

"Hah," says Dino. "That's great. You are a genius. A fucking genius."

Dino is using "genius" in the conventional Wall Street sense, which means that Mac has found a way to improve his pay dramatically. He's probably looking at over a million a year, maybe closer to one and a half, and for two years, guaranteed. The guarantee is essential, because it means that he doesn't have to worry about any First Boston Hooky Duke, something that First Boston has been known for ever since the firm was taken over by the Swiss. The Swiss were apparently appalled that a number of traders and bankers in New York were making more than the chairman of the entire multibillion-franc firm, but when the chairman tried to cut pay, those same bankers and traders ran for the door, and there was no one left to make any money. Now First Boston—still owned by the Swiss—is handing out guarantees like the rest of the Street.

The elevator arrives, and we ride up to the security turnstiles. I can't help feeling jealous of Mac. He's going to make major bucks, probably four times what I get.

"Hey, Dino," he says as we walk through the security turnstiles to the next set of elevators, "seeing as this is my last day, can you pay me what you owe me for commuting?"

"Sure," Dino says, "but I don't have any cash on me. I'll send you a check."

Mac wastes no time once on the floor. He doesn't even bother to log on to his Sun workstation, though I do see him checking e-mails on his PC. When Court Harvey appears on the desk at quarter to eight, he and Mac go into the office, where they stay for over an hour, right through a government announcement of the most recent GDP figures.

"Hey, Meat," Vollmer says, once activity quiets down, "what's going on in there?"

"Mac's leaving."

"What?" Vollmer loses his color. Unlike Chip McCarty, Stevie Vollmer obviously doesn't have a backup plan.

"Ah, fuck me," Vollmer says. "We've got to get him to stay. Where's he going?"

"FOB."

"Shit!" Vollmer throws down his headset. "I heard they're giving away two-by-twos."

Two-by-two: two million dollars a year, guaranteed, for two years.

"I wouldn't get too upset," I say. "Mac's one less big mouth to feed. And now we're short-handed. Harvey needs you now more than ever."

"I don't want to work for that putz."

I shrug. When I look the other way, I catch Tom Carlson's eye. He nods, as if to remind me that I'm on his side.

"Did you know about this?" Court Harvey asks me in a whisper. He has just stormed out of his office and come up to me as if this were all my fault.

"He told me this morning on the way up to the floor," I say.

Court fumes. I know that he hates Chip McCarty, that he has been waiting for a chance to fire him, as he did Colin Dancer. Still, it's humiliating to lose Mac to a competitor. It displays a lack of dictatorial control. Isaac Hunt won't like it.

"So are you going to try to keep him?" I ask.

"Yes."

I spy Isaac Hunt slipping into Court's office. Mac is still in there. I have to bid some ten-year notes then, and then some five-year notes, as we no longer have a five-year trader. An hour and a half slide by, and then Court Harvey taps me on the shoulder. I was aware that he left the desk, but not that he has returned.

"Go talk to him," he says, meaning Chip McCarty.

"What do I say?"

"Remind him what loyalty means. You're his buddy. Try to get him to stay."

"Did you make a counteroffer?"

"Yes."

"As good as FOB's?"

"More or less."

I don't laugh at this, but it takes effort not to. "More or less" means less, and less means Mac won't stay. Chip McCarty has spent the last eleven years of his life as a trader, and to him this is just another transaction. He has value because he has performed well and survived. He sees his success as his own. To him, the firm has not made him. If anything, it's his main foe. Why, he will ask, should I stay and work here for less? Why should I feel loyalty to you when all these years you've been paying me less than I have proved I'm worth? I will sell my services to the highest bidder. Either pay market rates, or I'm going to trade away.

Also, I can't see how it helps me to have Chip McCarty stay at the firm. If he leaves, then only Vollmer, Carlson, Glover, and I remain below Court Harvey. In other words, I'll be closer to the top. In addition, First Boston is throwing money around. Maybe someday Chip will send for me.

"Hey," I say when I walk into Court Harvey's office. Mac stands at the window, looking down on the construction.

"Would you look at that, Barry? Just like I said. They're actually tearing up the street again."

I walk up next to him and feel a breeze from the HVAC unit. Mac is right. The three straight lanes we enjoyed over Christmas are now torn up, rerouted, and gridlocked. There's a crane rearranging cement barriers. I can hear honking, in spite of the sealed window and driving rain.

"They want you to stay for less money," I say. "They seem a little desperate. I mean, Court asked me to come talk to you about loyalty. I guess they don't have anything else to offer. You'd be a fool to stay. I don't know why you're still here."

"It's just part of the drill, Barry. Besides, I want them to grovel. I want it to hurt."

"Do me a favor," I say. "Next time they need a guy over there, give me a call."

"You got it," Mac says.

"We could carpool again."

He chuckles. "FOB's offices are midtown. I'll be on the train now."

We shake hands and promise to stay in touch, though I doubt we'll have much contact. I'll have to work at it. When Mac turns back to the window, I head back out to the desk.

"Well?" Court asks.

"No way."

Court smiles. He can't help himself. He knows Chip McCarty was a threat to his power. This business is like politics: incumbents keep winning. And what has Court really accomplished by forcing out Chip McCarty? He's driven away one of his best traders, the one guy who can get a great offer from another firm. Why? So he can eliminate any threat to his personal position. Chip McCarty is right. Somebody has to bring Court Harvey down.

About an hour later, Rachel calls. My mother has phoned. She needs me. She's in Vancouver, where the doctors are giving Ben a one-in-four chance of survival. So Ben has been telling me the truth all along. I wish I'd sent him more money. He probably would have spent it on illegal drugs and alcohol, but now I know he doesn't have much time and who was I to deny him those pleasures?

Rachel has booked me on an early-morning flight.

"You're the best," I say.

"I've told you that," she says.

"You gonna be all right with the kids?"

"Like always."

"Chip McCarty quit today," I tell her.

"Really? What's that mean for you?"

A few years earlier, she might have asked why, or how it happened, or what Mac was planning to do, but now Rachel has learned to think, as I have, in Wall Street terms: *What does this mean for me?*

Clear skies arrive with the dawn. I am riding to La Guardia in the back of a Town Car, its interior thick with the driver's candy-factory-fire cologne, my window cracked enough to make breathing bearable. When we finally crest the Whitestone Bridge, I can see how the city is surrounded by water, and how that water is reflecting the morning light. The sun is now high enough to shine against the thousands of windows of Manhattan, several miles to the west, making the whole island glitter and wink. There's something momentous about the sight, all that human bustle crammed so closely together. Even the little houses squeezed along the water's edge in Queens seem poignant. It's beautiful.

With the three-hour time change, I make it to Ben's hospital room a little after eleven in the morning. My mother sits in a chair by his bed. The Vancouver paper rests in her lap. I give her the *New York Times* I brought—she's an avid fan of the paper—and kiss her on the cheek. I feel powder and smell something odd. Hairspray, perhaps. There is no talking to Ben, whom I would not have recognized. What is left of his hair is gray. His face is sunken, ashen-colored, his lips thin, the color of skin. An IV hangs from a stand and snakes its way into his arm. The topography of the hospital blankets display an almost stick-figure outline of his body. I doubt he weighs much more than a hundred pounds.

"He's supposed to be getting better, but he's not," my mother says.

There's an accusatory tone in her voice, and I know she blames the hospital for this. As a former nurse, she toggles between utter faith in the medical profession and complete distrust. She looks to Ben, and I to her. My mother has always been older than my friends' mothers, but now I see that she is just old. She sits with her knees together and the paper on her lap, her back hunched slightly forward in the way of some older women. Her turtleneck sweater runs up her neck right to her jaw and appears to be helping her to support her head. She looks very thin, and wobbly.

I borrow a plastic chair from the patient next to Ben, who has no visitors and is unconscious, anyway. By the window there's a third patient, mouth agape, snoring. The room itself is painted a yellowy white. Above, fluorescent lights buzz behind ice-cube-tray-styled covers, which are built into ceiling recesses. There's a smell of floor polish and antiseptic. It's no wonder most people despise hospitals.

"I'm sure they're doing what they can," I say to my mother.

"Since when is doing what they can enough?" she says. "He's not supposed to die before I do."

I get out of my chair and kneel beside her, putting my arm around her back. After all the time I've spent thinking about and worshiping Ben, I know I should feel more for him, but I don't. I can't shake the feeling that he's brought this on himself. Cancer. It's as if there was always something rotten inside him, and now it's finally showing itself. I know this is mean, at least to Ben, but I have to believe it. I don't want to live in a world where lives are taken randomly, especially the lives of children from their parents. Were anything like this to befall Sam or Jane, I don't know what I would do. I could never explain to them what would be happening. How can you offer to your small children no understanding but that life is often unfair and cruel?

My mother always taught me there was a reason for things. She believed you could control your own fate, and maybe she was right, but only to a point.

Later, I am able to convince my mother to go back to the hotel by promising to stay at Ben's bedside. She knows he is going to die, she says, and she wants family to be with him when it happens.

I watch her shuffle from the room with the *New York Times* cradled under her arm. The room is quiet, and soon I find myself thinking of a large ten-year-futures position I have. I debate in my mind the possible outcomes of this trade, think and rethink how much pain I will take if it goes against me, how soon I will cash in if it goes my way. Waking dreams of trade outcomes are a hazard of the job.

I hear the sheets rustle, and look up. Ben has stirred. It's the first time he's moved since I arrived. I get out of my chair and stand over his bed.

"Ben," I say. "Ben. It's me, Barry. Can you hear me?"

I get no response, so I squeeze his shoulder. It's bony, still. I lean over the bed, hold both of his shoulders. "Ben," I say. "Ben."

He opens his eyes. It is said that eyes are the windows to the soul, but I know better. There was never anything real to be seen in Ben's eyes, just as there is nothing to be seen now. They are big and dark, the kind of eyes that fool people, that make them think that they know him.

"It's me," I say. "It's Barry."

I've often wondered how he turned out so differently from me. Has he done what he's done out of laziness, or did he have some other idea? Does he feel any remorse for what he's done to our mother? What, exactly, did he think he was doing, or did he think about it at all?

"Careful," says a nurse, with what I think is an Irish accent. I jump and turn, and before me is a short woman, with freckles and amber-colored hair. Young.

"I'm his brother," I say.

"Yes," she replies, using that simple affirmation to scold. *What are you doing,* she seems to be saying, *jostling the patients?*

"I'm his brother," I repeat, and know that I'm oddly proud to say this, dubious distinction that it is.

Friday, around lunchtime, I dial the firm's 800 number, then punch in the code that puts me through to the government desk. Tom Carlson answers.

"It's a shit show," he says. "Producer prices jumped over a percent, and the market is coming off like a prom dress. Court is only putting numbers on trades he feels like doing, and with you and Mac gone, that leaves a lot of ground between Stevie and me. Then the Bundesbank has been trading up a storm in bills today, and we still haven't hired a fucking bill trader. The Krauts are killing me, Barry. You back Monday?"

"I think so."

"Hurry, man. I tell you, we really need you here."

I call Rachel next.

"Things are fine," she says.

"And you?"

"Okay."

"I'll be home soon."

"When?"

"I can't say, exactly, but Sunday, probably."

"So—how's your brother?" she asks.

"Not so good. He never recovered from the operation, and he's not going to. He's already like a corpse. We're on a death vigil here."

"I'm sorry."

"Don't be sorry. I don't know what to think or feel anymore. My mother, though, has fully adopted the grieving-mother role. Not six months ago, she said she'd written him off. Now she can't leave his room."

"She is a mother. Oh, that reminds me. Gretchen Barnes called here for you. She wants you to call her. It's something important at work."

We hang up and I again dial the firm's toll-free number, then go through the switchboard to reach Gretchen. A male voice answers the phone.

"Who is this?" he demands.

I tell him.

"She's on a line. I'll take a message."

"I'll hold."

Two other men come on and ask me whom I'm holding for before Gretchen picks up the line.

"You must be slinging a lot of stock," I say.

"I'm having a real problem here," she says. "Court's been calling me once an hour today. He's going mad. I've had to get our new associate to screen all of my calls. Can you imagine, not being able to pick up your phone in this business?"

"Tell him to cut it out."

"I have, and he called right back. Do you know that he got inside my building two nights ago? He was waiting for me when I got off the elevator. I was scared to death. My nanny is scared shitless. And twice in the last week I've caught him following me on the street."

Court Harvey, managing director in charge of worldwide government trading, former top athlete, is a stalker. It's a startling idea. "Have you called the police?" I ask.

She hasn't. She wants me to talk to him, to get him to back off. She's adamant about not calling the police, or telling anyone at the firm. "Do you know what happens to women in this business who make those kinds of complaints? I'm not ready to retire and sit around for a decade, hoping I hit the lawsuit lotto."

"I don't know, Gretchen. I think you have a legitimate gripe. He used a work phone, called you at work. He's toast."

If she makes this charge, Court will be gone. Not even Court will be able to survive a sexual-harassment charge. The firm fears sexual harassment more than it fears financial panics or Democrats in Congress. The field is wide open. All I need is a little help from Gretchen.

"I just want him to stop," she says. "Can't you talk to him?"

"I'll try, but it sounds like you might have to do something official."

"Just talk to him," she says. "I gotta hop."

I check my watch. It's a little before four in New York. I call the desk and get Vollmer. "Court left," he says. I can almost see him sneering. "On account of all the extra people we got around here."

"How much longer can you stay?" my mother asks. It's Saturday night, and we're eating takeout Chinese at Ben's bedside.

"I really can't stay any longer," I tell her.

"I need you to stay. I really do, Barry. You've been such a big help."

"But I'm needed back at home, Mom."

"Your brother is dying. Can't you stay for this next week? He won't make it much longer."

"I don't think I can," I say. "We're very shorthanded at work, and Rachel and the kids need me. I'm sorry."

"I need someone, Barry. I don't think I can face this alone," she says, looking down into her lap.

I think about my decision the whole plane ride home, justify it in my mind. The stakes for my life are too high. I am on the edge of an incredible opportunity, the kind that might come along only once. Chip McCarty is gone. I see a chance to bring down Court Harvey. With Gretchen's help, it shouldn't be hard. I can't let this pass. A couple of years at the top and I'll be able to write my own ticket. We'll even be able to move back west, where Rachel and I and the kids can get back to the place where we've been heading all along.

I don't reach New York till just before midnight. The weather is clear, and the plane makes its approach from the south, traveling almost directly over the Statue of Liberty, then tilting left and giving me a clear view of the firm's building. All the lights burn on the trading floor. Those lights are always on. The plane continues over Brooklyn and then Queens, and Manhattan passes by my window. When we finally touch down at La Guardia, I have an odd feeling that, at that very moment, Ben has died. I shake it off. I've never been one to believe in odd connections or unlikely coincidences, and, besides, I need to get home and get some sleep.

12. Nothing to Say

Dino is waiting for me when I pull into the Park and Ride the next morning, though I'm several minutes early myself. There's a mist so heavy that he's running his wipers as he idles. Something about the way those wipers move back and forth, a one second pause before each swipe, makes me think he's been waiting a long time.

"You sure you don't want to ride in the back, like royalty or something?" Dino asks when I jump into the front seat. It's our first morning commute together with Chip McCarty permanently gone. "I mean, I know you're not used to the front."

I recline the seat. I notice that it's heated, a nice touch, especially from a country as warm as Japan. "This will do," I say.

Dino guns the car, and we're soon doing our typical eighty-mile-an-hour shimmy down I-684.

"I applied for a parking sticker," Dino says after several minutes of silence. "I'm twenty-eighth on the waiting list."

"You made senior vice-president?"

Dino nods. "They gave it to me at year end, in lieu of a respectable bonus."

"Why didn't you say anything?"

"I was too pissed off. Is there anything worse than being bought off with a *title*?"

Dino suddenly slams on the brakes and veers left, to the Mobil service station in the middle of the Hutch, the same station he never stopped at for Mac. Four years they rode together, and Dino never once gave in. Dino's character runs deeper than his glibness; underneath he's quite tough and, I suspect, pitiless.

"Let's get some coffee," he says, jerking to a stop at the curb.

Five minutes later, I'm walking back to the car, my face turned from the wind and drizzle, a double-cupped serving of Colombian roast in my left hand. "Hey, look at that," Dino says. He points to a Lincoln Town Car, its driver filling it up at the pump. In the back is the unmistakable figure of Charles Blatts, the chairman and CEO of our firm, reading the *Journal.*

"Should we go over and say hi?" I joke.

"That's the life," Dino says. "Thirteen sticks a year and a driver. Too bad he doesn't have a piece of fluff back there with him. We'd both get a raise."

On the highway, I ask, "Suppose you really did have some dirt on your boss. What could you do with it?"

"What do you mean by dirt?"

"Dirt."

"Well," Dino says, pushing back his black curls, "if it's something like he's married and you catch him cheating on his wife, not much. If it doesn't happen at work, the firm is not going to care, and he could hang tough. Besides, for all you know, his wife doesn't care. Meanwhile, you still got to work for him. No, it's got to be very serious. Something illegal. I mean, you could catch Court Harvey marching naked in the Greenwich Village Halloween parade, and I doubt it would do you any good."

"What would work?"

"First, let me say that he better not be having a great year, because they'd protect Heydrich, Himmler, and Adolf himself if they were making a lot of money."

"Court's having a decent year, like always, but nothing off the charts."

"Then you need something that could cost the firm money if it became public."

"Like, say, shtupping a summer intern?"

"I was thinking more of insider trading, or, in your department, messing with the treasury auctions, like Solly did, but, yeah, sex might work. Big discrimination liability, I would think. Did Court give it to that redhead you guys had last summer?"

"No."

"Too bad," Dino says. "Looks like you're just going to have to work, like the rest of us."

The trade inquiry this morning is relentless. Court Harvey never emerges from his office, where he is no doubt attempting to find another five-year trader. Lord knows, with all the mergers and cutbacks we've been through in the last few years, there is plenty of talent around, though most of it has the stigma of being discarded. Wall Street hates discarded things, no matter the intrinsic value. Every once in a while some lunatic (later called a visionary) will pick up something discarded, as Michael Milken did with junk bonds, and become rich, and then rich and famous. Most who try this get fired first. No, discarded issues and people are too risky. Wall Street likes to hire other people's traders, just as it likes to risk other people's money.

Tom Carlson, Stevie Vollmer, and I handle the flow as well as we can, but, in truth, the three of us are doing what six guys did when I started at the firm almost four years earlier. I wonder if this is by design. The government-bond market is shrinking. It would make sense to eliminate employees and cut costs. In such an environment, there is security in being management. Of course, there's always security in management, it's just that security is more important now.

About eleven-thirty, I call Isaac Hunt's secretary. "Shirley," I say. "This is Barry Schwartz. I need to see Isaac today."

"I'm afraid he's booked up for the next couple days."

"This is an emergency."

"I can't very well rearrange his schedule, can I?"

"Listen, Shirley. When I say emergency, I mean it. Millions of dollars are at stake."

I realize immediately that this is a poor choice of words. I've already traded almost two thousand million—two billion—dollars since I walked into work. Millions of dollars are at stake with everything we do. Millions of dollars are as common as rain.

"Look, Shirley. Put me on his schedule. A situation has developed that could prove not only very costly financially for the firm, but a major public embarrassment as well. It involves sex. You don't want this thing to explode onto the front page of the *Daily News* just because you wouldn't put me through."

At four that afternoon, I'm sitting in Isaac Hunt's gloomy office. The light coming in the window seems to do so reluctantly, and with great fatigue; the sky is irrepressibly gray and drab. Isaac Hunt sits behind his desk, head slightly crooked, as if to question preemptively whatever it is that I think could make the front page of the *Daily News. All right,* he seems to be saying, *this had better be good.*

Soon, he agrees with me that it is. He wants to meet with Gretchen, whose name he still does not know. I tell him it won't be easy. I paint a picture of a reluctant but very threatened woman, someone desperate, capable of lashing out. I suggest that we might keep the thing quiet, were we able to make certain promises.

"Promises? What kind of promises?"

"That you will get rid of Court."

"On what grounds? Nothing has been proved. Or even accused, except by you."

"Once she makes a public accusation," I say, "the cat is out of the bag. You'll have to get rid of Court, and worry about a settlement. And deal with the negative publicity. My way will save you that. I'll bring her to you. If she convinces you, you take action. If not, fight her. But I think you will find her convincing."

His mouth turns down at the corners. He is angry, apparently with me, but we set up a meeting for the next day at five.

"How do you know all this?" he asks. "About Court, and the woman?"

"I know the woman. She came to me for help."

He tilts his head back and rests his chin on his hands, which are still held together at the fingertips. "I see," he says.

I walk upstairs to the equity floor, look out across the tops of the hundreds of computer screens, and see Gretchen standing at her desk. She stares off into space, gesticulating with her right hand, which holds a pen, and talking into her headset. Sales: it's all about talking, telling stories, building relationships. The firm is big on the word "relationship," as if it can somehow mask the zero-sum game involved in every trade.

I head toward Gretchen. She wears a lavender blouse and black skirt. She is surrounded by men in white shirts and dark pants. I wear the only blue dress shirt on the floor. I might as well be wearing a sandwich board that says "Bond Trader." Bill Klune, the Isaac Hunt of the Equities Division, has made it clear that he believes in white shirts, and the men of the Equities Division believe in Klune—or at least in his power to affect their pay.

As I walk toward Gretchen, I notice that the equities floor has recently been remodeled, an apparent gesture to the run up in equity prices. Confidence is coming back into stocks, and into the employees who work on this floor. The most glaring feature of the remodel is the new ceiling tile, white as all the dress shirts. The ceiling tiles on the fixed-income floor are tawny with age; each air vent wears a beard of black soot. Equities file cabinets are made of richly stained wood, whereas bond traders have to look at metal cabinets the color of army khaki. Equities carpet tiles are new, a burnt-orange color similar to the Schwartz family Explorer. Equity salesmen have flat-screen monitors. I don't doubt that beneath it all there is the same blatant grab for money, but at least here it seems more refined.

Gretchen sees me and holds up a finger. I wait. Eventually, we find an office that overlooks the West Side Highway, already gridlocked with the afternoon rush hour. Dino and I will soon be fighting our way through that mess. Gretchen takes the manager's seat, props her elbows up on the desk, and cups one hand around the other's fist. It's an aggressive and, I think, practiced posture.

"I thought we weren't going to be seen together," she says. The office is lined with framed newspaper headlines of history's various stock-market debacles, including the one from last spring. This is unusual, in that most managers decorate their offices with posters showing the upward march of stock prices over time. I find the disaster approach rather comforting. "It happened before, it'll happen again," those headlines seem to say. Why get all worked up about it?

"This is important," I say.

"What is it?"

"I can get Court off your back," I tell her, "with your help."

"What kind of help?"

"I need you to talk to Isaac Hunt. Just tell him your story. He's looking for an excuse to get rid of Court, and you can give it to him."

"No way. I told you. I don't want to go public."

"This isn't going public. That's the whole point. Hunt doesn't want it to go public. Basically, the deal is this: you don't make a public charge, and Hunt will get rid of Court and not bring you into it. You'll get just what you want."

"Does he know my name?"

"No. I'm giving you the chance to control the situation."

"Leave me out of it, then. Getting Court fired hardly solves my problem."

"It'll help," I say.

"No, it won't."

"Gretchen, I can't leave you out of it."

"Why not?"

"Because I can't."

"Why can't you?" she says.

"Because I can't," I say. I feel my face burning. Hold steady, I tell myself. All your life you've shied away from moves like this. Don't let this chance slip away.

"Do you have any idea how many times guys have tried to get Court fired and failed?" Gretchen asks. "Everyone says he always makes a lot of money. You can't get rid of someone like that."

"No one can fight sex discrimination," I say.

"I'm not getting involved," Gretchen says. "Therefore, there is no discrimination. You're a man, Barry. You don't understand. Once I make an accusation, I'm fucked."

"Gretchen, the firm will still have to act. Think about it. If Court does this again to someone who does make a stink, then it will probably come to light that he's done it before and the firm knew about it, and then there will be hell to pay. The firm has to act now. It will act now. So—I'm asking you. Don't make me go forward alone."

"You could stop, Barry. You don't have to 'go forward.'"

"Yes, I do. I can't sit around and think about what might have been."

She looks at me a little sideways. "If you do this, Barry, I won't back you up. I can't. That makes it my word against yours."

"Like I said, the firm will still have to take the accusation seriously. You'll be involved."

She pauses. Her eyes seem to be following the action on the trading floor. "I thought I could trust you," she says.

Don't get emotional, I tell myself. Think like a trader. Do what is necessary.

"If you go through with this, Barry," Gretchen says, "I'm calling Rachel."

My heart skips.

"That's right. I've got leverage. Did you ever think about that?"

I haven't. I can't let Rachel find out, but I also can't let this opportunity slide by. My first inclination is to take the risk. Every once in a while you've just got to roll the dice. Perhaps Gretchen is bluffing. It won't be easy for her to make that call, and if she does I can deny everything. Rachel will want to believe me. I'll be able to argue that Gretchen has a reason to lie. I decide to call Gretchen's bluff. It's the trader's way.

"Five o'clock tomorrow," I say. "Isaac Hunt's office." I stand and leave the office, before I can change my mind.

Tom Carlson stops me in government gulch, on my way to my chair. The row is starting to take on a locker-room smell. Carlson most likely has something to do with this. He looks as he always does late in the day: hair askew, revealing his bald spot; shirt untucked, dangling like a curtain off his enormous belly; face greasy and damp.

"Where the fuck have you been? Every goddamn call has been for you since you left," he says. "Call your wife. She's called four times. Some emergency, she said. And some guy named Dan Connelly called twice."

I dial Rachel, wondering if Gretchen might have called already. No, I decide. She doesn't yet know what I will do.

"Where have you been?" Rachel says. "Ben died. Last night. Your mother wants you to fly back out tomorrow. I made a reservation."

"I can't go," I tell her. Rachel was asleep when I got home last night, asleep when I left the house this morning. This is the first conversation we've had since I've returned home.

"Why not?" she asks.

"I can't explain now, but I can't go."

"Well, you call your mother and tell her that."

"I can't go tomorrow, is all. Trust me, Rachel. I'll explain it all when I get home."

"I just don't understand you anymore," she says.

"I can explain. Tonight, when I get home."

"When will that be?"

"Normal time. There's one more thing, Rach. Maybe don't answer the phone for a few days."

"What? Why can't I answer my own phone?"

I don't know what to say. The suggestion just came out. "Never mind. Do what you want."

I hang up and look over at Carlson's desk. He runs a small drugstore there. Lately he's been stocking a big yellow bottle of Listerine, two bottles of Maalox, one of Pepto-Bismol, and a family-size bottle of generic aspirin.

"Looks like you got heartburn problems," I say.

"I tell you, man, it's getting worse and worse. Sometimes I get it way up here"—he pounds on his chest—"like I'm having a goddamn heart attack."

"An ulcer? Maybe you should see a doctor," I say.

"Waste a time. The advice is always the same: lose weight, take it easy, stay out of pressure-filled situations. Yeah, right. Besides, I gotta make some money here. Can't do that sitting at a doctor's office."

I try to remember the last time I went to a doctor. It was high school, for a football physical. "I've got a headache," I say, which is the truth. "Can you spare me a few aspirin?"

"Help yourself," he says, tossing me the bottle. "By the way, did you hear who Chip McCarty hired to trade tens at FOB?"

"Who?" I swallow four aspirin dry, thinking, Mac hired a ten-year trader? What the fuck. I'm a ten-year trader. He didn't call me.

"Colin Dancer."

"Really?" Fuck. That's what I think: Fuck. Spend enough time on the floor and you even swear in your mind.

"Yep. Can you believe it? And we're still working here. Right now those guys are sitting up there laughing at us."

"Did you see the Nasdaq today?" Dino asks. He pounds on his horn. We're stuck in the gridlocked traffic on the southbound West Side Highway. Our plan is to head north on the FDR, but first we have to round the southern tip of the island, a task similar to what faced Magellan, now that the Brooklyn-Battery Tunnel has traffic backed up to Stuyvesant High School.

"Why do you pound on the horn? No one can go anywhere."

"It has nothing to do with them. It's all about me. I pound, therefore I am."

"The Nasdaq had a good day," I say.

"Digicom," he says. "Up seventeen on twelve today. I'm telling you, man, you got to get involved. This thing is about to explode."

"What's Digicom?"

"They make circuit boards for cell phones."

"You own it?"

"Two thousand times, baby."

"What?" I ask. "You mean to tell me that you made thirty-four grand today on some stock you own?"

"Yep. Gotta hunch? Buy a bunch."

"Digicom," I repeat. There's always someone making a buck you don't know about.

Dino pounds on the horn. "God help me," he says, "I love making money."

All I Could Get

I spend the rest of the ride home trying to figure out how to explain to Rachel that I'm not going to Vancouver, and that Gretchen may call. My mind seems frozen. I can think of no good way to couch it. The truth is that I can't leave town because I'm trying to get Court Harvey fired. I'm making the kind of hard-nosed play that does not allow for another life. No illness, no problems, and certainly no death.

All the lights are on downstairs when I look in the dining-table window. I can see the movie *Dumbo* playing in the living room, but my family is not in sight. I stand there for a moment and breathe in the smell of damp earth and rotting leaves. There's no rain, but it's a wet and chilly evening. Water drips from the roof and the trees and hits the leaves on the ground with an intermittent patter.

I walk inside to find Rachel at the kitchen sink. She asks if I can help her move something in the bedroom. I follow her upstairs.

"Can you please tell me what is going on?" she asks in the bedroom. There's nothing to move. She stands in the middle of the room, arms crossed, wearing a sweatshirt that the firm gave me when I got hired. It's like getting pulled into the office at work.

"What do you mean?" I can't tell if Gretchen has called.

"Why can't you go to Vancouver?"

"Because I'm about to become head of the desk."

"How? You just started. You're still new."

"I'm still standing, Rachel, and that's what counts right now. Don't you realize what this means? You went to Court Harvey's house. Do you realize what men in his position make every year?"

"How are you going to get rid of Court?"

"He's been stalking Gretchen. He has to go."

"He's been doing what?"

"He's been stalking her. It's bizarre, but true."

"Has he harmed her?"

"No." I tell her about Court following Gretchen on the street, and sneaking into her building. Rachel backs up and sits down on the edge of the bed.

"Well," she says, "even if you get rid of Court, why would they make you the head guy? And what makes you think that if they do they'll pay you what they paid Court, even if you get his job?"

These are good points. The top spot is up for grabs. And they didn't give me what they paid Colin Dancer when I replaced him. Still, I'll make a lot more than I make now.

"Okay," I say, "so I make a million a year, instead of one eight. I mean, Rachel, c'mon. Don't you realize what this means for our plans? We'll be set up in no time."

"But couldn't it wait a week, Barry? One week? Your mother needs you."

"I can't leave this week, Rachel. I just can't. But I'll be able to take care of my mother for the rest of her life."

"This isn't about money, Barry. It's about family responsibility. It's about the kind of person you are."

And, I think, the kind of person I want to be, which is someone who doesn't want to think about money. Ever. I try to explain this to my wife. "Look, Rachel, I just cannot go. Everything we've worked for is coming to a head. We can't expect to achieve our goals without sacrifices. The easy thing for me would be to abandon my plans because of this, and later say what a good person I am for not letting work get in the way of family responsibility. Well, that's pretty much what work does. I'm tired of being a working grunt. I am tired of being bitter. I'm sick and tired of rationalizations for failure. I just want success, and success is not always pretty."

"Isn't there some way, Barry, that you could . . ."

Her words trail off as I shake my head no.

"There's one more thing, Rachel. Gretchen, she doesn't want me to say anything. She thinks it will hurt her career."

"So why are you going to do it?"

"For us, Rachel. For our plan. I'm trying to stick to it."

"I don't think it was our plan to abandon your mother on the death of your brother and screw over someone who's been your friend for fifteen years and helped you get this goddamn job in the first place."

"It wasn't," I admit.

She shakes her head. "Is that really what you're going to do tomorrow? Get up, put on your suit, go to work, screw your friends?"

"I wouldn't put it exactly that way," I say, though it does sound bad, the way she puts it. I wonder for a moment if maybe I shouldn't call the whole thing off. And then I think of the dirt-stained carpet of our old place in Colorado, and of carrying the phone and rent bills in my pocket, and I decide I can't back down. I've got to see things through.

When I look at Rachel, I see her staring at me with a look of the most profound disappointment that I've ever seen on her face. I open my mouth to ask for her understanding, to make her see that I'm doing this for us. There can be no going back to duct-taped fenders, secondhand clothes, sheets hanging on the walls. Rachel would see me as a failure, as I would see myself, and I don't think our marriage would survive it. Success, then, even if it means "screwing" my friends, is the only option. I'm still standing with my mouth agape, trying to find the right way to express this, when Rachel rises to her feet and walks out of the room.

I can barely breathe the next day as I walk across the floor to Isaac Hunt's office. It's odd, but, the closer you get to Hunt's office, the farther you get from trading activity. His part of the floor houses the mathematical geniuses who create our various pricing models, guys often so out of tune with the physical world that they forget to brush their hair, zip their flies, or even change their clothes. They work in silence, and tend to look at traders as overpaid idiots, which, compared with them, we are.

Gretchen and Isaac Hunt are already in the office when I arrive, as well as another man. I've seen him before in the building, but I have no idea who he is. His hair is completely gray. He wears a neatly pressed blue shirt with French cuffs. It's five o'clock in the afternoon, and he shows none of the beat-up look that traders have late in the day. Also, traders get fired or retire long before they go completely gray. I take him immediately for a lawyer, and he is. Sabin Devers, firm council.

"Ah, Barry," Isaac Hunt says. He introduces me to Devers, then says, "I made some arrangements ahead of time, so that this can be done very quickly."

I sit in the one vacant chair. Gretchen still has not acknowledged that I have arrived. She won't even look at me, and, looking at her jaw, I wonder if she isn't clenching her teeth. I accept a two-page paper from Devers. He gives a different and thicker set of papers to Gretchen. Isaac Hunt explains that the papers recognize a problem with Court Harvey's behavior, and state that the firm is taking action. Court's employment will be terminated. Gretchen states that she finds this an acceptable and complete action on the firm's part, and that she will not disclose the terms of the agreement. The firm promises that the episode will not become part of her permanent record, nor will there be any consequences in regards to her future employment. As for me, I promise not to disclose what I know of this matter, which strikes me as a small price to pay for what I stand to gain.

"Does Court know about any of this?" I ask.

"No," says Isaac Hunt.

"I can't emphasize enough," says the lawyer, "just how delicate this matter is. Everyone involved will be served best by not mentioning it to anyone."

Gretchen shoots me a look.

"So, then," Devers says. He rubs his palms together, as if his hands were cold. "Let's bring Shirley in to notarize. Everyone can sign, and we'll move on."

It is very quiet as Gretchen signs, just the scratching of her pen and a distant horn, perhaps a tugboat on the Hudson. I glance over at Hunt, who is staring at Gretchen and fingering one of the Lucite tombstones on his desk. The tombstones are little trophies that commemorate corporate-bond offerings that the firm has managed. Such offerings earn the firm fees, which is to say risk-free money. Hunt probably has some formula worked out in his head as to what each tombstone is worth to his personal comfort. The Wal-Mart deal put a new wing on his Connecticut mansion. The Dupont deal put a new Mercedes in the garage . . .

When Gretchen finishes signing, she stands and leaves without looking at me. I notice that Hunt watches her till she is out of sight, beyond the rocket scientists. I take up a pen, stare at my name on the page, and sign. I'm back at my desk in two minutes.

"Hey, Meat," Stevie Vollmer says. "Where you been?"

"I could tell you, but I'd have to kill you." I see light flashing on my phone board. It's a general government-desk number, a call that could be for anybody. I answer it to avoid talking to Vollmer.

"This is Shirley, from Isaac Hunt's office." She has no idea she's talking to me. "Mr. Hunt would like to speak with Court Harvey, please."

I put her on hold. "Anyone know where Court is?" I ask.

"Office."

I walk over to the office and glance through the vertical blinds. Court has swiveled his chair around so that he faces the exterior window. He's leaning way back in his chair and tossing a ball up and catching it with his right hand. The ball is painted like a globe. We all received them the year before, when the firm was making a big push to be thought of as global. Court is talking to someone on his headset. It occurs to me that this bare office is the one place he relaxes, the one spot where he feels at home. I pause, to give him a few seconds, and then knock on the glass. Out the window, the late-day sun is coming in low across the rooftops of Hoboken, throwing long shadows.

Court swivels back around in his chair. He is smiling. He waves me in.

"Isaac Hunt on forty-six," I whisper.

He nods, mouths the word, "Thanks." He laughs, then laughs again, harder, at whatever had been said on the other end of the line.

"Yeah, right," he says into his headset. "And Chip McCarty is a fucking genius."

I go back to the government desk, look down the row, breathe deep the hot, stale air. Isaac Hunt will never make a guy as short and fat and sweaty as Carlson the boss. Stan Glover is too quiet. This leaves Vollmer and me.

Dino has a traders' meeting that runs late, and I am left to sit on the desk as the traders and salespeople turn off their squawk boxes and screens, and the trading-floor din ebbs, till it is almost quiet, save the buzz of the lights and the whirr of the computer fans.

I wonder if Gretchen will really call Rachel. I think that probably she will, but that I'll be able to deny it. I've laid the groundwork with Rachel. She may have her doubts about me, but I will be convincing in my denial and true to her from now on, so that even the denial will, in effect, be something close to the truth, as if a different person did those earlier things, not me. Isn't that, essentially, what redemption is all about? Over time, Rachel's doubts will fade. It is the actual power play at work that is likely to stay with her, that will make her wonder just what kind of man I am. I have doubts myself. Do I really need to play it this way? Might not success come to me if I just keep my nose to my computer screens and not make a fuss? Probably not. And things staying the same could spell ruin for me. There's danger in not acting, too.

A light flashes on my phone board. Probably a wrong number. People in the know rarely call this late, but I answer it anyway. For me, answering phones is a habit.

"Are you happy now?" Gretchen asks.

I'm startled; I hadn't expected this. I wonder if she's called Rachel yet, or if she's just warming up for that call.

"You think you've protected me from Court?" she says. "Well, did you ever wonder how being unemployed might stop him from hanging out at my building? Did you?"

"I'm sorry, but—"

"Great, Barry. Just great."

"At least you won't have to see him at work." I cup my hand over the headset wand and hit the privacy button on my phone console. No one's around, but I'm taking no chances.

"Running into him at the firm was never the problem," Gretchen says. "You've solved nothing for me. Nothing. Except that now I've got to be looking over my shoulder even more than before."

There is silence on the line. This is the moment when I should mention the affair, but I can't. I feel convulsions in my throat.

"Gretchen," I stammer, "haven't you ever done anything at work to get ahead that caused others some pain?"

"I've always been fair," she says after a beat, which sounds self-serving to me.

"I don't think your fears will be realized," I say. "I'm just trying to get ahead, just like everyone else. Just like you. Can't you see that?"

The line goes dead.

Rachel is flipping through catalogues when I come in the door. She says hello without looking up, or any emotion at all. I trudge up to the bedroom to change out of my suit. At the top of the stairs there's the smell of smoke and I see that Rachel has built a fire in the fireplace, though now it is almost out. We were very excited about that fireplace when we bought the house. We almost never use it now, though, because the chimney draws poorly, and smoke often pours back into the house.

I decide that if Gretchen called Rachel won't bring it up till Sam goes to bed, and right now he's reading a comic book in his room. I stop at his door.

"Hey, Dad."

"Hey, Sam," I say. He's sitting upright in bed, two pillows behind his head. His bare knees stick out through his oldest and favorite pair of pajamas. "How's the book?"

"Good. How was work?"

I pause. "Good," I say.

He looks up from his book at me, wondering, I suppose, if anything is wrong.

"Did anyone call on the phone tonight?" I ask him.

His brow creases, angled to the center of his head, just like his mother's.

"Uh-uh. I don't think so. You mean like Tokyo or something?"

I go to change out of my suit. Then I walk back to Jane's room, open the door, and step inside. In the dim light I can see that she's asleep atop her blankets, her little bum up in the air. I lean over and kiss her head. Still asleep, she raises an arm and places it around my neck. I hold still till she moves again, and the arm falls back to her side. I slowly slide the blanket out from under her, cover her, and stand watching her sleep. I know I could go downstairs and try to make peace with Rachel, but I wonder if maybe I should give her some distance and let her come to me. Certainly this seems easier than a confrontation. I leave Jane's room, head for the bedroom, and crawl into bed without any supper. When my alarm wakes me the next morning, Rachel is not beside me. I find her asleep on the couch, wrapped in a fleece blanket, a twenty-five-year-old episode of *McCloud* on the television.

Court Harvey appears on the desk that afternoon at four. He wears a charcoal suit, including the jacket. This means he's not staying long. Only visitors and job applicants wear suit jackets on the trading floor.

"Hey, guys," Court says, "meeting in the conference room. Right away."

Carlson, Vollmer, Glover, and I stand up and leave the market to do its jig without us. We walk down to the conference room. It's a windowless interior room, with a fake plant in one corner and phone speakers built into the dark wooden conference table. On the wall are sepia photos of Wall Street from the distant past, when men carried trading tickets in their hatbands. We take seats at the table.

"Where is everyone?" Glover asks, as if he's just looked up from his computer after two years. Back then, a desk meeting meant ten to twelve guys. Now there are four. During those same two years, every other business at the firm has grown by at least 10 percent.

We wait several minutes; then Court enters, followed by Isaac Hunt and Charlie Sullivan, who runs corporate-bond trading. They stand by the door, all of them with their hands clasped behind their backs. I happen to glance at Carlson, whose eyes are bugging out, his brow glistening with sweat. It occurs to me that he thinks we might all be fired.

"Look, guys," Court says. "I've decided to take some time, for personal reasons. I've been coming here every day for more than sixteen years and I think I need a break. I want you to know that I've enjoyed working with all of you, and that I take many good memories with me."

"It will be very difficult to replace Court, as you know," Isaac Hunt says immediately. "For now, Charlie Sullivan will oversee governments, until permanent arrangements can be made. Any questions?"

Sixteen years, seven as the head of the desk, and we get a twenty-second explanation. No one says a word. I look over at Vollmer. He has the stunned but happy look of a man who has just won the lotto. Carlson is slumped back in his chair, as might a man who has just narrowly avoided a car wreck. His great stomach bobs up and down.

"Well," Isaac Hunt says, "that's it."

There's a moment of stillness—so uncommon on this floor—and then I stand up. The others follow my lead. Court positions himself at the door, so that he can shake hands with all of us on our way out. I step aside, to be last. I can sense from Court's expression that he is genuinely saddened to be leaving. This is a watershed moment in his life. Perhaps he's wondering, now that he's no longer head of the desk, just who he really is. His eyes look moist. He must have loved this job. It even appears that he feels affection for Carlson, Glover, and Vollmer. Perhaps he really doesn't know how deeply they hate him.

"Good luck, Barry," Court says when we finally shake. "You've been a good friend. I really owe you some thanks."

I find myself looking through the open door to the foreign-exchange row. I can't wait to get back to the desk.

"What are you going to do now?" I ask.

"Take some . . . time."

"Time?" I ask. I've seen Court take a lot of things—money, pride, advantage—but I doubt that he will ever take time. He has no idea what he will do. He hasn't thought a moment past this meeting.

"Time," he says firmly.

Time, I think. Court Harvey will drown in it.

"I can't believe it," Vollmer says back on the desk. "Can you believe it? Can you?"

"Sure," I say.

"He resigned? Court Harvey resigned? Just like that. How did we get so lucky?"

"What makes you think it's luck?"

"Meat, are you telling me that it wasn't luck? They canned him?" Vollmer's face flushes as he struggles for understanding. "Ah, fuck, whatever. This is the best news around here since they put those toilet-seat-cover dispensers in the bathroom stalls."

"Yeah, resigned," I hear Carlson say into his headset. "Just now . . . No, resigned. I don't know, work on his watercolors, who cares? . . . Fuck, yes. I am fucking happy."

I hit a light on my phone board. Dan Connelly is on the line. We haven't spoken for three months.

"Barry, what is up with you? Why don't you return my phone calls?"

"I've been busy, Dan. Hey, I hear you bought a house in Aspen."

"Yep. The deal, you know. Had the money."

"Why didn't you tell me?" I ask.

"I was going to, Barry, but, well, I decided to wait. We're remodeling. It's not ready yet, and, frankly, I wasn't sure how you would take it."

"What does that mean?"

"I know you want to buy something there, and all."

"Okay, I'm jealous," I tell him. "But I'm happy for you, too."

"Good," he says. "What else is new?"

"You know what, Dan? The shit's flying around here. I gotta hop. I'll call you later."

I hang up the phone. I've ended a man's career. I didn't kill him, and I don't doubt that he deserved what he got, but still I feel bad about it. I hadn't expected to; guilt is not something I've felt before on the trading floor. I wonder if Court felt that way when he moved out whomever he moved out. Probably it never occurred to him.

Next to me I can hear Carlson talking to someone new. "Fuck, yes," he's saying. "I'm fucking happy."

"You did that, didn't you?" Dino asks on the car ride home. I glance to our right, across two lanes of traffic, to the Yonkers racetrack. There's a light drizzle, little more than a heavy mist. A single horse trots on the track, pulling a buggy.

"Did what?"

"Got Court Harvey canned."

"Where did you get that haircut?" I ask, trying to divert the conversation. I don't want to talk about Court. Dino still has black curls, but now they're trimmed and shaped. They weren't this morning.

"Went downstairs after futures closed. Shampoo, cut, quick massage, forty bucks."

"Forty? What do they massage?"

"Blow me. Tell me about Harvey. You got him canned, right?"

"How would I do that?" I ask.

"I remember that conversation we had yesterday morning. You had something on Harvey and you found a way to use it. I mean, bully for you. But now you got Sully. Jesus, who did Sully blow to get himself made the head of governments? He's totally over his head in corporates."

"Hunt says it's only temporary."

"Sully will still probably get another boat out of it."

Charlie Sullivan, Dino's boss, never finished college, but he once was the regular caddy for the former head of the Fixed Income Division, back when caddies and babysitters could still get hired, and a kid from the mailroom could sometimes work his way up and change the business, as Lewie Ranieri had at Salomon Brothers. Sully hasn't changed anything but his net worth. He owns a seven-thousand-square-foot house on Long Island Sound, where he moors four boats. He is thirty-nine years old. This drives Dino mad. Though he's only seen the boats in photos on the wall of Sully's office, they are physical evidence to Dino that, no matter how hard he works, no matter how well he trades, he will never be as rich as Charlie Sullivan.

We ride in silence, leaning from side to side as Dino plays slalom with the traffic on the Cross County.

"You know, Barry," he says, "I must say, I'm surprised. I didn't think you had that kind of move in you."

"Why not?"

Our wheels squeal as we angle left to pick up the Hutch. Dino sighs. "Yeah, you're right. Why the hell not?"

I feel relieved when I get home that night. I need a drink and a little sanctuary.

It's a little after seven-thirty. I don't bother with the window, just walk in the door to see that the dinner table is set for only one person. I find a plate in the microwave with a piece of chicken, some rice, and string beans, all of it covered in cellophane.

The house is eerily silent. I walk upstairs, almost fearing what I might find. Perhaps Gretchen did call, and Rachel has scooped up the kids and fled.

I find Sam belly-down on the floor of his room, playing with his fleet of toy cars. I take a deep breath, feel my knees wobble with relief. Rachel and Jane are in the master bedroom, where Rachel is folding laundry.

"You guys ate?" I ask, the first words I've spoken to her in two days.

"Yep."

"And?"

"And what?"

"I'm here at the normal time."

"The kids couldn't wait," Rachel says. "They can't wait. This is too late for them to eat dinner. It's not fair."

"You ate with them?"

"I was hungry," Rachel says.

"Daa-dee," Jane bleats. She waddles over and grabs me by wrapping her arms around my knees. I pick her up. Her hair smells of orange-scented soap. She puts her arms around my neck.

"So," I say to Rachel, "I guess I'm wondering what you're really saying. Do you always want to feed the kids early, or is this just for tonight?"

"I think we should try it this way. The old way wasn't working."

"The old way meant that I got to have dinner with the family, which was really important to me. It was my one joy of the day, the one I count on."

"I'm sorry, Barry, but there are three other people here. And there seem to be more and more nights when you are out." She says this without looking up. Maybe Gretchen did call. Rachel is matching up socks, and folding them into balls.

"I've just gone through a bad run," I say. "I'll be home more often now. Besides, we've been doing it the old way for almost four years."

"That doesn't make it right."

"Please, Rachel," I say, "I can't get home from work any earlier. You know that."

"I'm sorry about that, Barry. I really am."

I stand there a moment, and then decide that I'm too tired to take it any further. I set Jane on the carpet so I can change out of my suit. I feel a burning in my chest, and I pound on it to make it go away, though it leaves a rancid taste at the back of my throat. Jane, watching this, turns to Rachel and says, "Daa-dee sick."

Rachel stops with the clothes and finally looks at me, as if to say something. I hope for some bit of tenderness, of kindness, and for a moment I think I see in her eyes that she wants to give it, but then she looks down again, and goes back to the laundry.

13. Polluted with Money

A month passes, and then Isaac Hunt calls me into his office. It's early evening, and most of the floor is empty, though the rocket scientists are still hunched like elves over their computer models. I wonder if someone has to remind them to go home.

Hunt's office is dark, except for a reading lamp on his desk. He has rolled up his shirtsleeves, and is studying a research report on corporate bonds. His face is a study in concentration and interest, and were he reading Balzac or Tolstoy, or some other author from a literature course I never took, I'd think him an intelligent and serious person. But he's reading a research report. It's clear that there is nothing at this very moment that matters as much to Isaac Hunt as what is in that report. This makes me question whether I have what it takes to succeed in this business. I doubt I could ever care that much.

I clear my throat and Hunt motions for me to sit. He sets the report down gently, sacred document that it is. "Have you ever thought," he asks, "about what this country is really good at?"

Spending is the first word that comes to my mind. "Lots of things," I say.

"Sure, but, say a thousand years from now, what will historians write about the United States?"

A thousand years? I'm worried about getting paid this year, and he's contemplating an entire millennium. I suppose this is the luxury of being a manager.

"I have no idea," I say.

"C'mon, Barry. Certainly music. Jazz, blues, rock and roll, these are all American art forms."

"Okay," I say.

"And money. No country on earth has ever created wealth like the United States. You want to know why?"

"We have the natural resources, we escaped most of the devastation from war, we have lots of people."

"Mostly, it's the people," he says. "The type of people. Americans will work hard, extremely hard. Americans are crazy that way. Upstairs we've got investment bankers working a hundred hours a week, week in and week out. You can't get the Europeans to do that. They won't do it. But Americans will, because they can see the reward at the end."

I nod.

"So now I'm going to need you to work extremely hard, and you will reap a large reward at the end."

"I am working hard," I say, "and I will continue to work hard."

"Barry, I'm talking about the future. I am making you head of the desk. I've thought about our talks and I've decided to give you a chance. Charlie Sullivan is too busy where he is, and I don't want an outsider. Your colleagues respect you. But it's unprecedented, this move, someone as junior as you. I have high hopes. You will report directly to me, and I want to hear from you frequently, especially at the start."

"Sure," I stammer. I feel a wave of panic come over me. Head of the desk. My plan actually worked. I have no idea what to do next.

Hunt is thinking along the same lines. "So," he asks, "what's your first priority?"

"I'll have to move fast," I say, improvising. "I'm going to make Duane Rizzo, my checkout guy, the bill trader. I'll hire a new five-year guy. And can you get me two M.B.A.'s for the summer? I'll need the bodies, with guys taking vacations and whatnot. If one of them works out, I'll look to add him the following year."

"Fine," Isaac says. "Those details can be handled over the next couple weeks. Have you thought about Steven Vollmer and Tom Carlson? They have both approached me for the job I am giving you. There will be resentment. They will both be upset."

"Well, why not make Vollmer manager of the long-end? It's only two guys, but that might mollify him some. We can do the same with Carlson and the front-end. That way, Carlson will feel responsible to help Duane in bills. But you have to tell them this. Coming from me, it will only piss them off."

"In this business, people are always pissed off. But if they had something better," Isaac Hunt says, "they'd have left already."

In other words, they just have to take it.

Over a month has passed since Gretchen's threat. She hasn't called, and I think that things might be softening with Rachel. We talk now, sleep in the same bed, and sometimes touch. Last night, when I brought her flowers, she smiled at me in a way that nearly brought tears to my eyes; I realized the extent to which I am starved for her affection. Now I jog across the empty trading floor, feeling the bounce of the floor tiles. I call and tell her the good news.

"Well, that's great," she says. "I know it's what you wanted."

"Yeah," I say.

"Do you know what you're doing?"

"I'll figure it out."

"Isn't there someone you can ask, someone who can help you? Isaac Hunt, maybe?"

"It doesn't work like that here."

"Barry, you need to be careful. Maybe everybody hated Court because he was the head guy. Maybe now they're going to hate you."

"You know I'm not Court."

"I'm just trying to figure out if that's a good thing or a bad thing in regards to your new position. Court was tough."

"And you're saying I'm not tough enough?" I ask. "That I should be more like *Court*?"

"Just be careful," she says.

"Hey, Barry," Vollmer says the next day. I sit up in my chair. He has never called me Barry. "Congratulations."

We've just come out of a desk meeting with Isaac Hunt. I am officially the boss.

"I'll need your help," I tell him. And to make him feel better, I say, "I had some luck. Like you said, sooner or later that M.B.A. would be good for something."

"You're not Court Harvey," he says. "Everyone is thankful for that."

The market trades actively that day, but I really can't concentrate on it. Instead, I scribble down a list of all I have to do: promote Duane to the bill seat; refine a list of potential five-year traders; meet privately with each of the traders about their new roles and, invariably, pay expectations; find out what everyone made in previous years; meet with Richie Perlmutter, who's been named sales manager; set up meetings with our top ten accounts; come up with a better market rap, because I am now the main commentator; try to act like I know what I'm doing while I try to figure out what I'm doing.

"You ready, motherfucker, you ready? Looking for a Levi's departure," Dino says on the phone. A Levi's departure means we leave at 5:01, after the style of jeans.

"No way," I say.

"Dude," he says in a whisper, "Sully just told me something about you, and I don't know whether or not to believe it."

"Everything you've heard is true."

"You son-of-a-bitch. I guess that means you can leave when you want."

"Just the opposite."

"Well, when can you go?"

I tell him I'll get a broker car.

"Barry," he says, "I want you to know I'm very happy for you, but I gotta be honest. You, running governments? This has got to be one of the most fucked-up places, management-wise, in the universe. How could this happen?"

"I worked this hard, Dino. I saw an opportunity, and I took it. What are you getting at?"

"You're unprepared and exposed. You have no friends over there."

"My wife made a similar point."

"Smart woman."

"What about you?" I ask.

"Me?"

"Make sure your privacy button is on," I whisper. We all have privacy buttons. They prevent someone else from hitting our lines and listening in on our calls. I once heard a story about a convertible-bond salesman who got caught having phone sex. A cautionary tale. Most of us worry about getting caught talking to a corporate headhunter, which is a far more serious offense.

"Privacy on," he says.

"I'm going to put an idea in your head," I tell him. "You don't have to answer now. Just think about it."

"Okay."

"Five-years."

"As in notes?" he asks. "As in U.S. Treasuries, be a monkey, carry a banana in your briefcase, sixteen to the quarter, a billion up, what do you want to do?"

"Like you said, I need some friends over here."

"Sully will be pissed. Pissed. That is blatant, in-your-face poaching."

"It's still my honeymoon," I tell him. "Isaac Hunt will give me a poach or two."

"Don't even think about involving me till it's a done deal. I want to claim complete and total ignorance. More than that. I want to be the Sergeant Schultz of the fixed-income trading floor. But I'm in, if you can get it done."

I order a car to wait for me at ten to six, even though I know I will not be ready to leave at that time. The idea is that I want the car ready, so that I won't have to waste a moment when I am ready to go, which happens to be six-thirty-five. For once, traffic is clear on the West Side, so that I reach the Park and Ride just an hour and ten minutes after I leave work. Amazing. It's dark, and the Escort is cold. I kick off my shoes, turn the car over, and head out.

I check my watch. It's quarter to eight, and I know I have to race home if I want a chance to put Jane to bed. This has always been part of my fatherly duties, and it's especially important since Rachel stopped making the kids wait for me to have dinner. I gun the car down Route 172, then run the red light at the entrance to I-684. I now have a long, clear straightaway ahead. I get the car up to sixty before I shift out of third gear, the engine whining from the speed and the cold. At the same time, I take stock of myself, mark myself to market. On a personal level, I'm trading at a heavy discount. I've raised myself up at work by bringing down Court Harvey, and I know I didn't do any favors to Chip McCarty. I misled Tom Carlson. I let Gretchen down. I've cheated on Rachel. I've barely given my kids the attention I pay to Carlos at the food cart. This is all self-evident, obvious. The real question is: Could I have gotten where I am any other way? Have I not done what was necessary to achieve what I have achieved? At least I can say I didn't flinch. I've brought us out of subsidized housing, acquired family health insurance and the promise of financial security. Are these not part of being a good father? Do they not offer some basis for redemption?

Being part of your children's lives is part of being a good father. If I want to be there to put Jane to bed, I have to make it home by five to eight.

Ten minutes to make the trip is adequate time at six in the morning, but it's a challenge at night. I pass two cars on Route 172, each time ducking back into my lane just ahead of the oncoming traffic, the engine a siren, the car shaking with the speed. I pray Bedford's finest are on coffee breaks. I manage to pass a silver BMW on the uphill stretch of McClain Road (it isn't Chip McCarty), and then cut through the Mobil station at 117 to avoid getting caught at the light. I force my way as the fourth car making a left on the red light at the Manufacturers Outlet Center, and speed over the Preston Street Bridge. I'm in Mount Kisco now, and only six minutes have passed. It's a miraculous performance.

I pass the Ford dealership doing seventy when, ahead of me, a car pulls into my path from the Sawmill Parkway exit. It's a Volvo, seven or eight years old, a square box of a car. If the Volvo veers left at the fork, I'll be okay, but a right will mean that I'll have to pass it on the tight and uneven streets that skirt the horse estates en route to my neighborhood. As I close on the car, I pray for a left. I just want to get home unimpeded. Please.

The car goes right.

I pound on my steering wheel before downshifting to make the turn. I'm on his bumper in seconds as we travel up the Croton Lake Road hill. I check my speedometer: twenty-two. I pull out to pass, but he pulls into the center of the road, which is barely the width of two cars. He then eases back right when I fade back. I again try to pass, and he again blocks me. I check my watch: 7:53. I'm a mile and a half from home. At the top of the hill I get around him, but then a strange thing happens. He gets on my tail and stays there, even when I run the Escort at fifty down the bumpy dirt of Meeting House Road. He follows me right into my driveway.

I slide my loafers on and get out of the car ready to swing.

"Are you a kid or an adult?" he asks. "An adult," he adds when he sees me. In the darkness I can make out that he wears wire-rim glasses. He has pudgy cheeks and reddish, frizzy hair. He looks like the kind of guy who works for a nonprofit.

"What are you doing in my driveway?" I say.

"Do you always drive like that? I live around here, man, and that's no way to drive. I'm your neighbor, you know? Kids live around here. That's no way to drive."

"Okay," I say. I take a step toward him. We're still fifteen feet apart and I am ready to fight, but he retreats to the safety of his Volvo. I watch as he gets in and backs the car out of the driveway. It takes him two tries. It's a steep driveway with a curve at the end, and backing out is a matter of faith and practice. With the Volvo on its way, I check my watch: 7:57. I sprint to the house.

Rachel and Sam are sitting at the dining table when I burst inside. Rachel is tutoring. She looks up briefly and I feel a chill. "There's tuna fish in the fridge," Rachel says. "If you want to make a sandwich."

"Is Jane in bed?"

"Yep."

Damn, I think.

They go back to Sam's math. I stand at the door, feeling invisible.

"Aren't you going to ask me about my first day as boss?" I ask.

"Later, we can talk."

I'm not hungry, but I eat two tuna-fish sandwiches. It's a habit of mine, at the first sign of stress, to overeat. At first I think Gretchen has called, but if it hasn't happened yet, it probably won't.

I chew my sandwiches and watch as down at the other end of the table Sam finishes up his work. He's run his hand through his hair so many times that he now has a cornice of sandy locks hanging over his forehead. Rachel's hair is pulled back in a bun, the way she wears it when she's doing a serious cleaning of the house, and I must admit that the place looks neat. The kitchen counter gleams; Janie's toys are neatly stacked in her box in the living room; her shoes and Sam's boots are lined up at the door. I stare at Rachel—she's wearing an old L. L. Bean turtleneck frayed along the shoulders—but she won't look at me. I try to think back to when we first met and couldn't stop looking at each other. How could I ever have imagined it would come to this?

"It's not working," she says, once Sam has been packed off to bed. We're still sitting downstairs, at our dining table.

"What's not?"

"Us, Barry. Our marriage. This life."

"I'm trying, you know that, Rach. I'm trying, I really am."

"I'm not sure trying is enough. You're always saying that you're doing all this for us, but you'd do the same thing if we weren't here. You've got something to prove, I think, and it has nothing to do with us. The truth is, we're not doing well. I've lost my companion, and I don't just mean you're never around. Even when you are around, you're different. Barry, you left your mother alone to deal with your brother's death. You're all she has in the world, and you abandoned her like she and Ben never existed. The Barry I knew would not have done that."

"It was a means to an end," I say. My eyes find her right hand, for some reason. It rests on the table, the nails shiny, the color of pearl. Rachel has been to the nail salon today. "Look," I say, consciously catching her eyes, "things will get better now. I'll get better now. I know what you're saying, and you're right. I feel bad about those things, and about the time I'm away, all of that. But I'm trying to see this through. Just once in my life, I'm trying to stick something out till I really succeed. I mean, think about it, Rachel. I never really stick to anything."

"What about me?" she says. "Why don't you feel the need to stick to me?"

"I do. You know I do."

"That's not how it's been. Ever since we went to Philadelphia. And here it's only gotten worse," she says. "Much worse. That's why I'm pulling out."

"Pulling out? What does that mean?"

"We're going back west, Barry."

Did I hear that right? No, she must have meant something else. "The kids?" I stammer.

"Well, they can't stay with you. You're certainly not capable of taking care of them. I'm taking them with me."

"Taking them? What about Sam? He's still in school."

"I've enrolled him out there. It'll be tough, sure, but it's *been* tough. This is not working for us, and we all need something that works."

"What does Sam say?"

"You and I will talk to him tomorrow."

"For Christ's sake, this is insane. You can't leave. We are building something here. We are so close."

She shakes her head. "Building something? We had something. We were a family, once. I don't blame you completely. I didn't stop you. I was like the alcoholic's wife. What do they call them? The enabler. That's what I was: the enabler."

My stomach clenches into a tighter knot. I feel hot and dizzy. "Please," I say. "Don't."

"It's all arranged. This may actually be good for you. You've gone off in another direction, and now you can go there without guilt or outside responsibility. You'll be free."

"I don't want to be free. I want my family. I want my kids. You're proposing to take them two thousand miles away. They won't have a father."

"They don't have one now. When did you last see Jane, or really spend time with Sam? And now, with your new position, it will be even worse."

I don't doubt the truth of what she is saying; right now I'm paralyzed with it. I feel desperate and panicky. Everything I've worked for seems to be slipping from me at the very moment I am about to attain it.

"I'll be honest," Rachel is saying. "I don't know if I still love you. It hurts me to say that, but it's true. I never thought my feelings for you would change, but they have. And it makes me so sad, because I know that deep inside you, somewhere, is that person I fell in love with. That kind, sweet, caring person. But I can't find him anymore. And I can't keep going through the motions, hoping he comes back."

"I'm still the same person, Rachel. I am."

"Maybe, but I doubt it." She stands up, heads for the stairs, and starts to cry. "That's why I have to go. I'm really starting to doubt it."

I am left sitting at the table, staring out the same window I look in every night. I can make out nothing but my own fuzzy and dejected reflection.

That night I set up my alarm on the coffee table by the downstairs couch, where I sit for most of the evening. Maybe I sleep an hour or two. I don't want this to happen, and at the same time it seems too late. At times that night I think it's for the best, and then scold myself for such sloppy thinking. *Everything's for the best, it's meant to be, God's will.* These are the thoughts of the weak and the simple-minded. It cannot be for the best. Family dissolution, fatherless children. It's a disaster.

Yoshi calls once. I'm awake. We miss a trade. Later I doze, but am up again by two-thirty. At three-thirty I unplug the alarm and go for a jog in our dark and empty neighborhood. Upon my return I shave, then shower, then sit on the couch in a towel till it's time to dress and go to meet Dino at the Park and Ride.

At quarter to nine I call Rachel. I know that Sam will be off to school. "You don't have to do this," I tell her. "We could make some changes."

"Barry, stop it. Don't keep going on like that."

"You're breaking up the family."

"I'm not getting into the blame game, and you shouldn't, either. You might lose."

"But why, Rachel?"

"Barry, this life, it's just not me, and, more important, it's not us. I've told you this over and over, begged you to make a change. But the change you made was in the other direction."

"Rachel, you have to be realistic and look at what I've just pulled off here. You said that yourself. Please, hang in there."

"I've been hanging a long time, and now I'm hung. I'm telling you no. That's all there is to say: no."

She hangs up.

At eleven-thirty I have Mickey O'Hara send up steaks from Peter Lugers. It's my first gesture in the reign of Barry. Just the thought of food makes me queasy, but I have to make grand gestures for the guys, try to get them on my side. Not that it's that hard at the start. People have been sucking up to me all day. All the brokers have been offering to send up lunch once they heard of my ascension; I'm now their meal ticket. A few bond-floor managers, like Ryan Hauptman from mortgages and Terry Finnick from high-yield, call to offer congratulations. Finnick wants to meet for a drink, and Hauptman suggests dinner in Westchester. These are smart and successful men. Savvy men. They want an ally wherever they can find one.

The steaks arrive at twelve-thirty, thick slabs of beef atop greasy romaine leaves, packed in individual tin pans covered with a clear plastic top. There are two vats of scalloped potatoes and little Styrofoam containers of creamed spinach, a large shopping bag filled with crusty bread, and a dozen new bottles of A1 steak sauce.

"Oh, baby," says Tom Carlson as we all crowd around the food. "Keep it coming, Barry. Keep it coming."

"An army travels on its stomach," Vollmer says.

"Can I have one?" Duane asks. As a checkout guy, he was not entitled to broker food, unless it was sent specifically to him. Now he's a trader, but as wobbly and unsteady as a newborn fawn.

"Don't ask, take," I tell him. Good, general job advice.

"Aren't you eating?" he asks.

"Don't worry about me," I tell him.

At one I call Dan Connelly, only to find that he's left his job. This means his e-mail no longer works. I leave a message on his answering machine at home.

Chip McCarty calls a little after three. "You can tell me," he says. "Charles Blatts is really your uncle, right?"

I do my best to laugh.

"Congratulations," he says. "Really. You're size now. So—tell me how you got rid of Court."

"He left of his own accord."

"And I'm Alan Greenspan's love child. C'mon, Barry. Somebody—you, I'd guess—had to push him out. You got something on him. Was that rumor about him importing young hairless boys from Asia actually true? C'mon, what was it?"

"He left of his own accord," I repeat.

"Okay. Look, we ought to have dinner. How about next week?"

Mac wants me to have my secretary call his secretary to schedule the meal, and I agree. I release the phone, then look down at my to-do list, and move hiring a secretary to the top.

At ten to five, Stuart Konig comes over and sits in Court Harvey's old seat. He holds out his hand, and offers congratulations. "Incredible," he says. "You are going to be rich. I mean, you'll be absolutely polluted with money."

I ask him to call me. I want to have a private conversation, and on the trading floor this is best done by talking on the phone, even if the person you want to talk with is in the next seat over. When Stuart calls, I offer him a job.

"Not now," he says. "I'm having too good a year. Talk to me when I'm down and they're coming around to pick at my carcass."

I want to tell him about Rachel, but I can't. Stuart and I go back to business school, where we met and shared our plans and dreams. We traveled together to New York to look for work, and exchanged information on banks and recruiters. More than anyone, he knows where I'm trying to go. So I can't tell him about Rachel, because I am too ashamed of the failure.

"We'd better have this talk with Sam," Rachel says when I walk in the door. It's six-thirty, and she's already cleaning up from dinner. Hamburgers, from the smell of it.

"Where is he? And what about Jane?"

"Jane is watching a video. Let's go see Sam. He's in his room."

I first sneak a look at Jane, who's sitting on the couch, her mouth wide with a smile. On the screen an elephant is giving her baby a bath in a wooden tub, mother and child playing with delight. Jane giggles. I wipe a tear from my eye.

Upstairs I find Sam on his knees, making piles of his belongings.

"Whatcha doing?" I ask.

"Mom wants me to sort out the stuff I don't care about."

The don't-care-about pile is a fifth the size of the other. I look at Sam. He's wearing shorts and a Yankees T-shirt. He's a big kid, with sandy hair and a smattering of freckles about his cheeks that give him a mischievous look. He has Rachel's high cheekbones and all of her expressions. People often comment that it's hard to tell that I've been involved.

"Mom and I need to talk to you," I say.

He looks up, innocent as the child he is. I get down on one knee and talk to him as would a coach in a Little League huddle. "We're making some changes," I say. "We're going to move."

"Move where?"

"Mom and you and Jane are going to move back to Colorado."

"What about you, Dad?"

"I'm going to stay here and work."

"But I don't want to go to Colorado," he says.

"It's for the best," I tell him, though the words trip in my throat, and he notices.

"Colorado sucks. All my friends live here. My school. I want to stay here with you."

"It's not possible," I tell him. "You know I've got to work all the time. Who would drive you around, take care of you? And you'll love Colorado. You were born there. There are great mountains and places to bike. You'll make lots of new friends. You'll love it."

He looks past me, to Rachel.

"Do I have to, Mom?"

She nods, as she always does when he asks if he "has to," a nod that acknowledges whatever protest he might make, and dismisses it, too. "You do. We need you, Janie and I."

"But why don't you and Dad want to live together? Isn't that what you're supposed to do?"

"Yes, but it's not always possible," Rachel says.

"Dad, you told me that you and Mom would never split up."

"I did?"

"Yeah, remember? When Tim's parents had that fight, you said you and Mom would never do that."

"We're just going to live in different places for a while," I say.

His teeth are clenched. He's not fooled, not one bit.

"Can't you and Mom make up? Please."

"We're doing what we think is best for the family," I tell him. I notice that his eyes look watery, and that he's wrinkling up his nose. "You don't have to cry. It'll be okay," I say.

"I'm not crying," he snaps. And, with that, he starts to sob. I walk over to him, kneel to the floor, and rock him in my arms, feel his bony shoulder blades and his weight against me. I know Rachel is still at the door, probably thinking that I'm putting on an act to show that I care, but it's no act. I don't want to let go.

The movers are coming on Friday to take the furniture that Rachel wants. "I'm leaving you the TV, the couch, the coffee table, and all the stuff in your office," she tells me on Wednesday night. She also set aside two sets of dishes and silverware, and a few old pots and pans. Later, I find that she's left a fondue maker, still in the box, an unopened wedding present.

I set up on the couch again for the night. I doze in short intervals. Sleep just won't take with me. I drink a scotch, then another.

I listen to the house sleep. There is the buzz of the refrigerator and the humidifier we run in Jane's room as much for the white noise as for the moisture. When nothing changes for ten minutes, I go upstairs. Furtively, like a burglar, I stick my head into Rachel's room. She is asleep, and I breathe easier. I go to Sam's room. He snores, as he almost always does. The light from the hallway catches and reflects off the Scotch tape hanging from his walls. There is still clutter all over the floor. I close my eyes and just listen to him snore. I try to commit this sound to memory. It's something to carry with me. Then I walk to Jane's room.

The humidifier drowns out all sound till I get down on the floor by Jane's crib. I put my ear to the bars. She sleeps on her stomach, with her knees pulled up and her backside high. She breathes steadily, with a little ripple of a snore. I put her to bed on this night. She understands nothing of what is about to happen to her. Probably, she will remember nothing of one of the most important events of her life, as the loss of my father was for me. I again feel tears come to my eyes as I listen to those soft, innocent breaths. I'm not sure if I'm crying for Jane, Sam, or myself. I put my hand over my mouth to stifle any sound, and in this way I regain my composure. I lean my head against the bars of Jane's crib, and with time I am able to doze to the sound of her breathing.

Saturday arrives like a hanging day, cloudy, with some low-lying mist. I watch from my spot on the couch as daylight fades in. In the last week, the trees in our back yard have sprouted buds. A bushy-tailed squirrel runs along the railing of our back porch.

Rachel comes downstairs early, before the kids wake. She's dressed in jeans and a turtleneck, her hair pulled back into a ponytail. The movers have cleared the house the day before, and the Explorer is packed to its ceiling with personal belongings.

Rachel asks me to wake the kids while she packs up the food. "And please don't look at me like that. Let's just get on with it."

Upstairs, I shake Sam awake in his sleeping bag. He groans and lets out a long sigh. Rachel has laid out his clothes, and I instruct him to put them on. "Okay, Dad," he says, and I have to leave the room to keep my composure.

I rub Jane's back till she wakes, then lift her from the crib that

Rachel will leave behind. Jane nestles into my neck. Just the smell of her hair is enough to make me think that my heart might stop, right there. I move about the room dizzily, till I find my bearings well enough to lay her on the changing table and put her in her clothes.

By the time I have strapped the kids into their seats and kissed them on their heads, the bile is bubbling up my gullet as if my body were a volcano. I close Jane's door, walk around the back of the Explorer, and retch on the driveway. My insides produce a watery and foul-smelling yellow liquid. I haven't eaten much the last couple days. I walk to Rachel's window, where she looks at me through mirrored sunglasses.

"You've broken my heart," I tell her.

"We're even, then."

With that she expertly backs the vehicle out of the driveway. In seconds my family is gone.

14. The Way of the Buffalo

The next two months drag on like one long workweek. I travel up and down the Eastern Seaboard, then to Chicago and the big clumps of money on the West Coast, lodging in three-hundred-dollar hotel rooms where I lie awake thinking how much Rachel might have enjoyed taking such a trip. In New York, I work constantly, often staying late to have dinner with clients or simply to sit in my office (Court's old office, its walls still bare, like a holding cell), and contemplate the desk numbers and various reports that I receive daily. Carlson, Vollmer, and Glover are all making decent money, slightly more than they made the year before. Duane proves to be a timid bill trader, but at least he frees Carlson to make money trading twos. When I look at the numbers, the only trader who clearly is failing to pull his weight is me. Try as I might, I'm making only half of what Colin Dancer made the year before. It doesn't help that I spend so much time off the desk, but this is hardly an adequate excuse. I make sure that the daily profit-and-loss report is no longer printed out and left on my desk, where anyone can snatch it. I don't want the other traders knowing how little I'm contributing to the bottom line.

In July, *Bloomberg Magazine* puts out an article on bond trading that makes many of the same points about the business that I made to Isaac Hunt, plus a few that I hadn't thought of. The gist of the piece is that the business just isn't as good as it used to be, and it's going to get worse. The writer titles the article "Going the Way of the Buffalo."

Carlson cuts out the title and tapes it to his computer, right next to the specifics of his latest diet and the article that claims that monkeys can think.

One evening, hot and humid as they come, I run into Gretchen at the security turnstiles. I think we both would be happy to pretend we didn't see each other, but we're only a foot apart. I have a car waiting to take me to a desk dinner, and I offer to give Gretchen a ride. It's the first time we've spoken since the day of the meeting in Isaac Hunt's office.

"I don't think so," she says.

"C'mon. A ride. Don't be silly. You might as well take it." I'm not sure why I want Gretchen to accept the offer. Up to this moment I'd been hoping I would never see her again. I suppose I'd rather she didn't go through life hating my guts, though I'm not sure, exactly, how this ride will change that.

Gretchen's face is showing plenty of hatred, but she gets in.

In the back of the Town Car I can smell her perfume. Like many smells, this brings back memories. She's wearing a white blouse. Her hair shines in the light from the street.

"They want me to go to London, Barry."

"London?"

"Yeah, London. Klune is all over me about it. I don't want to go. I can't go. I've got Buster to worry about, and my parents."

"Things worse with your parents?"

"Yes. My mom, especially, has been sick a lot lately. I don't want to leave. And once the firm gets you over there, you don't know how long it will take to get back."

"So say no."

"I did. But they're not going to take that for an answer. They keep on you. If you keep refusing, they stop paying you. And, look, we're two-thirds of the way to bonuses. I'm screwed. I just lost this whole year. Don't you see, it's the Court thing. The whole thing makes them uncomfortable."

"You think Isaac Hunt told Klune?"

"Of course he did."

"Well, the thing is over, anyway. Court's gone."

"It's not over. It will always worry them. Especially Klune. He was a Green Beret in Vietnam. John Wayne and all that. He doesn't like women on the trading floor. Do you know what he once asked me? He said, 'Why do you want to work in a place like this?' Do you think he asks that question of men, Barry? No, women make him uncomfortable, and now he's forcing me out."

"He's not forcing you out," I say. "He's sending you to London."

"He knows I have a child, and I've told him about my parents. I'm a single mother. There are four single guys in their twenties he could send, if he needs bodies over there. Normally, they send single guys because it's cheaper. But this time he picks a single mother? No, he wants me to leave the firm, and he knows it's too dangerous, legally, to fire me. So this is what he's going to do."

I don't know what to say. It's certainly believable.

"You fucked me over, Barry. I told you this would happen. I had my life pretty much how I wanted it. I liked working here. I had things set up well for Buster and me. Now I'm going to have to find another job. From now on, stay the hell away from me."

We're on the Upper West Side, and Gretchen tells the driver to pull the car over. As we slow to a stop, I say, "Rachel." I stop myself. I am going to tell her that Rachel has left me, but there's no sense in that.

"What about her?"

"I want to thank you for not calling her."

She stares at me for a moment. "I did call her," she tells me. "She didn't seem surprised."

Gretchen shakes her head in disbelief or disgust, jumps out of the car, and slams the door.

It takes the next half-hour to traverse Central Park. Ah, hell, I think. Rachel knew. She knew and she left without ever bringing it up. How could she not have said something? I wonder if she can forgive me, and I ask myself, had she done that to me, could I forgive her? I think I could. Maybe at some point in a marriage you have to be ready to forgive everything.

I finally make it to my dinner on the East Side. Carlson, Vollmer, Glover, Dino, and Duane are there, along with Brian Zigfeld and Eamon Foley, Ziggy's boss. Every time there's a management shift, the broker bosses appear, to make sure the gravy will keep flowing. For me it's a good way to feed the troops.

I take the open seat left at the table, between Vollmer and Ziggy. I count six open bottles of wine on the table.

"Guess who just got the job of head government trader at Cutthroat?" Ziggy asks while Foley is ordering the food.

"Who?" Vollmer asks.

"A guarantee, too," Ziggy says. "I'm hearing two sticks a year."

Vollmer and I look at each other, and we both know who it is.

"Christ," Vollmer says. "He's a customer now? We'll have to be nice to him?"

"Court's not so bad," Ziggy says. "You just have to know how to deal with him."

I will have to call Court Harvey. A customer is a customer. He stayed away from the markets a few months. At least he knows himself well enough not to spend too much time alone. Or maybe he tried it and didn't like it. I drove past his place in Bedford on Sunday and saw a for-sale sign. I was on my way to a matinee in Bedford. I didn't want to spend time alone, either. I spent Sunday praying for Monday.

Soon dishes are cascading onto the table, at least three times the food needed. At the end of the meal, we sip cognacs and coffees and suck on cigars the size of relay batons. I'm just about ready to ask for a car home when a waitress walks into the room carrying a piece of chocolate cake with a candle stuck in it.

"Happy birthday, Barry!" Ziggy says.

"No shit," Vollmer says. "How fucking old are you?"

I'm thirty-six, and have been for a while. "It's not my birthday," I whisper to Ziggy.

"It's not? I thought it was." He pulls out his Palm Pilot and punches a few buttons. "You're right," he whispers back. "It's Court's birthday. Sorry."

Meanwhile, everyone on the desk is singing, off-key and out of time, to my happiness.

Twenty minutes later, all eight of us are standing outside the restaurant, waiting for broker cars, while Eamon Foley berates the dispatcher on his cell phone. "Do you know who you're talking to? Do you have any idea?"

A beggar approaches from halfway down the block. His hair is cut short but unevenly, as if he snipped it himself without a mirror. He wears a thick overcoat on what is so warm a night that all of us traders wait in our shirtsleeves, suit jackets thrown over our shoulders or folded over our arms. The beggar also sports two brown gloves and a pair of oversized mukluks, not of a pair.

"Spare any change?" he asks when he reaches us.

Duane Rizzo, who is standing closest to him, hands him some coins.

"God bless you," the beggar says as he heads off.

"What the fuck are you doing?" Vollmer demands.

"I had some spare change," Duane says.

"Listen, putz. First of all, he's just going to drink it up. Second, you give him money, it encourages him to beg, which is a pain in the ass for everyone. And, most important, you get nothing for it. *Nothing.* You want to give to the poor, give to an organization. At least you get the tax write-off. Don't you get it, Duane? You don't give money away. You just don't. It's a bad habit. You'll never make it as a trader that way."

Duane stands mute, eyes wide, still baffled that giving money to a beggar can make him a bad trader.

I fly to Denver that Friday, rent a car, and drive up to Aspen. I've proposed trips twice before, and each time Rachel has put me off, saying that they are still settling in, still not ready, that it could be disruptive to the children's transition. She knows I'm busy with work and thus weak, and I came away from both of those calls hating her for putting me off, hating myself for letting her, hating my job for beating the stuffing out of me. Now I know that Rachel has put me off because of Gretchen. Still, I haven't seen my children since they left in the spring. It's time.

I take a room at the Hotel Jerome, the town's original hotel from the silver-mining days, when Aspen boasted a railroad, four breweries, and triple the current population. The Jerome is an exceptionally expensive hotel, but there's a small hedge fund nestled on a mountain of red rock overlooking Aspen, and I'm going to visit its traders on Monday. The travel-and-expenses guy back in New Jersey will thus cut the reimbursement check without question. I shower, wrap myself in the plush white bathrobe I find in the closet, and call my family. Rachel answers.

"I'll get Sam for you," she says. I've been making it a practice to call every other night, or almost, so that Sam and I can stay close. Sometimes Jane gets on the line, after which Sam comes back and tells me what she said. Jane has discovered the joy of using words and grown fond of her tiny, throaty voice. It makes me happy to hear her and Sam, but I begin to feel rather insignificant when I realize how easily their lives go on without me.

"Wait," I say to Rachel. "I need to talk to you."

"What is it?"

"I want to see you and the kids. It's been all summer, Rachel."

She pauses. "Okay. When?"

I surprise her when I tell her that I'm in town. Though her apartment is just down Mill Street from the Jerome, we make plans to drive out the next night to the Woody Creek Tavern. After dinner, Rachel will take the kids home, put Jane to bed, and have a neighbor keep an eye on Sam, so that Rachel and I can talk alone. The very idea that I'm so close to them quickens my breath, and, with the high altitude, I have a hard time slowing it down.

The next afternoon, I dress and leave the hotel by five, my heart fluttering with the thought of seeing the kids and Rachel. I drive out Cemetery Lane to McClain Flats—nothing like the road of a similar name in Mount Kisco—and then descend toward the river. Halfway down the hill, I pass the W/J Ranch, where Rachel, Sam, and I once lived. I have time to kill, and decide to pull in and have a look around. Not much has changed. The road is still dirt, dry and dusty from baking all summer. The buildings still look like log cabins. A private plane flying out of the airport buzzes overhead. I park my rental car by our old unit, and then walk over to the Rio Grande Trail, the defunct railroad bed from a century before. Straight ahead, up the Brush Creek Valley, I can see the trails of the Snowmass Ski Area, and, beyond that, the craggy peaks of the Elk Range.

The trail is rock-hard, though there are footprints and mountain-bike treads and a couple elk tracks baked into the dirt. Olive-colored sage bushes and green scrub oak cover the plateau. The sage is fragrant, though at times the wind shifts and blows east to west, and this brings with it the stench from the sewage-treatment center just over the berm to my left. My eye catches a flash up the trail, and after a moment I notice it's a pair of mountain bikes coming toward me. The riders wear typical bike gear, which is to say that they look like peacocks. I have stepped to the side of the trail to let them pass when the lead biker stops at my side.

"Barry," he says. It's Dan Connelly. Had he not stopped, I might not have recognized him. He's lost a lot of weight, so much so that his cheekbones have reappeared on his face, for the first time in almost twenty years. He's tan, and his teeth are very white. Amy, too, has been spending a lot of time in the sun.

"Hey," I say, genuinely happy to see him. With Dan I can feel like the same guy I was in high school, when we used to cruise around in my mother's Chevrolet wagon, a vehicle as big and maneuverable as a barge, and look for beer and girls. Often we found neither, but we were happy just to look—and to have a companion to lose with. "You look great," I tell him.

"He hired a personal trainer," Amy says, teasing him, though no doubt telling the truth.

"I'm lazy," he admits to me. "Only crazies like you can work out at four in the morning."

"No choice," I tell him. I start to explain what I'm doing in Aspen.

"We know," Dan says. "We have Rachel and the kids over when we're in town."

"You do?"

"We love them. Great kids," Dan says.

"That little Janie is some cutie," Amy says.

It hits me like a punch in the gut that I have to hear about my children from someone else.

"Well, maybe we can get together back east," I say.

"You haven't told him?" Amy asks.

"Told me what?"

"We moved," Dan says. "We live in the Bay Area now. That start-up I told you about, it had to be out west. It's where the action is."

Life may not be a race, but it feels like one now, and my best friend has just left me completely in the dust. I feel as if I'm about to collapse.

"Hey," Dan says, putting his arm around my shoulder. When he speaks, it's a whisper. "Hang in there. I know how you feel, but things come around again, just like that Johnny Cash song says."

"Don't give in," I say.

"Exactly. We'll talk. Amy and I leave tomorrow. I'll call you when we get back to California," he says. "We better get moving, before we stiffen up."

Amy clips on her pedals and starts moving away, but Dan pauses, as if to fiddle with his bike but really to speak to me.

"We're not telling anyone yet, but Amy's pregnant."

"Congratulations," I say. "That's great." So the fertility doctor paid off.

"Hang in there, bud," he says. He clips onto his bike and heads off toward his wife. I turn back to my car.

The tavern is made of wood, backed up to the Woody Creek Trailer Park, where a lucky sliver of Aspen's working-class clings to life in the upper valley. I park across the street, on the baked dirt at the roadside. A stuffed boar stands guard over the entrance. I turn to make a quick check of the parked cars (the Explorer is not there), and then walk past the patio tables, under the boar, and into the restaurant. My eyes, unadjusted to the darkness, can make out only the glow of the Rockies game, which plays on both televisions. Eventually the pool table fades into view, and the dining tables, the bar, and the new leopard-print carpet. Anyplace else, this carpet would look ridiculous, but here, beneath the mounted Tennessee boar and buffalo head and the framed Annie Leibovitz photo of Hunter S. Thompson and the many Polaroids of the tavern's patrons, it works.

I feel nervous. It has been so long since I've seen my family. I go over in my mind what I will ask Rachel for: an end to the separation. I will admit to the affair, and make it clear that it was a mistake, a huge mistake, and that it's over. I'm a changed man. If Rachel wants to stay in Colorado, that's fine. I'll fly back and forth every other week. I'll spend two more years on the Street. I figure this will establish our financial position.

I'm sucking on a Dos Equis at the bar when Sam climbs up my bar stool and hugs me. "Daddy, Daddy," he yells. Jane is right behind him, yelling the same thing. I soon find myself down on the leopard-skin carpet, hugging my children. My senses seem to overload, the feel of them in my arms, their smell, the sounds they make, the familiar way each fidgets. For me it's a feeling of pure joy, as if I've been made whole again.

Rachel stands at the door, smiling. She's wearing jeans, and a gold-colored blazer with brownish lapels. Her hair is pulled back and braided. She looks lithe, tan, fantastic. She's been spending a lot of time outside in the mountains.

"You look great," I say.

"Thanks," she says. I want to kiss her then, but I'm not sure if this will be allowed. I hesitate, and she gives me a peck on the cheek. "Let's eat," she says.

Sam does most of the talking at the table, telling me about his baseball team and his new friends, and how he can ride his bike all over town. "You can go outside all the time here," he says. "And at school, we have outside recess all year round. Even in winter." School started the previous week.

Jane, meanwhile, has found the toy police car, and brought it to my lap. She climbs up herself, and sits on me the entire meal, eating French fries off my plate.

"So, Dad," Sam asks finally, "are you going to come live with us?"

"I don't know," I say.

"C'mon. You'd love it here."

"I know. I used to live here."

"You did?"

"With you," I tell him.

"Can't he, Mom?" he asks Rachel. "Pleeeeeease."

"Cheeeeese," Jane says.

"Nothing has been decided," Rachel tells him. "Remember what we talked about?"

Sam is quiet after that.

After dinner, I strap Jane into her car seat, say good night to her and Sam, and drive back into town. I park my car at the Jerome, then walk over to the Little Nell Hotel, at the base of the ski mountain, where Rachel and I plan to meet.

The bar is lined with photographs of skiing greats from the fifties and early sixties: Anderl Molterer and Toni Sailer, Christian Pravda and Toni Matt, Buddy Werner and Jimmy Huega. I order a scotch and watch the people. It's the last night of the summer season. At the tavern, people wear jeans or biking clothes, and some of the clientele comes from the trailer park. At the Nell, one needs money to drink, and its patrons seem incapable of dressing down. I see leather pants and rattlesnake boots, a pressed fuchsia shirt, rubies and diamonds. Cell phones chirp repeatedly, as if keeping some intermittent kind of time.

I've just finished my first scotch when I notice a woman by the bar with long tawny hair, streaked by the sun or a hairdresser, or both. She's wearing a leather jacket over a pair of linen slacks of a greenish-gray, unnamable pastel color. I haven't seen her face, but I know she is beautiful, and I wonder where her man is. A woman like that turns up in the Little Nell bar because there is a wealthy man to meet her. Heads turn as she walks my way, and it is several seconds before I realize that it is Rachel.

"Hi," she says, and my heart jumps, just as it did when I first spied her in Aspen, a hundred feet and ten years from this very spot. I wish we could go back there.

We chat about Aspen and the kids and expenses. I want to bring up

Gretchen, but now I find I can't. It's too painful to admit to, even though I know Rachel knows. I am so embarrassed, and feel so let down, that I can't really admit it to myself. It's as if some other person did those things.

Meanwhile, Rachel is telling me she plans to work on the mountain again when winter arrives. "I know the money is pathetic, but I need to do it for me. I'm good at it, and I want to do something I'm good at. It should count for something."

"It does," I say.

"So—how is it being the Court Harvey of the desk?" she asks.

"I wouldn't call myself that, exactly. But it's weird. I've got all these personalities coming at me all the time, always for money. I haven't been trading well. The truth is, I feel like an impostor. I mean, there are guys who could make the jump and never look back, but every day I keep wondering when it's going to end. Like I'm an impostor sure to be exposed. Do you know what I mean?"

She leans her head and that beautiful hair against the wall. "You're no more an impostor than anyone else," she says.

"I guess that's a comfort," I say.

She smiles at me.

"Rachel, this is crazy, you here and me across the country, and . . . well, I want to make this work, for us, and for the kids. I know some things have gone terribly wrong, but I'm devoted to you and the children."

There's no more smile. She looks down at her drink, speaks to it.

"Don't do this, Barry. I came out here because it's where I belong, and because I needed space. You say you're devoted to me, but how am I supposed to believe that after all those years of watching you devote everything to your job? It's like you expect to have it both ways. What did you think would happen when you took us there? You knew what it would be like. Or you must have had some idea. It was a terrible risk you took."

Well, I think, she's right about that.

"I share the blame," she says. "I should have questioned you. I shouldn't have gone along so easily. I'm at fault, too."

"So let's make it work," I say.

"No, I can't. Just because we both made mistakes doesn't make it equal. This isn't some bond math equation. It doesn't work like that."

"So what does that mean?"

"I'll be honest. I've seen a lawyer about a divorce."

"You have a lawyer?"

"I just wanted to know what my options are."

I can't imagine Rachel going and getting a lawyer. "What about the kids?"

"What about the kids? I could have asked you the same question every day for the last five years. Look, I haven't made any final decisions. I really don't know what to do. But I want you to give me some room. You seem to think we can just put the pieces back together again, wind back the clock, and act like nothing happened. Well, we can't. We can't just go back and be like we were before."

"But, Rachel, I still love you. Do you know that? I really do."

She looks at me, her expression blank. And then I feel it coming out.

"I know you know about Gretchen and me," I say. Immediately, the air comes into my lungs. It's as if the life force itself is connected to admitting what you've done to those you've hurt, those you love. It wasn't hard admitting my transgressions to myself; I've learned how to live with that kind of disappointment. The thought of seeing the same disappointment in Rachel, though, scared me into silence.

Now Rachel doesn't even blink.

"All I can say, Rachel, is that I'm so sorry. If I could change one thing about my life, that would be it. I don't really understand why I did what I did, but I know I will never do anything like that again. The thing about Wall Street is, it finds your weakness and that's the thing that takes over your life. If you're greedy, you become more so. If you're mean, you become meaner. If—"

"So, Barry, what is your weakness?"

"I took you and the kids for granted. You might say I lost track of myself."

She rubs at her eye.

"I want to still love you, Barry—but I can't take you back, just like that. You've hurt me, hurt me in a way that I never thought you would. I'm not the same person I was when we left here. I believed in you. Now I need some time to be alone, and figure things out. I need some space." She lifts her hand, pushes the hair from her face. I look for and see her wedding ring, am thankful for that one bit of constancy. "But your kids need you. Why don't you come by around ten tomorrow and take them out to brunch."

"Brunch," I say. I think of the Sunday mornings when I used to get up with Jane and Sam and take them to the bakery in Mount Kisco for hot egg-everything bagels. Now brunch will be an obligation for them, like Sunday school.

"What do I tell the kids, Barry? They're going to wake up tomorrow, just like they do every day, and I'll have to tell them something. Will you be there, or not?"

I will. If there's one thing I'm still certain about, it's that I want to be there. I imagine how it will be when they wake tomorrow, Rachel shaking Sam, who'll bury his head in his pillow and kick his feet so that it looks like ferrets are fighting beneath his blankets. Jane will watch all this from the notch in her mother's hip, and maybe when she's older she'll still have this memory of watching her brother wake on one of the few mornings when they went out to brunch with their dad.

15. Plan B

In New York, we hit that two-week period when the leaves change, and the beauty of Westchester takes me by surprise. The leaves turn, and the trees alight in yellow and green, orange and rust. On weekend mornings I sit bundled up on the back deck, drinking coffee and watching the sparrows, finches, and blue jays fight it out for the birdseed I put in the feeder. I've read that when it gets cold the little birds must eat every evening, or freeze to death in their sleep.

Mostly, I work. Late in October, I have two meetings with Isaac Hunt about desk compensation. Desk-compensation meetings have a martial quality to them, akin to a planning session for a great D-Day-like invasion. For managers like Isaac Hunt, the "enemy" is the traders, who are to be softened up with a verbal barrage ("We worked very hard to get you to this number"), and then stuck with, well, as little as the firm can get away with. Our desk revenues are down a little over 20 percent, and Hunt cuts the bonus pool by 35. My role is to fight for my traders, and I do, with about as much success as the Poles had with the Nazis.

"I've got businesses growing by twenty percent," Hunt says. "Businesses that demonstrate growth get a bigger share of the pie."

"It's a transition year for us, and you know it," I say. "We've had turnover and we have fewer people. Given what's gone on, we did better than could be expected. In big years we don't get the full bump, so we shouldn't take the full hit now. Hell, last year we had a blowout year, and we got killed at year end. We are owed."

I think of Vollmer, and how he made a similar argument to Court Harvey, and where it got him.

"Owed?" Hunt says. "You are owed nothing. You're new at this, and you don't have any idea what the process is about. Ryan Hauptman doesn't come in here and argue like this."

"He doesn't have to."

"No, he doesn't, because every year he puts up spectacular numbers. His desk made six times what yours did. *That's* how you get paid."

I stand to leave, but Isaac Hunt tells me to sit back down. He wants to oversee how I will divvy up the bonuses. I make suggestions; he frowns, then bumps up Vollmer and Dino's pay by taking it from Carlson and Glover.

Other managers, I'm sure, don't have to put up with this kind of meddling. When I argue the injustice of what he's making me do, Isaac Hunt raises one of his enormous hands, its palm as white as mine. "Don't sweat it," he says. "You think this is difficult, but once you tell everyone their numbers, you'll realize that there's really nothing they can do. They may argue or act like children, but at the end of the day, they just have to sit there and take it. Your job is easier than you think."

The next weekend, I fly to Colorado for Halloween. Sam dresses as Derek Jeter, the Yankees' shortstop; Rachel dolls up Jane as a kitten; and all of us together walk up and down Cemetery Lane, Aspen's prime trick-or-treating territory. With all the kids and parents on the street, there are moments when things almost feel normal, but then I notice how Jane has grown or hear a new saying that Sam keeps repeating, and I realize that I am nothing more than a visitor, some distant relative who comes to town to tell the children how much they've grown.

That night, after the kids go to bed, I sit on Rachel's couch while she takes to the reading chair, her feet covered in wool socks, stretched out on the coffee table. Things are going well, she says. Sam is adjusting to school and making friends. Jane likes her new day care. Rachel is starting up again with her music.

"Why did you ever stop?" I ask.

"I don't know. Having Sam changed everything for me. But, really, I think it was a lack of guts. Playing music in public takes guts."

"I never stopped you," I say.

"This isn't about you."

"I'm sorry," I say. "I'm defensive, I know. I'm not sure what to say anymore, but I want you to know that I want to make things right again."

"Barry," she says, "I'm seeing someone else."

My chest contracts. I feel a wave of panic, as if I'm suffocating. In the past, the idea of someone else touching Rachel filled me with rage, but what I'm really feeling now is a deep and terrible sadness, and a loss of hope.

"I want to be honest with you," she says. "I just need to try some new things. It's only fair."

"Is it . . . serious?" I manage to ask.

She laughs. "No, it's not. And that's the point."

"Just tell me one thing," I say.

"What?"

"Do we have any chance? Is there any chance we might make a life together? Maybe, sometime in the future?"

"Maybe, Barry, maybe. We'll just have to see."

A drab November sky settles over Westchester. The days continue to shorten, till it looks dim and gray at four in the afternoon, if I happen to glance out the window, which I often don't. I visit Rachel and the kids for three days at Thanksgiving. Otherwise, it feels as if I'm living underground.

December arrives, and bonus day with it. The day itself is warm and moist, with a low-lying fog that hangs in the darkness of my neighborhood as I make my way to the Park and Ride. It's an eerie sight. The fog and mist scatter my headlights. I feel almost as if I'm driving on the bottom of a murky pond. I focus on the ditches and stone walls along the side of the road, and make my way to the main streets of Mount Kisco by avoiding these obstacles.

Dino arrives five minutes late. When I open the back seat of the Infinity in order to throw in my suit jacket, I notice a case of Budweiser on the seat.

"What's the beer for?" I ask.

"It's from the deli. Depending on how my day goes, I might have to drink a few on the ride home."

We pull out of the lot and make the left onto the highway entrance ramp. Dino hits the gas, and we rattle down the highway at seventy, all the way to Manhattan, slowed slightly by the poor visibility. We approach the gate on the Henry Hudson Bridge, where traffic cops stand wearing clear plastic slickers with orange sashes. One looks in our car as we wait for the EZ-Pass to open the gate. We are all, I realize, under surveillance.

Dino sighs. "Grab me one of those suckers," he says. We're past the cops now.

"You really want a beer?" I look at his clock. It's 6:37.

By his silence I assume he's serious, so I give him a can, which he pops open and slurps loudly. The smell of beer fills the car.

"Just tell me how bad it is," he says.

I hesitate, then launch into his bonus talk, which involves my repeating over and over what a tough year it's been for the government desk. All I can think of is Court Harvey, and how he fed me the same line of crap every year. I wonder if it ever made him short of breath, the way it makes me, as if bald-faced lying takes more oxygen. "But," I say, "we—I've spoken about this with Isaac Hunt, who is following your transfer with great interest—we feel very good about your future as the five-year trader. With revenues down, there just is not as much money to go around this year, but we worked very hard to get you to your number, and we think you should feel good about it."

"We? Hey, Barry. Cut the 'we' crap. How many fucking people are there in this car, anyway?"

"You think it's fun giving out numbers, Dino?" I say, thankful

Dino has now freed me to say what I want. "I could pay you two million bucks and I bet you'd still bitch about it."

"No, Barry, actually, I'd be happy with that."

"Well, you actually made five seventy-five." This includes salary, bonus, and restricted stock; it's an 8-percent increase over what he made the year before.

"That sucks, Barry. You ought to think twice about giving a guy a number on the way to work. You could end up in an accident."

"You asked me for the number." My stomach is turning from the smell of the beer.

"You could have waited, especially since you knew how bad it was."

"It's not bad," I say.

"Bullshit. It's shit. Pure shit. I bet Chip McCarty made over a stick last year. I am not a cut-rate talent, and I shouldn't be paid like one."

Ahead, I can see the George Washington Bridge half gone in the fog.

"You made almost six hundred grand in a year. It's a small fortune," I say, with conviction. On Wall Street, it's amazing what people can find inadequate.

"Listen, Barry, I don't give a damn how good *you* feel about that number. I don't give a damn about next year, or the year after that, or my future at the firm or on the planet. Fuck the future. You think I did a good job, pay me now."

His anger is palpable. It's a side of Dino I haven't yet seen. I sneak a glance at him, his teeth clenched, his face set hard into a narrow-eyed mask of anger, a half-crushed Budweiser can in his fist. So this is Dino Corsetti, thirty-three-year-old deli proprietor and bond trader who has made—just from one job—twelve times the median family income. Twelve times. And for doing what? Playing Ping-Pong with a few bonds. Dino wasn't always like this. At one time he drank coffee in the morning, and he probably felt grateful and happy for the riches to be bestowed upon him. I promise myself that I will remember this tomorrow, when I get my number.

Glover and Vollmer express dismay at their numbers, and anger, but it's the normal dismay and anger of every bonus meeting. The anger is meant to hide disappointment. Even when you know you're going to get screwed, you still hope against hope that it will turn out better than you expected. Traders are weak that way, just like everyone else.

Only Duane Rizzo thanks me when he gets his number. He's too inexperienced, and poor, to be angry.

Tom Carlson comes in last, drops into a chair that squeaks beneath his weight. He wears his normal world-weary look; his hair is askew, his eyes are dark and sunken, his skin is sallow. The top button of his shirt is undone beneath his tie, and the shirt itself has a frayed hole at his left elbow. "Bonus shirts," we call them. The hole is supposed to suggest that the wearer isn't being paid enough to buy new clothes.

I give him my spiel, and then his number, which is $375,000, twenty-five thousand less than he earned last year. I consider this unfair—he made a fraction more trading this year, and this was a tougher year—but it was Isaac Hunt's call. I expect Carlson to howl. I wish I could put the whole thing off.

"That's horseshit!" Carlson yells. He jumps to his feet. "YOU . . . CAN'T . . . PAY . . . ME . . . THAT!" His eyes bulge from his head as if he is being garroted, the whites lined with red. His nose flares, and his mouth is lopsided and angry. Time seems to be slowing down. I look up at Carlson for the first time in the four years I've known him, and what I notice is that his teeth are chock-full of gold fillings. "I'VE NEVER HEARD OF ANYTHING MORE OUTRAGEOUS IN MY LIFE!" he yells, his voice cracking with emotion. He pounds his hand on my desk, hesitates, then plops back into his chair and slumps to his left side, as if he were an electric toy whose batteries have just run out.

I am frozen in my chair, holding tight to the armrests to weather his assault. I become aware of the air blowing in through the HVAC unit, and of a slight whirring from my Sun workstation as the live feeds flicker. Otherwise, there is no sound.

"Tom?" I say.

"Three seventy-five," he mutters. "I don't feel so good."

He tilts out of his chair and hits the floor with a thud. Outside the glass partition, heads turn. I jump from my seat and run around the desk. Carlson lies legs akimbo, his face scarlet, his bloodshot eyes rolled back in his head. Janice, the new secretary, comes to the door, and I tell her to call 911. Then I lay Carlson flat on his back, open his tie further, and search for a heartbeat. His skin feels clammy, and it takes a while, but I find a pulse in his neck.

I look up at the glass partition. Vollmer and Dino stand on the other side, along with a dozen or so other people from around the floor. I turn back to Carlson. He's staring at the ceiling.

"Hang on, Tom. Help is on the way."

"Not fair," he mumbles. "It's not fair." There's a hot, rotten smell to his breath. He grabs my forearm, and squeezes it with considerable might. I expect him to say something more, but he doesn't. I am left to wait with him till the paramedics arrive, all the while held fast to his side.

That night, I speak with Carlson's wife. It was a mild heart attack, and he is expected to "recover fully," she says. The doctors, however, don't want him to trade again, so even though his wife sounds hopeful, my guess is that the recovery won't be as full as Carlson might hope.

Really, it's surprising more people don't collapse on the trading floor. When your whole life is wrapped up in a job that respects only money, then getting your number is a true judgment day. You do away with any notion of self-examination, and settle for having a year of life boiled down to this one simplification, this one number that says it all.

Later—it's 1:17 in the morning—I give up on sleeping. I'm too wound up, what with the image of Carlson toppling over and the nervousness about what tomorrow will bring. It's impossible to lie alone in this empty house and listen to the bare branches of our maple scratch at the shutters out my window. I put on my clothes, grab a coat, and head out into the neighborhood.

The temperature has dropped at least twenty degrees. There's a breeze, and above me the sky is clear and dotted with stars, easily viewed through the leafless trees over the road. And then I spot it: a comet that's been getting a lot of play on the radio. It hangs in the sky, a fuzzy ball of sparkles, and I find myself transfixed by it, as men have been transfixed by comets for centuries, contemplating a distant light and our insignificance in the comings and goings of the universe. As I look at that comet, the obvious becomes clear to me: that I am not bound by large forces beyond my control, that there is nothing but the shame of admitting failure that keeps me here, that I can change my life if I want to. I can quit my job, go west, and try to reconstruct my family. I can try to repair the damage that I have done. There is nothing stopping me but my own will.

Of course, I am neither impractical nor improvident. There is real risk in going west. Rachel might not take me back. Whether she does or doesn't, I will still have to earn a living, and I'm well aware that as a family we are used to better than what we left, and it isn't likely that I'll find a job in Aspen that pays four hundred grand a year, or even a fifth of that. I don't want to go back to worrying what the total will be at the grocery checkout, to carrying bills in my pockets in the hope of finding money in the street. I fear being poor again, and have good reason to. I doubt Rachel and I would survive it.

In the end, though, I have to ask myself: Do I love Rachel? I know I would risk everything just to have her smile at me again. I can't imagine *not* sharing my life with her. And I want to be a father to my children. I'll wait for bonuses to be paid—no sense leaving a huge chunk of money on the table—but that's only weeks away, and in the meantime I can start to change my ways.

I stand another moment and watch that comet sparkle, thankful that it's there. Then I turn back to my house, making my plans for flight.

The next morning is clear and cold, the wind shaking the trees and kicking up leaves left from the fall. Dino is not at the Park and Ride. I give him ten minutes, then drive in alone. Now that my course is set, I don't have an ounce of nervousness. Whatever the number is, I can accept it. I'm leaving.

Shirley waves me into Isaac Hunt's office when I arrive five minutes early for my appointment. Isaac sits at his desk, bent over a piece of paper, his ebony scalp visible in a patch of thinning hair atop his head. "How are you doing?" he asks, without looking up. That question again. "Sit down."

"Fine," I say, sitting.

"That was something yesterday with Tom Carlson. I don't think that's happened here since '85 or '86. I heard you stayed with him, pulled him through. I commend you for that; it was very brave. If I'd been in your seat, I don't know."

"I don't see how I could have done anything else. You would have felt the same."

"Well, you don't know till you are tested," he says. "Carlson, though, he took terrible care of himself. He was a prime candidate for this."

It occurs to me that this is the classic management spin on a trader's failure: blame the trader. True, Carlson took terrible care of himself, but even the most obese slobs usually don't have heart attacks at thirty-nine.

"Anyway, Barry, let's move on. Given the somber mood here, what I have to say next is rather difficult, but I've been going over the numbers, and I must tell you that they are disappointing."

Disappointing? Haven't we had this discussion?

"We are getting it together," I say, not that I really need to worry about the future. I'm just playing a part. "Things have turned around."

Isaac Hunt is staring at the paper on his desk. "I gave you a lot of responsibility far sooner than many thought prudent," he says. "I don't think it was the right thing to do. I only need to look at these numbers to see that."

Okay, he's going to slam me, knock me down, pay me shit, and speak about opportunity. I know that. It's what I did all day yesterday. I'm actually looking forward to hearing him talk about my future at the firm.

"Government trading is too important to all the businesses of the department for it to crumple up as it has. I know you haven't been in the position long, but you have lost my confidence. I like you, personally, and think you are a bright guy with a bright future, and that you will land on your feet. Your bravery yesterday speaks to that, but we're not in the business of saving lives here, we're just trying to make money. Now, I don't doubt that you've made every effort, but effort is not enough. We're traders, and traders must show results."

"Of course," I say.

"So I'm going to put someone else in charge of your desk."

My first reaction is to argue, but what does it really matter? I just need this year's bonus.

"It's not only the numbers," he says. "I'm replacing you because you have lost my confidence, and I cannot have managers who have lost my confidence."

"You haven't given me any time to earn it," I say.

"No. You got opportunities that most guys on this floor dream of. You can only blame yourself," he says.

I take a deep breath. Think like a trader, I tell myself. Don't panic. Get the money.

"What about last year's comp?" I ask.

"Three seventy-five," he says. Carlson's number, exactly.

I hear myself screaming. I can't help it. "That's less than I made last year! It's half what I paid my top people."

Isaac Hunt leans forward over his desk. "Listen," he whispers, "your personal trading was barely half what Colin Dancer made for us. The desk revenue was three-quarters of what Court Harvey brought us. You know what that means? We didn't have to pay you one stinking penny."

It's starting to feel personal. I could leap across the desk and go after him. No, I tell myself. Stay calm. Stay calm.

"This is tough for you, I know," he says. "You have some decisions to make. If you stay with us, you can expect to go back to your old position. Or you can leave at any time. We will still pay you your bonus."

"My old position?"

"Bills," he says.

"You have a bill trader."

"I'll have the kid moved back downstairs."

"I quit," I say. This is better than I expected. I can leave now, without having to wait for my bonus. Besides, there is no way I could face

Vollmer and Glover and the rest as the bill trader. The shame would be too great. Hunt knows this. I also don't want to demote Duane, though I know that under different circumstances I might. The Street has taught me a lot about the decisions I'm willing to make.

"I understand," he says. "Let me remind you of the confidentiality agreement you signed in regards to the Gretchen Barnes matter. Should you break that agreement, you will lose all of your restricted stock, and we would have the option of seeking legal redress for damages."

I can hear myself breathing.

"Who would I tell?" I ask. I stand, and leave his office.

I feel liberated when I drive out of the building, unemployed. My God, it's exhilarating, all that pressure lifted, just like that, a big check (half of what I hoped for, but still big) coming my way.

Northbound traffic on the West Side Highway is light as I make my way north. I start to plan my phone call to Rachel. Even after taxes, I'm going to clear six figures on my bonus, and we'll probably get another fifty grand when we sell the house. That's a pretty good stake. We could start over. At least, we could try to start over. I'll find something out there, a job that will just be a job, one that will pay the bills, which won't be much. We can get rid of one car, live frugally, and still live well. I'll see the kids for breakfast, and be there for Rachel. So the whole trip east has been a bust. It's time to admit it, and move on.

At the house, I jog from the car to the kitchen, call Rachel with my coat still on, so excited I'm almost manic with the idea of it all, of going back and starting over.

I get Rachel's machine, and hang up the phone. I walk over to the dining area. I'm standing where our dining table once stood, where we used to have family dinners. The house is empty. It hits me then that I'm unemployed, alone, and miles from home.

That night Mickey O'Hara, my old broker, calls me. I still haven't gotten hold of Rachel. Mickey says he needs a favor, and I tell him I will grant it even before I know what it is. What can I really lose?

"Can you promise to do three hundred million a month with me? It's not much, and I really need it, Barry. I got seven kids at home that's got to eat and get dressed in the morning, you know? You've always been very fair with me, and I hate to come begging, but I need your help."

"I don't get it," I say.

"Chappy will take me on if I can promise them a certain volume."

"Why Chappy?"

"Because I don't have any choice. I've been a broker for fourteen years, and I don't know nothing else. I got no degree, no trade, no real skills. I do this, or I end up cleaning windshields on the West Side Highway."

"What happened at Brokertec? Did you get let go or something?"

"You don't know?" he asks.

It turns out that Brokertec closed its doors this afternoon. When I tell Mickey what happened to me, I can hear the breath go out of him, as if I'd punched him. He was counting on me. I wish him luck, and suggest he call Stevie Vollmer.

"I already have," he says.

It's not till the next evening, pitch black outside at five o'clock, that I reach Rachel by phone.

"You quit?" she asks.

"It was bizarre. I decided to quit after I got my bonus, and then they fired me before I got the chance. You were right. I had to get out."

There's a long silence on the line.

"Rachel?" I say.

"Yes."

I tell her that I want to go out there and start fresh. I lay out my plan, a life together. I will be satisfied this time, I say, with the simpler things. I understand what I've lost. I want to start over, get it right.

"If you want to start over, then you really have to go back to the beginning. You can't just come back where things went wrong. And, look, even then I don't know if I can be there for you. I don't know."

"Okay," I say. "The beginning."

"What will you do for money?"

That's the question. It seems it's always the question.

"I'll look for something out there," I say.

"Can you be a bond trader here?"

"Not exactly. But I'll look for something related. I'll give it a try."

There's a long pause.

"Rachel?" I ask.

"Okay," she says. "Like I said, you can start at the beginning. You can come to town and take me out on dates. I think I might like that. And you can be a father to your children. They need you. But you have to give me some space. We'll see what happens."

I agree to this. At least I feel there's a chance.

I spend the next six weeks trying to find a job out west. The Christmas and New Year's holidays make it tough, and the little employment interest I find is in Denver, where they won't even pay what a first-year M.B.A. gets in New York.

"God," Rachel says when I tell her, "I thought going to Wharton was supposed to mean something. Wall Street was supposed to mean something."

"It does, on Wall Street," I say.

The first week of February, the phone rings in the evening. The house is under contract, with a closing tomorrow. I'm heading west as soon as the papers are signed. The phone could be the Realtor, or perhaps it's my mother. We're back to talking once a week. She argues strenuously that Rachel and I should get back together. I tell her we're working on it.

"From opposite sides of the country?" she asks.

"I'm moving out there soon," I tell her.

Now I pick up the phone. It's Chip McCarty. We've talked once since I left the firm.

"How you making out?" he asks.

"Okay."

"Well, I have a proposition for you. Do you think you could come in with me tomorrow, spend the day, talk with a few people?"

"You got a job for me?" I sit up. I realize that I want him to make me a job offer. Meaningless as it is, I still want to be wanted in this way.

"In a word, Barry, yes. Look, I'll be honest. If you're not in the right frame of mind, it could sound, well, insulting. But it's not. You're looking for work, and I am dead serious. I really want you for this job. Colin likes the idea, too. I can't pay you what you were probably making, but I think you've got to look at this as a fresh start. Prove yourself. Re-create your career. Come along at the right speed. It may not feel like it now, but you've got a bright future. The key is to stay at it. Barry, I am telling you, you stick with this business, you are going to be a very rich man."

"Chip, I can't tell what you are offering me."

"Bills, Barry. I need a bill trader. You'll make two, two fifty a year, which is good for a bill trader. And you will be in line to move up."

"You want me to go back to bills?"

"Hey, it beats watching soap operas. Besides, you need to get back in the game. It's not good to stay away too long. You've got to say yes. This is just what you need."

Part of me wants to take the job, to prove that I can be a success, and to get the money. I look around my empty living room. All my things are packed into bags and set against the wall. I've given the furniture that Rachel left behind to charity, rid the house of everything else that wasn't attached. Tonight I'll be camping out in my own living room. I think Wall Street has been the most humiliating experience of my life.

"C'mon, Barry," Mac says. "What do you say? This is a great opportunity. I'll drive tomorrow, like old times. Come in and meet some people. I've talked you up all day today. The job is basically yours. Meet me at the Park and Ride, six-fifteen?"

I almost have an urge to say yes, but there's only one plan left to me.

"I can't make it," I say.

"What the hell, Barry," Mac says. "Where are you going to get a better offer than this?"

If Mac knew the whole situation, he'd probably tell me that I was crazy, that I was throwing away near-certain success for an uncertain future. It's a bad trade, he'd say, the risk/reward is all skewed to failure. Maybe he'd be right, but I can't worry about those odds now. In fact, I can't even play that game.

Later, well after midnight, when sleep still won't come, I go outside to pack up the Escort. In the driveway I pause to smell the air, which is cool and moist, scented with dead leaves. I can see a pile left from the previous autumn, spread at the base of the enormous oak on the front lawn. The house throws off enough light to turn the tree into a huge silhouette; it towers over the house. In these late hours, when you can't see the other houses or the road, or hear the other people, when the trees are more an idea than a vision, you can get a sense of just how awesome this place must have been, back before it got subdivided and carved up and anyone thought of picking up the leaves.

I turn back to the car and load it up. There isn't much: just two duffels and a garment bag. In the garment bag are five business suits, a pair of tasseled loafers, a dozen dress shirts, and as many ties. These are the material goods I've picked up in the East. I look at that bag lying in the hatchback and decide it really doesn't fit there. I carry it back to the house, then up the stairs, where I haven't walked in a week. There's an odd odor from having the carpet professionally cleaned. I feel as if I'm trespassing. I quickly glance into Jane's empty room, and Sam's, and finally go to the master bedroom. I leave the bag at the back of my closet, as though I've forgotten it.

ACKNOWLEDGMENTS

For favors large and small I'd like to thank John Price, Kurt Harrison, Rod Gancas, and Jamie Watkins; Andrea Beauchamp, Herbert Barrows, and Derek Green; Terry Zaroff-Evans; Xanthe Tabor and Alexis Gargagliano. For gargantuan efforts on my behalf, I'm deeply indebted to Jennifer Rudolph Walsh, Jordan Pavlin, and Deborah Lasser.

A NOTE ABOUT THE AUTHOR

Scott Lasser received an M.F.A. from the University of Michigan and an M.B.A. from the Wharton School. He is the author of *Battle Creek,* and was formerly a government bond trader at Lehman Brothers. He lives in Old Snowmass, Colorado, with his wife and two children.

A NOTE ON THE TYPE

The text of this book was set in a typeface called Times New Roman, designed by Stanley Morison for *The Times* (London), and introduced by that newspaper in 1932.

Among typographers and designers of the twentieth century, Stanley Morison was a strong forming influence, as typographical adviser to the Monotype Corporation of London, as a director of two distinguished English publishing houses, and as a writer of sensibility, erudition, and keen practical sense.

In 1930 Morison wrote: "Type design moves at the pace of the most conservative reader. The good type-designer therefore realizes that, for a new font to be successful, it has to be so good that only very few recognize its novelty. If readers do not notice the consummate reticence and rare discipline of a new type, it is probably a good letter." It is now generally recognized that in the creation of Times Roman, Morison successfully met the qualifications of his theoretical doctrine.

Composed by Stratford Publishing Services, Brattleboro, Vermont

Printed and bound by Berryville Graphics, Berryville, Virginia

Designed by Iris Weinstein